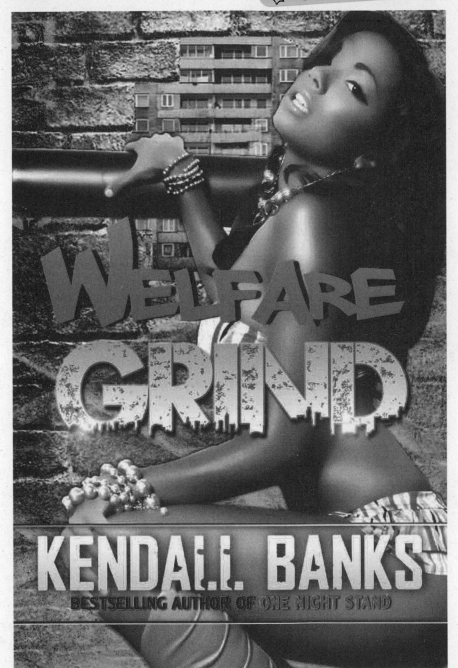

WELFARE GRIND

KENDALL BANKS

WELFARE GRIND

KENDALL BANKS

BESTSELLING AUTHOR OF ONE NIGHT STAND

Life Changing Books in conjunction with Power Play Media
Published by Life Changing Books
P.O. Box 423 Brandywine, MD 20613

Library of Congress Cataloging-in-Publication Data;

www.lifechangingbooks.net
13 Digit: 978-1934230381
10 Digit: 1-934230383

ACKNOWLEDGEMENTS

As always I want to start off by thanking my Lord and Savior Jesus Christ. I'm eternally grateful for all my blessings. To my mother, Roxie, thanks for always putting up with me. Even though you refuse to read any of my books, I still love you dearly. Your never-ending support is truly irreplaceable.

Because you've been pissing me off lately, I'm not thanking anybody in my love life right now. (You know who you are). Maybe next time...I still love you though.

To my BFF, Nycole, thanks for always giving me your honest opinion and great friendship. To the rest of my crazy fam, love you guys.

A special thanks to the group of professionals who always help me from start to finish. Kellie...wow, what can I say other than you outdid yourself this time. This cover is beyond hot! Thanks for always being there for me and the LCB team. Azarel, you truly helped me out with this project, sometimes even putting your own book aside to read my work. For that, I say thank you. I'm truly grateful for a publisher like you. Congratulations in advance on VIP. I know it's going to be a hit. LCB for life!! To Tasha, thanks for all your helpful input and ideas. You gave me insight to a world I knew nothing about. Oh, and just like I said in my last book...don't mess up any of my orders. LOL. To Tonya Ridley (Money Maker), you always give the best advice when it comes to my work. Thank you so much for helping make this project even better. Leslie, thanks as always. Lastly, thanks to the test readers, Aschandria, and Virginia.

Shout out to the LCB authors. Jackie D., Miss KP, Danette Majette, J. Tremble, Carla Pennington, CJ Hudson, Chris Renee, Mike Warren, VegasClarke, Tonya Ridley, Jai Nicole, Ericka Williams, and anyone else I've failed to mention. It feels good to be surrounded by such talented authors. Keep up the good work.

Thanks to all the book stores, who continue to pump my books. I appreciate the support.

Last but certainly not least…to the readers. Words can not express how good it feels when people come up and give me praises. You all truly enjoyed One Night Stand and Another One Night Stand, so hopefully I will not disappoint you this time. This book is a little bit different, but I'm confident you will find it just as enjoyable. However, don't worry, I haven't forgotten about Zaria. She will return! Thanks for the love.

Smooches,

Kendall Banks
www.facebook.com/authorkendall
Follow me on Twitter:@AuthorKendallB

ONE

"That's my shit," I said excitedly as Drake's face appeared on the seventy-two inch screen of my plasma television. 106 & Park was on as usual.

Rushing into the living room, I snatched the remote from the cocktail table and turned up the volume causing the music video to rise to an ear blistering level. My music always had to be loud. I couldn't enjoy it any other way. After setting the remote back on the table, my head bobbed to the song's throbbing baseline as I recited every single word to *The Motto* and made my way across the floor back to the bathroom.

In a pair of denim booty shorts so tight that my butt cheeks could easily be seen, I swung my hips from side to side in a rhythm that was always good for attention. There wasn't a nigga around right now to impress, but my hips had a mind of their own. They swung and swayed out of pure habit. My breasts, which thankfully had no sag to them, were pressed against the inside of my peacock blue tank top so tightly they looked like they'd pop out at any moment. And the soles of my Chanel flip-flops smacked loudly against the bottoms of my pedicured feet with each and every step towards the bathroom.

"Mommy," Treasure, my ten year old daughter called as she opened the door of her bedroom and poked her head out into the hallway.

"What?" I asked with agitation as I passed by, singing between my words to her. "Now she want a photo, you already know though, you only live once, that's the motto, nigga yolo," I sang, not wanting to be held up or interrupted.

"Cash won't do what I tell him to do," she whined.

"Cash, do you want an ass whipping?" I asked my four year old son loudly from the bathroom as I grabbed the lit blunt from the ashtray and began to inspect myself in the mirror. Taking my index finger, I rubbed my Marilyn Monroe mole on the left side of the face, a beauty mark passed down from my mother.

"Noooo," he said in his little squeaky sounding voice.

"Then do what your sister tells you!" I shouted as I hit the blunt and flooded my lungs with smoke from the weed. The last thing I wanted to deal with right now was whining and tattling from my kids. A bitch had plans.

"Mommy, where are you going?" Treasure asked, slowly trying to ease her way out of her room and towards me. "I wanna go with you."

Releasing the chronic smoke, I sighed annoyingly. *Here she goes trying to fuck my high up. Every time she sees me getting ready to go somewhere, she wants to go*. I pulled my shorts down and sat on the toilet with the door wide open.

"Girl, no," I said over the loud music coming from the living room. "Now, get back in your room. I'm busy, shit."

"But, mommy," she whined.

"I said, no. Now, close that damn door and watch your lil brothers like I told you to."

My two-year-old son Dinero was also in the room, most likely tearing up shit as usual. Shane, my boyfriend's sixteen year old son who was autistic was in his own room probably talking to himself or repeating some shit he'd heard on television.

Treasure folded her arms, poked her lips out, and pouted as she closed her door, knowing that asking again would simply get her a serious beat down. Shaking my head, I released a long piss, then took another hit of the blunt before sitting it back in the ashtray. A thin, gray cloud of smoke slithered towards the ceiling

2

as I stood up, looked in the mirror and ran a pinky finger across my newly arched eyebrow.

I was going to leave the kids alone for a few hours while I hit the bar and had a few drinks. Treasure could hold it down. She'd done it plenty of times before and knew the rules. She knew that neither she nor her brothers were to come out of their room until I got back. At ten years old, it was clear not to answer the phone. And not the door either. Children's Protective Services tripped nowadays on kids being left alone so Treasure knew that violation of *any* of those rules was an automatic ass whipping.

I never worried about anything bad happening when I left Treasure alone with her brothers. She was mature for her age and being groomed to be my assistant. Besides, my mother did the same to me when I was young. Instead of leaving me alone for just a few hours, she'd sometimes leave me on my own for an entire day or night. I got used to it though. That's just how shit goes down in the hood. You had to grow up quick.

My mother had raised me in Gilmour Homes, a public housing complex boarded by Fulton Avenue and near Druid Hills Park. Now, I was raising my own babies in aother pubic housing development called McCulloh Homes. My mother had made it out changing her life, and certainly expected me to do the same. Little did she know, I did have plans to roll out one day, but I just had to do the shit in my own time. The difference between me and other hoodrats is that I didn't let the projects hold me up or bring me down. It's like my home-girl always boasts, "It ain't *where* a bitch live, it's *how* a bitch live."

Yeah, I'm on welfare, but I know how to make the system work for me. I wasn't your average welfare recipient. I wasn't one of them air head broads who got money on their EBT card and cried broke three or four days later. Nah, I didn't get down like that. Shit, that's hustling backwards. I had a muthafuckin' plan.

Money was always in my pocket, and my lungs stayed filled with the best weed. Even my three bedroom apartment had top dollar furniture, and my Dodge Charger was almost paid for, which I keep parked a block over so the complex's front office didn't get suspicious of my finances. But I wasn't content with just having new things though. Bullets whizzed through the projects like killer bees. There was a new nigga dead around this muthafucka almost every night. But before one of those unlucky muthafuckas turned out to be me or one of my babies, we were getting out, headed to Arizona as soon as I could get enough money saved.

Grabbing the blunt between my slender fingers which were tipped with two- inch long fingernails that curled under, I was more than pleased with what I saw in the mirror. I was hot. Call me conceited, but I knew I was the shit. Blessed with naturally good looks, my walnut skin tone and high apple cheeks, I'd never had a problem with getting a man. As a matter of fact, I'd had a boyfriend since the third grade. Standing at 5'7, my body was well-toned and I wasn't slacking in the ass department either. Men definitely considered me a dime.

I headed out of the bathroom and back towards the living room as the newest Wale video was now playing from the television. My head bobbed to it. Once again I placed the blunt to my lips.

BOOM!!!

The living room door flew open.

I almost shitted on myself as cops wearing bulletproof vests with DEA written across them quickly flooded into my apartment. They each had badges dangling from their necks and guns in their hands.

"DEA!" several officers shouted.

"Search warrant!" another one yelled. "Get your ass down on the floor right now!"

I placed my hands on my hips. "I ain't getting on no damn floor!" I shouted defiantly, pissed at the sight of my splintered door and the cops tracking their nasty footprints all over my plush new carpet. My neck moved in full swing. "What the fuck is wrong with y'all? Why the hell did y'all kick my door in?"

"Bitch, get your black ass down on the floor!" one of the

4

officers demanded, quickly pressing closer.

"Who are you calling a bitch? Fuck you! I ain't doing shit!"

"Mommy, what's going on?" Treasure questioned, peeking out of her room and seeing all the guns pointed at me.

"Go back in your room, Treasure!"

Suddenly several officers were on me.

"You Keema Newell, right?"

"Get the fuck off of me!" I ordered, trying to fight, refusing to tell them they had my name right.

But my struggle was useless. They were too strong. In a fraction of a second I was laying on my stomach with two sets of knees in my back. Their weight was so heavy I could barely breathe. Moments later my hands were cuffed behind my back.

Several officers quickly but cautiously made their way through the apartment and into the bedrooms with their guns pointed. The sight scared me. I was terrified a gun would go off accidentally and shoot one of my kids, my investments.

"Get the fuck outta my house!" I shouted from the floor. "Get away from my kids!"

"Get on the floor!" I heard them shout to Shane as they entered his bedroom. "Do it now!"

By Shane having autism I hoped desperately he would do as he was told rather than do something abnormal, something they wouldn't understand. He liked to mimic people, always in a daze, and touched things that he had no business touching. His weirdest characteristic was to sit down and stand up randomly with his broad chest outward, causing people to view him as a threat. I hoped like hell he didn't do that shit today. Before long, all four children were brought out of their rooms. Shane was in cuffs while Treasure, Dinero, and Cash were in tears.

"Mommy!" Dinero screamed for me from the arms of the cop carrying him.

"Put my baby down!" I belted.

Each child was placed on the couch side by side and the volume of the television was turned down. Immediately, the offi-

5

cers began to trash my apartment. In every room they snatched out drawers, tossed pillows, flipped over tables, opened cabinets, shoved furniture aside, and anything else they could do to fuck my palace up. I could hear glass breaking from the back.

"Y'all gonna pay for my shit!" I yelled. "Everything y'all break, y'all gon' pay for it. I swear on my life!"

"I've got a gun back here, Sergeant Whitaker!" a cop shouted from Dinero and Cash's bedroom. He walked out holding a .380. "I found it underneath the mattress of the kids' beds."

My eyes widened at the sight of the firearm.

"Got drugs in here!" another officer yelled from the kitchen. Seconds later, he appeared with a pound of weed in a plastic bag. He walked up to the tall, bald headed man. "I found it buried in the bottom of a cereal box, Sergeant Whitaker."

Both men looked down at me. My heart raced. A gun and drugs definitely meant jail time.

"That shit ain't mine!" I blurted out. "Y'all planted that shit. I'm gonna sue you crooked muthafuckas. I swear on my kids I'm gonna sue!"

As my kids cried hysterically, Shane sat silently with his hands still cuffed behind his back. His eyes were staring off into space.

Another officer came out of my bedroom carrying a shoe-box. "Got some money here," he said.

"Awe shit!" I mumbled. That was my stash, I quickly realized. It was ten thousand dollars; the money I'd been saving to get me and the kids out of the projects.

"Got some more money right here," another officer said, coming out of the same bedroom carrying my boyfriend, Dupree's stash. I knew it was roughly thirty thousand.

Finally the tall cop, who they called Sergeant Whitaker, looked down at me again. "A gun, drugs, and money, huh?"

"I told you that shit ain't mine."

"Then whose is it?"

"That's your shit. Y'all planted that!"

"I don't have time for her games," the sergeant told a fellow officer. "Take her downstairs to a car. Then call Children's Protective Services to come get the kids."

"My kids?" I asked surprised. "Why do they have to go to CPS? I have people who'll watch them for me."

"Your lying ass is going to jail for possession of a firearm and possession of marijuana with intent to distribute. You're also going to be charged with Child Endangerment. Those children could've gotten hold of that gun or those drugs and killed themselves," Sergeant Whitaker blasted.

"But I don't know anything about the gun or drugs," I whined. The thought of losing my kids knocked the fight out of me. "I swear I don't."

Shaking his head and fed up Sergeant Whitaker told the other cop, "Take her downstairs."

"Okay, okay," I said quickly, as the cop pulled me to my feet. "I'll tell you who the stuff belongs to."

Every single officer looked at me, waiting for the answer.

I was more scared at that moment than I'd ever been in my life. Dupree would never understand my reasons for doing what I was about to do. He'd probably kill me. But I had no choice. I wasn't going down for this shit.

"Well?" the sergeant questioned. "Whose is it?"

A small lump formed in my throat. I swallowed hard and said, "It's Shane's."

"Who is Shane?" Sergeant Whitaker questioned.

Out of shame, I couldn't turn around and look in Shane's direction. "He's the one you've got handcuffed on the couch. He's my boyfriend's son."

As the sergeant glanced at him, Shane immediately stood up with his two hundred twenty pound, buffed body looking like he was ready for war. It took just two seconds for all the guns in the room to shift his way. He didn't flinch or even speak. They could see something was off with him. I knew it as my heart beat hoping Shane wouldn't get blasted right before my eyes. All the officers looked at each other and then back at me.

"I swear to God it's his," I said, with tears forming in my

eyes. "Please don't take my kids."

"Son, is that stuff yours?" Sergeant Whitaker asked Shane.

"Son, is that stuff yours?" Shane repeated.

He continued to look off into a space of his own, a space that his disease always seemed to make him feel safe in. His days were almost always spent like that. The shit was annoying most times. He looked like an oversized, shell shocked space cadet.

"Of course he's not going to tell you it's his," I said. "But, it really is. Don't let that silent treatment he's using fool you. He does that all the time."

"Fuck it," the sergeant replied in frustration. "Take both of them down stairs and call Children's Protective Services to pick up the others."

TWo

I've heard people brag about going to jail like it's summer camp or a badge of honor. They talk fondly about it like going to jail ain't shit. Treasure's daddy was on year eight, doing fifteen years in The Feds for armed bank robbery. He regularly sent flicks home of him and some of his buffed up homeboys posing for the camera like they were lounging at a health spa. Before getting shot and killed, even Cash's daddy couldn't seem to stop running his dumb ass in and out of there like it was the fun place to be.

Please!

A person had to be smoking crack to think spending even half a second in that shit hole was okay. I mean seriously. What was so cool about having someone tell you when you can eat, sleep, and shit? What was cool about being around a bunch of funky bitches who didn't want to get in the shower and wash their asses? What was so good about any of that nonsense?

Fuck all that. I didn't care what any of those jailbirds were talking about. Jail ain't a place a bitch like me could ever get used to. Nah, I wasn't about to do no time. That's why as soon as the judge set my bail in court this morning I headed straight to the phone, made a collect call to my home girl Imani, and told her to hurry up down here with the money. I also made sure to tell her to keep the shit on the low. The last thing I wanted was for word to get back to Dupree or his brother, Rick. Shane was still locked up and until I could figure out exactly what to tell Dupree, shit had to stay quiet.

The early afternoon, spring sunshine beamed down from the ocean blue sky as I made my way down the courthouse steps in the same clothes they'd arrested me in the day before. My skin felt nasty. I wanted a hot shower badly. The downtown Baltimore traffic was super busy as my flip-flops reached the bottom of the concrete steps and my eyes began to quickly search the street for Imani's Honda Accord.

"Keema!" someone shouted.

I looked across the busy traffic toward the direction the voice had come from and saw Imani's car parked across the street at the curb. Quickly, my feet jogged across the street. As soon as I reached her car, I went around to the passenger's side and hopped in. A Nicki Minaj song, blasted from the speakers.

"Girl, please hurry up and get me up out of here," I said, turning her radio down and leaning back into the seat. "My weave is itching like crazy!" I told her, pulling the eighteen-inch wavy tresses up into a high ponytail.

Imani looked behind her before pulling away from the curb and out into the traffic. Her eyes were fire engine red like she'd been crying for days, but I really didn't want to question her about it though. The last thing I wanted to hear right now was a bunch of sob stories. I had my own problems.

"Here is your phone," she said.

"Thanks so much for bringing it with you. And thanks for stopping by my crib. I'm so glad you still have a key. My shit has probably been ringing all night."

"It has."

"I still can't believe the police ran up in my shit. Now, I gotta go home and clean up."

At that moment, I looked down and noticed I had eight missed calls. As I began to see who they were from, I decided to tell my friend about my horrible experience. "Girl, you wouldn't believe the kind of stinking ass broads they got up in there," I told her. "It's like they had permanent funk sticking to them or something. The shit was so nasty."

"Keema, we gotta talk," Imani said with a worried look on her face.

"Don't worry about the bond money," I assured, assuming that's what she wanted to talk about. "You know I got you. I'm gonna pay…"

"Nah, Keema," she said, interrupting me. She threw her senegalese braids back behind her ear like those old ass braids still looked good. "I'm not sweating the bond money. It's not that."

Imani's appearance didn't look too good either. Usually she was just as fly as I was, but right now she looked terrible. Her whiskey colored skin looked like it hadn't been washed and her deep set eyes were extremely puffy. I figured maybe she'd just gotten out of bed.

"Then what's up?" My hands were up in the air.

Imani glanced at me with a strange look on her face before she spoke. "I've been having some real crazy nightmares lately." She reached to grab a lit cigarette from the ashtray, placing it to her lips with visibly trembling fingers.

"Nightmares about what?"

She took the cigarette from her lips and exhaled a cloud of smoke ahead of her. "About that shit we did, Keema," she said, switching to the left lane without even looking.

I shook my head with annoyance. This bitch just had to bring *that* shit up.

"Look, Keema, I know you not tripping, but I can't help thinking about it, girl. It's stressing me out."

The Mother Teresa sounding shit kinda worried me. I'd watched enough episodes of *CSI Miami* to know talk like that almost always led to somebody's black ass getting tossed in jail.

"So, what the hell does that mean? Are you thinking about going to the police or something?"

I eyed her carefully. If she answered wrong, I wasn't quite sure how I'd handle it at the moment. All I *did* know was the foul shit we'd secretly done could never get out to anyone.

Nobody.

It was the type of thing a bitch had to take to the grave.

One of them secrets you kill for.

"Quit looking at me like that," Imani said, noticing the disapproving stare my eyes were giving her. "And no, I'm not thinking about going to the damn police," she added.

"Then what the fuck are you thinking?"

Imani took another quick and nervous puff of the cigarette and exhaled while gliding back into the right lane. Suddenly, someone blew the horn causing her to jerk the car slightly. Her nerves were totally rattled.

"I don't know what I'm thinking. I'm just saying the shit got me fucked up in the head, okay?"

She shook her head.

I shook mine back repulsively.

"I can't sleep an entire night without waking up in cold sweats. I keep seeing that nigga's face in my dreams and hearing that damn gunshot. It's giving me the creeps, Keema."

My eyes narrowed. I focused on the small earring in her pudgy shaped nose as my voice became extra tense. "Did you tell anybody?"

Imani looked at me like I'd lost my mind. "What?"

"You heard me. I said did you tell anybody."

"Hell no!"

Another horn blew since we were driving so slow down a two lane street.

"You didn't tell anybody? A preacher, reverend, your momma, *anybody*?" I grilled, not totally convinced.

"No," she said point blankly, glancing at me then back to the windshield like I was crazy.

"Are you sure?"

"Hell yeah, I'm sure. Do you think I wanna go to the penitentiary for the rest of my life?"

"I don't know. You the one sitting here talking like you ready to confess and shit."

"It's not like that, Keema."

"Then what the fuck is it like, Imani? Please explain."

"I'm just saying the shit got me nervous. I never did no shit like that before."

"Well, we did it, bitch! Now, get over it."

She took another nervous puff of her cigarette, exhaling the smoke quickly. The sight looked nerve racking. I couldn't take much more.

"And quit smoking that damn cigarette all crazy like that," I told her. "You look like a fucking crack head chain smoker. You making me nervous."

"How is *my* smoking making *you* nervous?"

"Bitch, I don't know, but it is…so stop."

Imani shook her head and put the cigarette in the ashtray.

"Look," I told her, "as long as you keep your mouth shut, everything will be all good. Nobody knows nothing so we're not going to jail."

"It's not jail that scares me, Keema. That's not what I'm worried about."

"Then what are you tripping off of?"

She gave me a look of uneasiness.

"Spit it out."

"Girl, I'm scared of going to hell."

I couldn't believe this bitch. All I could do was shake my head and turn it toward the buildings that raced past by my window.

"I know you think I'm bugging, Keema, but I'm serious. We committed the ultimate sin."

"The ultimate sin?" I questioned in disbelief as I turned back to her. "What are you talking about?"

"Keema, you don't understand."

"Nah, Imani, it's *you* who don't understand. I don't want to talk about this shit any more. It's done and over with. Fuck that nigga. He's gone. And he ain't coming back." I turned my face back toward my window, done with the conversation.

Imani stared at the cars ahead. Her hands gripped the

13

wheel tightly as she made a fast turn causing the car to tilt back and forth for a few seconds. There were no sounds inside the car, and no words between us for several seconds. And now my nerves were bad all because of this hoe. Right now I had much more important shit to worry about like Shane sitting in jail for both the gun *and* the drugs. It also didn't help my conscience knowing the gun and the weed were actually mine. I had no idea whatsoever what I would do if and when Dupree showed up. He was missing…but that was nothing new. Our relationship had always been a see-saw. The nigga showed up on a Monday and sometimes came back on Thursdays. But whenever he surfaced again, how would I tell him that his autistic son was sitting in jail on gun and drug charges all because of me?

I turned to gaze out the window again, but this time my eyes were met with death. A nigga in all black, gripping what looked to be a pistol with a scope on it had me in a trance like state. He hung from the back driver's side window with a gun in hand perfectly balanced as his driver zig-zagged to get closer to the Honda. I gasped then attempted to hit Imani on the leg hoping she'd press forcefully on the gas giving me a chance to live.

Everything seemed to move in slow motion like some shit I'd seen in the movies. *Boyz in the Hood* was the first to come to mind. From the corner of my eye I could see the black Crown Vic less than four feet from my window, riding side by side like a nigga wanted to play bumper cars on the highway. My heart skipped twenty beats as I thought about what Imani had been saying. Was this some retaliation type shit for what we'd done? Maybe my girl had a reason to be paranoid?

My eyes zoomed in. There was only one driver and one assailant who thought he was an acrobat. He kept signaling for us to pull over yet he never took the big, black firearm off of me. I knew I had to get Imani to see what I was seeing without having this scary bitch panic and crash the car all at the same time. So, I figured I'd tell her under my breath so my assassin wouldn't fire off a few rounds after trying to read my lips.

Somehow my words had gotten stuck in my throat and I

14

couldn't even speak. I couldn't warn her.

My nipples hardened.

And the feeling of vomit rose from my stomach.

This nigga is tryna kill me, I thought.

And he would if we didn't pull over like he said.

"Imani, speed up!" I finally shouted. "This nigga got a gun!" Fear filled my voice and adrenaline exploded throughout my body.

"What!"

"Speed up! That nigga got a gun!" I repeated.

My head swiveled from Imani to the gunman then back to Imani.

The car now jerked. Then swerved from our lane to theirs. Suddenly, my body felt the Honda take off like a space ship being deployed.

Imani screamed to the top of her lungs as the car rammed us and my body hit the floor. Who woulda ever thought I'd go out like this?

THREE

Heavy breathing.

Then more breathing.

Then crying.

She's always crying.

I found myself crawling from the floor onto the seat as Imani pressed her head against the steering wheel howling like a wounded dog. She kept talking to herself, repeating all kinds of crazy shit and saying nothing was ever gonna go right for her in life.

I was pissed. Once I realized the guy who I thought had a gun really had a video camera just tryna film some bitches, I became enraged. But not at myself, at Imani. It was all her fault. Her paranoid ass now had me suspicious of every nigga I saw. I'd never hallucinated like that before. We'd run off the road into the gravel making fools of ourselves and would possibly be on You Tube within a fucking hour for free.

More crying followed from Imani as I sat back in my seat, still ranting.

"Toughen the fuck up! That crying bullshit ain't gonna get us nowhere!"

"I can't help it, Keema. I know I'm not gonna make it to see my twenty-fifth birthday."

Now, she was sniffling.

Imani and I had been friends since middle school. Always

in the same class, all the way to the eleventh grade when I decided to drop out. I knew her like the back of my hand and realized this shit was really getting to her. She'd never been so fragile with her feelings or ever let shit bother her this way. I was use to us hitting up all the parties in the hood and hitting niggas pockets that I hated to see her any other way. The fact that she'd pulled the trigger had her ass gone, and it was now driving me crazy. I thought about jumping out of the car into the middle of the street because she wouldn't stop ranting. Getting hit by a car would've been better than listening to her whining ass.

"Imani, get the fuck back on the road," I demanded as my cell phone rang. I recognized the number immediately.

"Awe shit," I mumbled as Imani put the car in drive.

The bitch was still staring off into space like a damn zombie.

"Hello," I said unenthused. It was time for my weekly sermon.

"Keema, where have you been?"

"What do you mean, where have I been? In my skin, Ma!"

"Don't use that tone with me. Now, I'm trying to better my life more and more each day, but you know how I can get down," she quickly threatened, then brought her voice back down to a comforting one. "I've been calling you for two days now."

"I've been busy. Smoking weed," I added sarcastically.

"I'm sure you're telling the truth. How many job interviews have you been on this week?"

"Twelve."

"You're lying," my mother fired.

I sighed heavily. "Then why are you questioning me?"

"Because my job as a mother is to get you on the right track. It was my fault for letting you drop out of school and I realize that. But I will not let you spend the rest of your life on welfare and throwing away your children's lives, too."

I wanted to tell her about my plans of moving to Arizona, but I wasn't sure if the time was right. If I told her I had plans on opening a slew of Day Spas she wouldn't believe me. She would say I couldn't do it, bringing a bitch's morale down. The crazy thing was that a part of me believed it was all to make her proud. I wanted to show her that I could make it out of this fucked up situation just like she did. But I decided against it all when I heard her ask about the kids.

"So, how's Dinero?"

"He's fine."

"Did you see about getting him in that early childhood program that I told you about?"

"Yep." I lied with a straight face.

"Okay. At least you did something right," she professed like I'd won an award from her. "I have something in the works for Cash and Treasure, too. As a matter of fact, I'm picking Treasure up from school today. I'll bring her home afterwards...gotta surprise for her."

My jaw hung low. *Picking up Treasure from school*?

I had to think...quick. My mind raced. I had to come up with something that made sense. My mother was witty just like me. It must've been a family trait. She wasn't old and slow like some of my homegirls' mothers. She was always on her toes. Then it hit me. I'd use her age as an excuse. It was the most believable bullshit I could come up with.

"Ma, don't do that, Treasure won't like it," I confessed with emotion. "I never wanted to tell you this but now you causing me to shoot straight from the hip."

"What are you talking about?"

"Look, Treasure told me she's embarrassed by you. She said everybody in her class got real grandmas, and that you too young."

"That's stupid, Keema."

"No, it's true." My voice hardened. "I mean, think about it. Whose grandmother is thirty-eight?"

"Keema, maybe you should focus on getting off welfare instead of entertaining silly ass remarks," she shot back. "My age is not a problem."

I had to think hard, ready for her next comeback. Imani

still had me fucked up and the way she drove crazily had my stomach churning with anxiety. I knew my mother couldn't say much about the age factor. Hell, we were only thirteen years apart which meant the bitch was fucking in the seventh grade if not before I was born. Now, she'd become this high achiever acting all high and mighty like she hadn't just lived in the same apartment building that I do now just two years ago.

"Look, Treasure's not going with you today. I gotta go. Bye," I said, abruptly ending the call.

All that talk about Treasure had me thinking again about how my kids were sitting down at CPS. That was most likely sure to mean I wasn't going to get my EBT card refilled this month unless I got them back beforehand somehow. It was also safe to assume white folks were going to be swarming all over my damn business, running in and out of my apartment, piss testing me, asking me all kinds of annoying questions, and asking my kids all kinds of crazy shit. It was going to be hectic.

This situation had thrown a huge monkey wrench in my plans. My upcoming move to Arizona was looking so close I could taste it before yesterday. Shit, I was honestly thinking about leaving Cash and Dinero's asses behind. What the fuck would I look like in hot ass Phoenix with a bunch of whining babies? Those two cock blocking lil niggas would just hold me up. Yeah, I was definitely hopping in my car and leaving at least one of them behind. But now my plan was on stand still. The police had my ten G's and my weed. They'd gotten Dupree's money too so I couldn't steal it from them as planned.

In my head I began to calculate all the shit I was getting from Social Services. I'd been doing pretty nicely with my EBT card, and WIC vouchers. Getting $300.00 per child, along with $200.00 for myself $1,100.00 was added to my card every month. But that didn't include what I got in food stamps. That was another $700.00, so altogether I cleared $1600.00 from the state. Dupree had even signed Shane's disability check over to me on top of the money he was paying me to take care of him. Plus, he had to give me extra money for Dinero since he was the only one of my three kids that was actually his. He'd even bought me the Dodge Charger so I could get Shane and the kids around easily. That boy needed around the clock supervision and Dupree's hustling didn't afford him enough time. Shane's mother had also bailed out on him when he was only three years old so besides Dupree, all he had was me. But now all that money I was making was being compromised. Besides the money I was making selling weed on the side, the kids were the nucleus of my finances. Without them I had a problem.

The turn of events pissed me off, but I wasn't going to roll over yet. In fact, my mind was already at work on conjuring up a new plan. I'd always had that talent when it came to money. Glancing over at Imani and seeing how somber she looked, I apologized for snapping on her. When she finally snapped out of her crazy ass mood and forgave me, I told her to stop by Dupree's strip club.

My mind was conjuring up a lie the closer we got to Frenchie's. I needed some money and the club always had some. Frenchie's was a legendary spot, started by Dupree's oldest brother Frenchie who was now dead as a door knob. But it made plenty of money, all day and night which meant Dupree was making money all day and night…on top of everything else he was involved in.

It was only 1:30 in the afternoon, but the strip club's parking lot was already filled with a few dozen cars when we pulled up. After parking only a few feet away from the front door, me and Imani hopped out of the car and headed inside. Moose, the club's bouncer and doorman, charged a dude ahead of us ten dollars to get in.

Looking around at all the dudes roaming about, I quickly calculated the money taken in at the door, the money from the bar, the dancers' pay out, and the money to rent the private rooms. Even this early in the day the club was still making a killing.

"What's good, Keema?" Moose asked over the sounds of Lil Wayne's song, *She Will*.

Moose was so black he was nearly purple. He stood about 6'5' and weighed a solid three hundred and twenty pounds. A nigga would've been crazy to fuck with him.

"Nothing," I replied looking inside. "Where my baby at?"

The club was filled with cigarette smoke as some thick bodied bitch in a g-string worked the stage real trifling and nasty like. Me personally, I never understood what made a dude get off on strippers. Them disease packing bitches sucked tons of dick every night, but men still loved to give up their money. I watched as niggas stood throughout the club clutching their drinks and watching her nasty ass as they talked shit to one another.

"Shit, I was just about to ask you the same question," Moose said.

My eyebrows crinkled. "He's not here?"

"Nope."

"That's odd." My mind quickly refocused on the money. "So, how much cash do you think y'all have pulled in so far today?"

Before Moose could answer my question, Rick, Dupree's brother, strolled up wearing a pair of dingy black sweat pants, a plain white t-shirt, and a pair of Prada tennis shoes. He wasn't known to be the best dresser, but his jewelry always made up for what lacked. Around his neck were two platinum chains filled with glittering crushed diamonds.

"Yo, Keema," he growled my way. "Why the fuck you askin' Moose some shit like that?"

"Because I'm part of the family business, right?" I questioned, then strolled in like I owned the place.

"Yeah, you fam, but you don't own shit."

All I could think about was how Rick and Dupree were the sole owners of about ten different businesses, thanks to the empire their brother left behind. They were paid….with no worries in life. Yet kept their money tight, never squandering on bitches. I needed to be the exception. My hand was out.

"Rick, I need some money, bad…can't wait either."

"Where's Dupree?"

I shrugged my shoulders. "I don't know. You know how he likes to pull disappearing acts on me all the damn time. That nigga can go days without calling sometimes. I came here hoping to find him because I need some moulah. But since he not here, you the next best thing."

Rick ignored my request. "Ain't nobody seen that nigga in a couple of days."

I shrugged again. "He might be with some of them other chicks."

"Go 'head wit' that shit, Keema. You know you his main girl. And besides Shane, and the club is his pride and joy. So, it's real odd for him not to come by and at least check on the finances."

"He ain't been by the house in a couple of days either," I revealed.

Rick shook his head, then breathed a little harder proving that if he kept gaining weight he'd surely die of a heart-attack by winter. It amazed me how he and his brother reminded me of Gerald Levert in the face, but Rick was just the sloppy, extra big one in the family.

"Knowin' that nigga, he probably made an out of town run," Rick advised.

It is possible, I thought to myself.

Dupree always made spur of the moment trips out of state to chase money. But something about this particular time had me thinking otherwise. I thought about schooling Rick about a previous threat, but quickly decided against it. Now wasn't the time.

"How my nephew doin'?" he asked protectively.

"Damn. You always asking about Shane like Dinero don't exist."

"Awe, don't even go there, Keema. You know Shane the one I gotta worry about. Dinero gon' be alright."

"Yeah, okay. Whatever, Rick. Keep treating my baby wrong. Shane's good," I lied. The lil nigga was probably getting bullied for his lunch tray as we spoke.

"Where he at?"

23

"With the baby sitter," I responded.

"Well, when you pick him up, tell 'em his uncle said what's up and I'll be ova to see 'em later in the week."

My heart damn near stopped.

"I hear you. But what about that money?"

Rick breathed a heavy sigh then whipped out a knot thicker than a double- decker sandwich. I watched as he peeled a few twenties off making me horny which each second that passed. After handing me the money, he stuffed the rest back inside his front pocket.

"Nigga, this is only two hundred. What am I supposed to do with this? I got four kids to take care of?"

"Keema, take that shit up wit' Dupree. I never fucked you, he did. I gotta run to check on the car wash," he told me right before packing up his shit.

"Fuck you, Rick," I told him with an attitude. "I'ma own this bitch in a few years."

Moments later me and Imani were headed back out to the car. My mind wouldn't let go of the fact that Dupree hadn't been to the club in a few days so I pulled out my cell phone and called him. Just as I thought, there was no answer. As soon as I pressed the end button and stuffed the phone back in my pocket, it rang. Quickly I snatched it out and answered.

"Hello."

"Hello," the caller on the other end said.

It was my caseworker at Social Services.

My eyes rolled, knowing she was calling about the kids.

"Keema Newell?"

I blew my breath. Hard. "Yeah, it's me."

"We have a problem," she blared.

I clowned the bitch. "Yeah, yeah, yeah. What's new?"

"A lot, Ms. Newell. It seems as if your monthly disbursement could be affected this month?"

That shit got my attention immediately. I sat straight up, ready to listen. They'd had my kids only one day and was already geared up to fuck with my money. Sure enough, she wanted me to be downtown at her office bright and early the next morning.

"Yeah, alright, whatever," I said, hanging up the phone before she could finish her final sentence.

FOUR

After rolling onto my stomach and wiping saliva from the corner of my mouth with the back of my hand, my eyes opened groggily to look at the alarm clock beside my bed. The surprising bright red digital numbers made them open wide and in fear.

"Shit," I said, quickly slipping from underneath the sheets naked and jumping out of the bed. I was running super late for my appointment with my case worker.

Quentin stirred in his sleep and farted as he lay beneath the sheets completely naked. I'd called him last night to come through and give me some dick. I made him pay for the pussy first though. Best believe I ain't ever been the type to let a nigga get his dick wet for free. Before a dude could get up in this good pussy, I had to get up in his pockets. That's real talk. Me and my kids needed shit.

Quentin was a trick. I mean a big ass trick. He hustled in the streets relentlessly, pushed a CL Benz, had plenty of money, and no problems spending it. He truly believed in sharing, which was my favorite type of nigga. I never had time for the stingy ones, just ones like Quentin, ones who didn't need much prodding and convincing.

I was taking a chance last night though by fucking him at my apartment. Usually I would fuck at a nigga's spot, Raven's house, or a hotel room. Shit, sometimes I'd fuck in the backseat of a nigga's whip if the money was right. Dupree didn't believe in calling before stopping by. He was the type who liked to just pop up so fucking dudes at my spot wasn't a good idea. He'd be ready to murk a nigga if he caught him up in here, and I definitely didn't need that. But last night I didn't feel like jumping through a bunch of hoops. My pussy was in need of dick and my pockets were in need of cash.

Last night I was simply going to fuck Quentin for an hour or so. Then I was going to put his ass out. But he wound up flipping the script on my ass. Quentin made me cum so many times that he literally fucked a bitch to sleep.

After walking to the bathroom and turning on the shower, I headed back to the bedroom and shoved Quentin's shoulder. "Wake up," I told him. "This ain't the Hilton. It's time to go."

"Fuck that," he groaned, turning over and attempting to go back to sleep. "A nigga tryna sleep. Leave me alone."

"Real talk, Quentin." I shoved his shoulder harder this time. "It's time for you to roll out. I got shit to do."

"Your ass ain't got nothin' to do. Quit lyin' and let a nigga sleep, damn."

This time I hit him with a pillow. "Get up, Quentin!"

"Shit!" He sat up and looked at me like he was about to make the fatal mistake of putting his hands on me. I didn't do that domestic violence shit. "What the fuck is wrong with you?"

"I told your ass I got shit to do. Now, put your clothes on and kick rocks."

"This is bullshit. What you gotta do that's so damn important?"

"I gotta go downtown to Social Services. I'm already late."

"You trippin'," he said, lying back down.

"Stop playing, Quentin! Get up!"

This time he sighed angrily and jumped up. As I opened my drawer to get some panties, he walked up behind me, grabbed my wrist, and turned me towards him with his dick poking straight at me. Beginning to kiss me around my neck, he placed a hand between my thighs.

"I want some more of this pussy first."

"Hell no, Quentin," I said, pushing him off of me. "I told you I'm running late. What part of that don't you understand? I gotta get my kids back, damn it!"

"Fuck all that!" He grabbed me again. "Just make another appointment."

"No, and stop grabbing on me like I'm your damn child."

"Bitch, quit all that jaw jacking. You know you like this shit."

He was all over me while lifting me up onto the dresser.

Fuck it, I thought to myself. The dick *was* good. But more importantly, it would give me the opportunity to get some more money out of his dumb ass.

"Alright," I said, placing my hands against his chest and pushing him back. "I'm gonna give you some more pussy but I need my loot first." I extended a hand for payment.

"What loot?" He looked at me like I was crazy.

"Keep playing dumb. You know I don't fuck for free."

"Bitch, you trippin'."

My hand was still extended.

"Damn, Keema. I gave your ass five hundred last night," he said.

"That was last night. We talking about now…morning pussy. A bitch gotta get paid. And I charge extra if it's before 11a.m."

He stared at me.

"Nigga, don't look at me like that. We both know you got it. And we both know you ain't gon' do shit with it but blow it on weed and the strip club. Shit, if you can make it rain on a bitch in the club who *ain't* giving you pussy, you can make it rain on a bitch who is."

He shook his head, knowing I had a point. "Damn, you a high priced bitch."

"Whatever."

He snatched up his jeans from the floor, reached into a pocket and pulled out a fat wad of folded bills. My eyes glimmered at the sight. He peeled off a stack of tens and twenties, placed the rest of money back, then walked back over to me. As soon as he placed the cash into my hand I began counting it like a bank teller, loving the feel of each bill as they slid between my fingers. It was about two-fifty, not my goal, but anything extra worked for now.

"Alright, Keema, it's time to fuck," Quentin said, grabbing my thighs and pulling me towards him.

Without even allowing me to put the money down he was balls deep in my pussy. The dresser started to rock back and forth with his power and rhythm. Leaning back against the wall I let my eyes close and my thighs open wide.

"Oh, shit," I moaned.

Our thighs slapped together loudly, echoing throughout the room. I could also feel his balls repeatedly smacking against my asshole. The sound and feel made me begin to fuck him back.

"That's right," he boasted, loving the way I returned his strokes. "Fuck this dick, bitch."

The dresser banged against the wall much louder now, sounding like it was going to knock a hole into it. It was also hitting the wall much faster now as our pace quickened. I opened my eyes to see his thick dick as it slid in and out of my nest over and over again. I loved that shit. Something about the sight always turned me on more and made me fuck harder. Now was no different. Seeing that dick splitting me wide open immediately got me wet. Fuck my appointment. *I'd get there when I get there.*

As usual the Social Services' lobby was packed with young hoodrats and their whining ass kids. Despite signs posted all over the place telling everyone "No Cell Phone Use," these bitches were carrying on the loudest most annoying conversations while their kids ran through the lobby like gang bangers tearing up shit.

I hated coming down to this place. But in order to keep

my government assistance, I had to come down here every several months to see my caseworker; rain, sleet, or snow. For about an hour I had to look in her damn face and listen to her ask me a bunch of questions about my personal business and how my job searches were coming along. My answers to the question were always the same. They never changed. Whatever it took to keep the money coming in. In my opinion, the visits were a waste of time. She could ask me whatever she needed over the phone.

Looking around at all these broads made me think about my situation. *Damn, I hadn't planned on being one of them for this long.* When I first got on welfare and began to learn all of the tricks of milking the system, it seemed like I'd hit the jackpot. A bitch didn't have to punch a clock or break my back. All I had to do was sit and wait for my EBT card to fill up with money every month. But eventually the shit grew tiresome and I saw it for what it was. Of course, my mother had been preaching the shit all along. I'd expected to be living much better by now; instead I was still in the projects, still fucking with no good niggas, and still having to answer to these white folks for my money. The realization made my eyes roll at the women sitting around me.

I was dressed in a white RIP Whitney Houston t-shirt, jeans, and a raggedy pair of Nikes. My hair was also pulled back in a plain looking ponytail. Obviously that wasn't the way I usually got down. My closet was filled with the latest Gucci shoes and Louis Vuitton bags. But in order to keep the money coming in, I had to come in looking like a bummy bitch, one who was definitely looking like life was giving her a hard time. I also made sure I parked my Charger a couple blocks away and pretended like I'd caught the bus. My case worker was *super* nosey.

As I chewed the tips of my nails, my eyes looked up at the clock for the fourth time. I'd already been out here waiting for nearly two hours. I guess her punk ass called herself trying to teach me a lesson for showing up late. It was so damn ignorant. If she was going to make me wait out here for this long, she could've had the decency to tell me. I could've had something important to do. Games like this one pissed me off. Every time I

31

came for my appointment the pathetic trick acted like I was here asking for *her* money, like I was trying to get in *her* pockets. The shit was unnecessary. I was here for The Government's money, which them greedy white folks had plenty of. All my caseworker had to do was quit hating and go ahead and set that shit out like her job dictated.

Finally the door to the back offices opened up. Ms. Vines, my caseworker, stuck her head out. She was wearing an out dated pant suit too tight for her fat frame, and a pair of cheap, Payless looking heels, which she seemed to have on each and every time I came. Her dark skin was dry and acne filled, which came from drinking too many of them damn Diet Cokes she always had on her desk. And today her short, bob styled wig was matted to the left side of her head.

"Keema Newell!" she called out.

"It's about damn time," I whispered as I stood from my chair and quickly walked past her, anxious to find out when I was getting my kids back and get this visit over with.

The two of us headed to her tiny office. As we walked I could smell a double cheese burger with extra onions seeping from her pores. Once we reached her office she plopped down behind her desk, opened a drawer and pulled out my case file. She opened it and sat it on her desk next to the half-empty bottle of Diet Coke.

"Was my Medicaid application accepted?" I asked sitting down. We'd discussed me getting full coverage during the last visit. I was hoping I'd be approved before the next disbursement, which should be here in ten days." I was always trying to milk her ass for whatever I could get. "Dinero's doctor really thinks he may have a disability. Oh, and don't forget you were trying to see if there were any openings at that nice public housing complex I keep hearing about called Orchard Ridge. I could use more room for my kids to run around in."

"Keema, right now the Medicaid application and new housing is the least of your worries."

Here this bitch goes. My eyes wanted to roll, but I forced

them to remain still. Despite how much I hated her, Ms. Vines approved my money so I had to be cool.

"We need to begin this visit with you telling me about why the children are in Baltimore City custody." Ms. Vines eyeballed me. "That's the reason I requested the meeting."

"The police kicked my door in two days ago pointing guns at me and my kids," I told her. "They told me somebody lied and said I was selling drugs out of my apartment. Can you believe that?"

"Why would someone do that?"

"You know how black people are, Ms. Vines. They nosey and always want to get stuff started. Just because I don't associate with none of them, they like to mess with me. I'm out looking for jobs everyday and they hating on that. That's all that is."

"Keema, the police don't just kick in doors for no reason. They do investigations before they do something that extreme."

I shook my head. "Not this time, they didn't. They kicked mine in for nothing."

Ms. Vines gave me a smirk and looked down at my case file. "Keema, the police found a gun and marijuana in the apartment," she said, raising her head to look at me.

"But it wasn't mine," I said, trying to sound convincing.

"Then whose was it?"

"Shane's."

"Your boyfriend's son?"

"Yeah, I didn't even know he had the stuff."

"So, you had no idea, huh?"

"I really didn't."

"But doesn't he have autism?"

"Yeah, that's why I'm so surprised. I'm starting to wonder if the autism thing is just an act. You know autism is a brain problem that makes it hard to communicate. But if he selling drugs his communicating must be fine."

"Keema…"

I cut her off since she hadn't been convinced yet. "His father told me that his autism only meant he'd have social impair-

33

ments and some mild character flaws, but this is too much. As a matter of fact, I'm thinking about telling his daddy he needs to find Shane another place to stay. I can't have that kind of stuff around my kids."

She stared at me for a moment, causing me to nibble on my nails again. I always did that when I was nervous. Right now I didn't quite know what was going through her mind, but the look on her face showed me she still didn't quite believe me.

"Ms. Vines, I miss my babies," I whimpered. "They're my world. I haven't even been able to sleep since the police took them." I stopped to sniffle before continuing, "And it's breaking my heart so bad I went to talk to my pastor this morning. He prayed with me. That's why I was late to see you. Oh God, Ms. Vines, when will I be getting them back?"

Ms. Vines leaned forward and folded her hands on the desk. "Keema, do you have any idea how serious this situation is? There was a gun underneath one of your children's mattress and drugs in a cereal box."

"But they weren't mine," I whined. "I didn't even know that stuff was there. I swear to God in Heaven I didn't."

"I find that hard to believe, Keema."

"Do you think I would actually have a gun and drugs around my kids?" I asked in disbelief.

"You tell me," Ms. Vines responded. "The police also stated they found a lit blunt in your apartment."

"That was Shane's, too."

"You mean to tell me that you didn't know he was smoking? You never smelled it?"

"I told you that autism thing may be a front. He's real slick."

She leaned back into her chair and looked at me strangely.

"I'm not lying, Ms. Vines. I would never put my kids in harm's way like that."

She exhaled. "Keema, I'm going to be straight forward with you. "You've been on assistance for several years, and haven't shown any urge to find gainful employment."

I slammed my hand on the desk. "I go on job interviews all the time!"

"Let me finish, Keema," she said sternly. "You're always late for our appointments, and you've failed multiple drug tests. To be honest with you, if it wasn't for the kids, I would've taken you off of assistance a long time ago."

I looked at her pitifully, biting my nails again.

"The system is in place to empower you, not enable you Keema," she preached.

"I know, Ms. Vines. That's what my mother tells me all the time. And I swear I'm trying my hardest. I've made mistakes in the past, but I'm a good person and I love my children."

She looked at me with no emotion. The fat bitch was pissing me off, but I didn't show it. I stayed in character despite the fact that she was trying to give me such a hard time.

"It's so hard out here for a single black mother, Ms. Vines." Tears appeared in my eyes.

Moments later, my cell phone rang. Recognizing Imani's number, I pressed the decline button and told Ms. Vines, "Me and my babies will be in the streets without assistance. Please don't make my babies suffer for *my* mistakes. I'll do better. I swear to God I will."

She stared at me for a moment. Finally she said, "I'm not going to cut your assistance, but you definitely need to get more serious about complying with the rules. As far as getting your kids back, that's up to CPS. I'm pretty sure they'll be in touch with you very soon."

Imani's ring tone erupted from my phone again. Once again I pressed the decline button. As Ms. Vines and I spoke more, Imani called again.

"Looks like someone's really trying to reach you," Ms. Vines pointed out. "It may be CPS."

I knew it wasn't but answered anyway with annoyance in my voice. "Hello."

"Keema," Imani said.

"Yeah, what?"

WELFARE GRIND BY: KENDALL BANKS

Ms. Vines stared at me.

"Someone's following me," Imani said nervously.

"What do you mean following you?"

"I mean there's a car behind me, Keema. It's been following my ass for the past twenty minutes. Everywhere I turn its there."

"Girl, you're paranoid. We went through that yesterday, right?"

"No, this is for real. Keema. Something's telling me it has to do with what me and you did. I can feel it."

"Look, I'm busy right now. Can you talk about this later?"

"Keema, wait."

"Imani, shit, I said I'm busy." My voice soared.

Ms. Vines' eyebrows rose.

"Now, quit fucking calling me!" I shouted and pressed the end button.

"Is everything okay?" Ms. Vines inquired.

"Yeah, I'm good. Now, about the kids and my Medicaid…"

FIVE

Thirty minutes later, my visit with Ms. Vines was wrapping up. We were discussing my Medicaid application and I was explaining how desperately I needed her to put a good word in with CPS so the kids could be back in my custody before the first of the month. If they weren't, that shit would interfere with my July disbursement.

My phone rang.

Glancing at the number and not recognizing it I figured it might be CPS, so I answered meekly. "Hello?"

"Keema Newell?" a female voice asked. She sounded white.

"Yeah, this her."

Ms. Vines stared at me again.

"Ms. Newell, this is Nurse Martin at Mercy Hospital. Do you have a boyfriend by the name of Devaughn Preston?"

My eyes widened. "Yes, I do. Why, did something happen?"

"Ms. Newell, I'm afraid, Mr. Preston has been in a very bad car accident. He's been heavily sedated for the past few days, but today his medication was finally decreased. He's been requesting to see you all day. He gave us your number."

Before I knew it, I was off the phone and telling Ms. Vines I had to go. After darting out of her office and out of the building, I dashed a couple of blocks over to my car, hopped in and headed directly to the hospital. As soon as I got there I rushed inside to the front desk and asked for Dupree's room. Blinding moments later I was at his bedside.

Dupree's thick, muscular arms were pierced with tubes that led to the machines beside his bed. His arm was heavily bandaged along with his shirtless body. Swollen lips, cuts and bruises were just the start to his visible problems. His hands, which had a tiny tattoo on each individual finger and knuckle, also had several cuts.

The sight scared me. I was always so used to seeing Dupree hustling, and running shit, seeing him like this was so surreal. He was never the type to rest or sit still.

"Dupree," I whispered as I neared his bed. My body shook and tears welled up in my eyes.

Dupree's eyes opened slowly at the sound of my voice. He looked startled and scared. I'd never seen him worried or afraid of anything. He was always calm and in charge.

"It's me, baby," I said quickly, placing my hands in his. "It's Keema."

For a moment he looked as if he was allowing his eyes to adjust to my face. "Keema," he finally said, looking relieved but still nervous.

"Yeah, it's me, sweetheart."

His face grew wildly animated again. He squeezed my hand tightly with his large, cold hand. "Did they hurt you?" he asked quickly. "I swear I'll kill them if they did."

"Baby, I'm okay," I assured him. "No one hurt me."

"Did they follow you here?"

He was starting to make me nervous. He kept rambling.

"Did who follow me here?"

"*Anybody*," Dupree said slowly, raising his upper body from the bed and staring wildly into my face. "Did *anybody* at all follow you here?"

The words were spilling from his mouth at a nearly rapid fire pace.

"No, baby." I glared at him even more so than before.

WELFARE GRIND BY: KENDALL BANKS

"Who would follow me? What are you talking about?"

"Look, Keema, you've got to take Shane, Dinero and your other kids away. Move out of your apartment, today."

"Why?"

"Because the niggas who tried to kill me may find out where you live and come after you guys. Everybody knows how much I love my boys."

My eyes expanded at the mention of the word *kill*. My heart stopped "Dupree, who tried to kill you?"

"Look, Keema, don't worry about that right now." He stopped mid sentence like it hurt to speak. After taking a couple of deep breaths, he continued. "I just need you to take my sons and move out of that apartment. It's not safe. If I wouldn't have gotten away, they would've killed me. I'm supposed to be dead right now. My car flipped two times."

Dupree had to be smoking crack if he thought I was just going to up and move out of my apartment on the spur of the moment because of some bullshit he'd gotten himself into. My rent was only fifty dollars a month; lights and gas included. Where else could I go in Baltimore and live like that? I was never leaving that good rent until my shit in Arizona was secured and ready for me to move there. Fuck that. I wasn't leaving my apartment.

"This shit hurts," he whispered.

"Where are you hurting?"

"Everywhere. The doctor told me I only fractured my ribs in three places and my arm, but my entire body is in pain. I can barely breathe."

I ran my fingers through his well maintained dreads. "Well, it definitely could've been worse."

Grabbing my arm he said, "Keema, you've got to go. I mean that shit."

I knew Dupree had money and was most likely offering to take care of me. He'd always talked about making me wifey. He would always picture himself coming home to a cooked meal every night and some good head after I'd put the kids to bed. All that was fine and dandy for some broads, but I wasn't ready for all that yet. My mind was still on heading to Arizona as a business owner- *single* and possibly minus a few kids.

Looking into his eyes I could see a deep seeded fear in him, like he'd seen the devil himself. For a moment he looked like a total stranger to me. My, firm, two hundred sixty pound Mandingo had gotten weak.

"It ain't safe to stay there," he continued. "These niggas ain't playing no games. If they'll try to kill me on a crowded highway, what the hell do you think they'll do to you and my seeds? They'll kill you guys in a heartbeat." He looked around the room quickly and then back at me. "Where's Shane?"

"Huh?" I asked dumbfounded, not quite knowing how to answer him.

He'd caught me off guard with the question. *Damn*, I thought to myself, once again reminding me of the dilemma I was facing. I still had absolutely no idea how I was going to break the news to Dupree. I hadn't really given it too much thought since getting out of jail. I'd been too busy trying to figure out a way to get my cash flow up to par.

Worriedly Dupree looked at me. "Where's my son, Keema? Where's Shane?"

"He's with Imani." I blurted the first lie that came to mind. "He's okay."

"Are you sure?"

"Yes, you know I wouldn't let anything bad happen to him."

"Keema, I'd loose my mind if something happened to my son. With his sickness, he needs extra protection. I'm not as worried about Dinero. You've got to get outta that apartment."

I turned away from Dupree, unable to face him after knowing what I'd done to Shane. After sitting down in a chair, I nervously grabbed a Glamour magazine someone must've left behind for the last resident. I began to flip through it, just needing to avoid eye contact with Dupree. I kept thinking about what would happen when he called Rick and told him to check on Shane. They loved that damn crazy ass boy.

Dupree leaned back into his pillows.

As he spoke to me my ears weren't listening. Whatever he was saying wasn't registering at all. Surprisingly as he laid there having barely survived a car accident, my mind was hoping Ms. Vines would be able to talk CPS into giving me back my kids within the next ten days before the next disbursement. Yeah, Dupree had problems, but I had problems of my own. And mine were my first obligation.

Suddenly, as my eyes looked at an ad for a pair of YSL pumps, an idea formed, one that made me lift my eyes from the pages and stare off into a distance for a moment. I now knew the perfect way to get big money fast. It would be risky though.

"Make sure you move soon," Dupree said, his words now registering clearly in my ears again. "Use some of the money I got stashed in the house. Don't spend it all though."

Funny. "I will baby. Did you tell Rick what happened yet?"

"Nah, you were the first person I had the nurse to call. I need you to tell that nigga what's up. Tell 'em to stay away. Just call me. And to watch his back."

Perfect. With my new idea in mind, I jumped up from my seat and tossed the magazine aside. "Okay, baby," I said, quickly walking over and kissing him on the cheek. "Just give me ten days and I'll be out of there."

"Keema, ten days is too long."

"I gotta go, baby." I headed for the door, refusing to let him break my stride. I had business to handle.

"Where you going?"

"I've got to go handle something, sweetheart."

"Keema!"

Letting Dupree's shouts go unanswered, I walked quickly out into the hallway and hopped onto the elevator. When I got downstairs, my feet briskly carried me across the parking lot to my car. Once inside I cranked the engine and pulled out of the lot, hoping my idea would work. Twenty minutes later, I pulled into Frenchie's lot. Happy Hour was in full swing. I hopped

41

out of the car and pranced inside. Music was playing loudly as Rick and Moose were conversing at the front door.

"What's up, Keema?" Rick asked.

"I need to holla at you for a minute," I told him.

He looked at me worriedly. "You okay?"

"Nah, I'm good," I assured him. "But it's important and it's personal."

"Alright," he said and led me to an empty corner of the club. "What's up?" he asked.

"I found Dupree."

"Oh shit. Where is he?"

"I can't tell you?"

Rick's face instantly twisted. "What the fuck do you mean you can't tell me? That's my brother."

"It was his idea, not mine. He told me not to tell you or anyone else."

"Well, is he alright?"

"Yeah, but he told me to come by and get the money out of the registers and make a deposit for him."

Rick looked tremendously skeptical. "What?" He frowned.

"Yeah, I know it sounds crazy," I told him after seeing his doubtful expression. "But Dupree told me to let you know it was important. He said he would tell you about it later."

Still looking unconvinced, Rick paused before speaking. "Why didn't he call me?"

"Look, Dupree never tells me anything about y'all business. I don't know why you haven't heard from him. All I know is that he told me he's doing this to protect you."

"Protect me? I beat niggas for fun, Keema. Why would I need protection? That shit don't sound right."

"Rick, don't you think I know that?" I asked, placing my hands on my hips. "Don't shoot the damn messenger. I'm just doing what I was told. You know he's the boss."

After several more moments of nerve racking questions and answers, Rick finally did what he was told but with reluctance. Handing me the money zipped in a rectangular shaped black leather bag he said, "Tell that nigga I said call me ASAP."

"I got you," I told him and headed towards the door surprised at how easily I'd gotten that off. *Damn, I should've thought of this sooner*.

"Alright, Keema," Moose said, sitting beside the door. "Watch yourself tonight."

"You too, nigga." I returned glancing at him. But as I glanced back at the bar just before walking out, I saw a face I recognized, an unmistakable face from my past. The sight made my blood run cold. He sat at the bar staring directly at me, his eyes silently broadcasting what he was going to do to me if I said anything to him in front of everyone.

"Shit," I said and dashed out of the door.

Six

I left Frenchie's mad as hell. I'd called Rayquan's ass over five times, back to back so I could find out what the fuck he was tryna pull. Of course he didn't answer. As my car did seventy on 695, I smoked the Newport just as wildly and nervously as Imani was smoking hers the other day. As both of my hands tightly clutched the steering wheel at that corny ten o'clock and two o'clock position they teach you in driver's school, they trembled nonstop. My heart began to beat like a drum against the inside of my chest at an unhealthy rate. Thoughts were bombarding my mind more than heavily and from countless directions. The pressure just wouldn't stop.

"Damn," I said, banging my fist against the steering wheel in anger at the most recent complication. *Was that nigga in the club waiting to talk to Rick*? I wondered. *Was he tryna set me up*? "I can't believe that shit!"

Minutes later, I quickly exited the highway with its Hemi growling, as I made my way through evening traffic to Lexington Market. I whipped and weaved anxiously in and out of traffic on Paca Street until I reached the parking lot's entrance and pulled in. It was packed from end to end and took me nearly ten minutes to find a car pulling out of a space. Unfortunately, a silver Buick Lesabre was waiting to pull into it. I'd had enough of riding around looking for a space and I definitely wasn't going to do anymore searching with this one staring me dead in the face. As soon as the exiting car allowed me enough room to maneuver my way into its spot, I quickly whipped my candy apple red baby right into the space, causing the old white lady behind the wheel of the Lesabre to angrily blow her horn.

"Fuck you, bitch! Your damn reflexes are too slow!" I shouted to her as I shut off the car, grabbed my purse, and jumped out headed directly towards the market while carelessly tossing my cigarette near the gas tank of a white convertible.

The old lady mumbled something to me as she slowly rolled past, forced to find another space. I simply gave the decrepit dried up hoe the middle finger and quickly kept it moving, never slowing or breaking stride. I had an appointment to keep.

I reached into my purse as I walked and snatched my cell phone out. Immediately my fingers began to press in that sorry muthafucka Rayquan's number again. I was so pissed off at him that my fingers kept jamming the wrong numbers, causing me to have to hang up several times before his number was finally dialed correctly. With the phone pressed tightly to my ear I listened impatiently to each and every ring.

"Hello?" he finally answered.

Just the sound of his voice annoyed me more than I already was. There was music playing in the background loudly. Voices and laughter could also be heard. I shook my head at the background noise on the other end. The dumb muthafucka was still at the Frenchie's. My blood pressure was about to fly through the roof. There was also a little skepticism brewing inside of me. I wasn't quite sure what the fuck he was doing there anyway. I just knew it was one of the last places he was supposed to be after what me and him had going on between us.

"Are you hooked on phonics, Rayquan!" I screamed into the phone, causing people walking through the lot to do double takes. Parents looked at me with twisted faces as they passed by with their young children.

"Bitch, watch how you talk to me," he ordered.

"Fuck that!" I returned fiercely, holding the phone to my ear tighter than before. My eyes glanced around to see more people staring. Usually I wouldn't give a shit about who heard me cursing someone out. This conversation was different though. Secrets were involved. "Damn nosey muthafuckas," I said, realizing I had to lower my voice.

"Fuck that," I repeated to Rayquan but in a much lower voice. The anger and fury was still there. "Do you need to go to a special school to learn how to kill a nigga? Do you need special classes? Huh? Are you fucking slow?"

"I slipped up," he admitted. "I was shootin' at the nigga, but he made it to his car somehow and drove off."

"You slipped up?"

"Yeah, but at least I made him flip in the car a few times."

"Muthafucka, how hard can it be to kill someone? That's your specialty, right?"

"Look, I just ran into a complication. That's all."

I couldn't believe this goofy muthafucka.

"That's obvious," I told him. "I realized that when I went to go visit the nigga in the hospital."

"Calm down, Keema."

"Calm down, my ass. And don't say my name damn it! I paid you good money to *kill* that nigga, not put him in the hospital so he could possibly find out later on that I'm the bitch who set him up. You know Rick and Dupree can be ruthless when they need to be."

"Just chill out. Damn. Calm…"

"Don't tell me to chill out. Fuck that bullshit. This can come back to bite me in the ass."

"I'm gonna handle it. I won't miss next time."

"You damn right! You betta not fucking miss next time. Don't play with me! I want the job done right. I want that nigga covered in six feet of dirt as soon as possible. If he ain't, I'm sending niggas after your ass to get my money back. You feel me?"

The doors of the market slid open as I walked inside.

"Ease up with them threats, Keema."

"Fuck you, Rayquan! Get the job done!"

"I said I'm gon' handle the nigga. Just relax."

"And why the hell are you at that damn club?" I questioned. Suspicion was beginning to peek. During the entire drive over I wondered if he'd been at the club possibly telling Rick what I had paid him to do.

"I had to meet somebody," Rayquan said as if it wasn't a big deal. "I'm leavin' out the door now anyway."

"There's a million different places in Baltimore to meet someone. Why couldn't you meet somewhere else?"

"Keema, you bein' too damn paranoid."

"Nah, nigga, I think I'm not being paranoid enough. Who did you have to meet?"

"Just chill out. It's nobody you need to worry about."

"Rayquan, if I find out you're trying to set me up…"

"Look, Keema, I'm just as deep in this shit as you are. *I'm* the one who tried to kill Dupree. Now, chill out and let me do what you paid me to do. I got it."

I wasn't assured but before I could respond he hung up.

I was so disgusted that I wanted to slam my phone against a wall as hard as I could. I needed to break something or hit somebody. My frustrations needed to be vented terribly.

There was so much riding on that job being handled, a whole lot of money, my future, possibly my life. The nigga Frenchie that me and Imani had killed set it all in motion.

Frenchie was Dupree's and Rick's older brother. He was a successful businessman and practically a millionaire. The nigga had a small string of clubs, detail shops, hair salons, cell phone stores, and other businesses spread out all over Maryland. The strip club Dupree now owned had also been his. He gave it to Dupree as a birthday gift, absolutely no strings attached.

I wasn't sure just how many businesses and properties had been left to Dupree and Rick or how much they were worth. Dupree never told me that. I was sure the net worth was somewhere in the lower millions though. What I was also sure of was that he'd designated both Rick and Dupree the primary beneficiaries of everything in his will, which included the businesses and properties. He'd also named both Dinero and Shane as the secondary beneficiaries, which meant that if Dupree and Rick died, the kids would get everything. And since I'm the children's guardian and care giver, everything would ultimately become mine.

Everything was going smoothly. Me and Imani had murked Frenchie real good. But the cops bussing in and unexpectedly taking the kids was the first road block. Now, with Dupree having survived the attempt on his life, shit was at a total stand still. Until I got those problems settled, I couldn't move forward at all.

After walking past countless shops and stands I saw Peppi waiting for me at the food court. He smiled brightly and waved me over. When I reached him, he gave me a warm hug and offered me the seat across the table from him.

Peppi was half Black, half Mexican with a gorgeous sun tanned complexion. He was tall, slender and handsome, and had long, jet black hair which he always kept in a pony tail. He was dressed in a starched, white button down, black slacks, and black Feragamo loafers. On his wrist was a platinum, three time-zoned Rolex.

"Hungry?" he asked politely.

"Nah, I'm good."

I was entirely too nervous to even imagine eating anything. Although I was facing him, my mind was still thinking about the conversation I'd just had with that damn idiot a moment ago. If he didn't get the second try right, I could possibly be in some huge life threatening trouble.

"You sure?" Peppi inquired. "It's my treat."

I shook my head. "No, thanks."

"Alright, then let's get straight to business. Peppi has got the greatest news in the world for you."

I hated that he referred to himself in third person most of the time, but I sure could use some good news. I leaned forward in my chair as the tables around us were filled with people talking and eating.

"Things in Arizona are moving very fast, much faster than I had expected. The build-out of the day spa is near completion."

He was animated as he spoke showing his perfect set of sparkling white teeth.

"I thought you said it would be several months."

"That was when it first started. Peppi had no idea the contractors would work so thoroughly. I've worked with them before so I know how good they are. But I had no idea they would knock this project out so quickly. It's far ahead of schedule. Peppi still can't believe it."

Damn, that was good news.

"Check this out," Peppi said, pulling a folder from the chair beside him. He pulled out several photos and handed them to me. "The place is fascinating."

I looked through the pictures and loved what I was seeing. I was speechless and felt all gooey inside. *My own place of business*. Originally the spot was just an abandoned field. Now, there was a two storied nearly completed day spa sitting there. Keema's Day Spa was what I would call it. The shit was like a dream, one that I never wanted to wake up from. Seeing something go from an idea to reality was an amazing thing.

"That's not it," Peppi said, looking like he was going to explode with enthusiasm. "Peppi has more good news for you."

I listened closely. Nothing around me existed.

He leaned forward, glanced around, and lowered his voice. "The dude I've been trying to hook you up with will be ready to meet with you as soon as you get to Arizona. He truly wants to do business. He wants to give you ten pounds of weed for three thousand dollars."

My eyes widened. Those prices were unheard of. Quickly, I did the math in my head. I'd easily make fifteen grand off the deal, I realized. I would be all the way set. My plan was coming together perfectly.

Peppi was the type of muthafucka who knew how to get things moving and how to get things done. He looked soft and like a pretty boy on the surface, but something about him made him a good person to know when you needed to flip dirty money. That's why I fucked with him. I needed a plan B just in case the Dupree scheme didn't work out. I'd met him a year ago right before my mother closed on her townhome. He'd been her real estate broker, and after giving me his card, I called him one day asking if he knew of any big money investments. That's when he told me about the day spa idea. Rich white women kept those spots filled, so I'd make my money back with no problem and then some. I could also use it as a front for my weed business.

I looked back at the pictures. "Did you tell the contractors about the nail area that I want to expand? You know I'm really into nails, so that area is super important to me."

Peppi leaned back into his chair and smiled. "Yes, Peppi told them everything. It's going down, Keema, just like I told you it would. But there is just a little bit of bad news." He grimaced at having to say those last words.

"What's up?" I found myself glued to the pictures, not wanting to put them down.

"You're going to need twenty thousand more for them to finish the work on the spa. The contractor is a little over budget. He says that if you can have it to him by next week, you'll be open for business by the end of the following *three* weeks."

I damn near couldn't believe my ears. The bad news meant nothing to me. Everything was coming together the way I'd hoped. A measly twenty thousand dollars more couldn't burst a bitch's spirits. Suddenly, I realized there was a problem...

My current situation.

All the good news had made me forget it for a moment. It was back and in living color now though. Everything with Peppi had all happened faster than I'd expected, but my pockets were nowhere near prepared. The thought deflated me, making me finally sit the pictures on the table.

I needed twenty stacks to finish the spa, another twenty-five hundred for the weed, and money to cover my living expenses in Arizona as I waited for my investments to begin paying off. Since the cops had my money and the state had my kids, I didn't have a whole lot of loot. I'd counted $1,800.00 from the money I'd gotten from Rick, but that with the other money I had only totaled close to three grand.

As Peppi spoke to me my mind was elsewhere. I couldn't focus on his voice any longer. I could only wonder and worry. Without money my dream was fading. Both my plans had crumbled. How could I have come so close just to watch everything fall apart? The shit depressed the shit out of me. I could only lean back into my chair dejectedly, only answering Peppi every now and then.

After nearly an hour an idea finally came to me. I perked up immediately. It wasn't quite over for me yet.

"Peppi, I'm going to get with you later," I said, rising quickly from my seat.

"Where are you going?" he asked. "Peppi wanted to take you to celebrate. There's a good Salsa spot on Charles."

"Another time," I said as I began to make my way out of the food court. "Just make sure you tell those contractors that I'll have their money for them by next week."

With visions of Keema's Day Spa floating around in my head, I reached into my pocket and called Imani.

"Hello?" she answered.

"I'm on my way over there. We got a move to make."

SEVEN

Pussy is *every* man's weakness and most times is his down fall. Niggas love and treasure it so much they'll follow it into a burning building or over the edge of a cliff. Men are just that dumb, stupid, and brainless when it comes to pussy. Maybe it's the smell of it that shuts down their entire brain, let alone their common sense. I was counting on that tonight with Paco, the dumb muthufucka I was sucking off.

It had been two days since my meeting with Peppi and every thread of my being was focused on getting that money up. Even as my knees ached and I devoured the dick before me into my mouth like a porn star, all I could think about was the money. With every bob of my head my mind was calculating numbers, decimals, and averages like a computer. The thoughts were nothing less than relentless.

Peppi's deal with the weed connect was just way too damn good to pass up. And seeing my day spa nearly completed definitely wasn't a reality I'd let go to waste. The spa was my baby. I refused to let either slip through my fingers. Why should I? I'd come too far, too close, and had made far too many sacrifices to give up now. Shit, I'd placed myself in harm's way. I had no other choice but to see this thing all the way through to the end.

I hadn't given up on the Dupree scheme either. I took the money that

I'd gotten from his club and retained a good family attorney. He didn't come cheap. He was one of them extremely high priced Italian muthafuckas in an expensive tailor made suit. Despite his high price tag, I had no choice but to fuck with him. I couldn't afford to take a chance on a lawyer who would possibly do a half ass job at helping me get my kids back. I needed one of them Johnny Cochran types; one of them muthafuckas who eats, breathes, and lives for courtroom battles. I needed a beast.

The attorney more than assured me that he could get the kids back. Fast. When I told him everything that had happened the evening of my arrest, he smiled and said this would be one of the easiest family cases he'd ever been a part of. He assured me that I didn't have to worry.

With that out of the way I thought back to my last conversation with Rayquan. He said the wheels were in motion, and that Dupree would be dead real soon. He also made it clear that the new plan for killing Dupree couldn't fail this time. Shit, Dupree was practically already dead. He just didn't know it yet. I'd been to the hospital twice to see him, once calling Rick from there finally telling him where Dupree was.

With all the loose ends being tied, the only thing left to do was step up my grind and get some cash flowing again and regularly. The attorney's retainer fee broke a bitch. I had to recoup and begin adding to a new stash immediately. Basically, my hustle and grind had to be more hard body than ever before.

Paco's dick was small, uncircumcised, and his balls gave off the mustiest stench I'd ever smelled in my entire life. The shit was nauseating, but I had to do what I had to do. I worked that little nasty, foul smelling, vienna sausage like it was one of those Philly Cheese steak sandwiches that always seemed to make my taste buds do cartwheels.

Paco wasn't cute at all. He was far from it. He was medium height, dark as midnight, weighed about two hundred sixty pounds, had lips the size of inner tubes, wore a played out ass perm, and rocked a gold tooth directly in the front. There should've been a law against that gold tooth shit. But for what he lacked in looks, he more than made up for in money. The nigga pushed a cocaine white 650 BMW, rocked more jewelry than Birdman, at any given time, and was always bragging that he never left the house with less than ten stacks in his pocket.

The nigga was hood and also a huge trick. I'd fucked with him several times before, making him cake me up each time. Since we had that type of history between us, it was easy to get the nigga to the motel room tonight. The muthafucka was so anxious to get some more of this banging ass pussy, he nearly tripped over his shoes while following me into the room. Once inside, I immediately made him take the gun he kept in his belt and put it in the top drawer of the nightstand.

Within minutes and with the lights off I had Paco naked and moaning louder than a pregnant woman in labor as I attacked his dick over and over again with my warm wet mouth, showing absolutely no mercy. Since he was so small, it was easy to repeatedly swallow him whole without gagging, making his knees nearly go weak.

As Paco's head rose to the ceiling, I let my eyes travel across the dark room to the closet. Its door was cracked open slightly, just enough for Imani, who was hiding inside to see what was going on without being exposed.

"Aww, damn, Keema," Paco moaned. "I can't take no more, girl. I want some of that pussy."

Ignoring him, I simply pushed him onto the bed, jumped on him, and took his dick back into my mouth again; this time sucking it more viciously than I'd ever sucked a dick before. His toes were curling up in his dress socks and his moans grew louder.

"Oh, shit, Keema!" he shouted.

My jaws were tightening and growing sore, but I didn't ease up. I kept working on his punk ass. With one hand I stroked his small shaft. With the other I softly massaged his musty smelling balls. The entire combination had his eyes rolling up into his head.

"Shit, Keema, I'm about to cum."

My mouth began to make slurping noises and I began to moan like I was enjoying it. The sounds were enough. He couldn't take it any longer. His dick exploded.

Paco couldn't even get a chance to enjoy his nut before the closet door suddenly burst open and Imani jumped out holding the 9mm. However, as Imani went to raise it, she stumbled and the gun dropped from her hand. Shockingly, it went off, brightening the room for just a brief second.

"Shit!' I screamed as I immediately laid flat onto the bed, hoping and praying I'd dodged the bullet.

Paco did the same. "What the fuck?" he yelled.

After a quick moment Imani picked the gun up from the floor and fumbled with it. She eventually got control and quickly pointed it toward Paco's chest.

I raised my head and looked at her. "Bitch, what the hell is wrong with you?"

"Sorry," she said genuinely. "My heel got snagged on the carpet."

I looked at her heels and then at her. "Why the fuck would you wear heels to a robbery?"

"A *robbery*?" Paco asked, not quite catching on yet.

"I don't know," Imani responded.

"You know this bitch?" Paco questioned me as I quickly jumped up and picked up his jeans from the floor. Ignoring him, I went through the pockets and found a stack of countless hundred dollar bills. My guess, about four grand.

"Keema, what the fuck is goin' on?" he asked with his nipples still hard and still in a frozen position.

"What part of the word *robbery* do you not understand? Now, take off that damn jewelry."

It finally dawned on him that this shit was no joke. With Imani pointing the gun at him Paco realized he had no choice but to come up out his Audemars watch, Jacob bracelet, and diamond encrusted chains.

"Toss that shit over here," I ordered.

Paco did what he was told with his face still bawled up.

After picking everything up I turned to Imani. "Alright," I said. "Kill him."

Imani looked at me like I was crazy. "Huh?"

"Kill him."

"What do you mean kill him?"

"Bitch, I mean aim the pistol at his ass and blow the shit out of him."

"Keema, that wasn't part of the plan. You didn't say anything about killing anybody." Her hands shook notoriously yet she never took her eyes off Paco who remained frozen. "You said we were just going to rob him. That was the plan."

"Fuck the plan. Plans change, Imani."

"Plans change, my ass, Keema. How are you gonna change the plans without telling me?"

Paco's eyes darted from face to face.

"Shit, Imani, does it matter why the plan changed? Just shoot the nigga!"

Imani shook her head quickly. "Oh, hell no, hell no, hell no," she repeated. "I'm not shooting him. Here, you do it." She tried to hand the gun to me with the nozzle pointed directly in my face.

"Bitch, are you fucking crazy," I snapped, quickly ducking and pushing the gun to the side with my wrist only. "Don't point that thing in my face." There was no way I was going to put my fingerprints on that thing. "What the fuck are you giving it to me for?"

"Because I don't want it."

"Point the fucking gun at him, stupid!"

My eyes darted back to Paco. We made eye contact. Surely he could tell Imani was a rookie type bitch, but he knew my work. I glared at him causing Imani to point the gun once again.

"Stop moving muthufucka," I blared.

He froze again.

"See, that's why you've got to kill him. He knows our faces and names."

"But, Keema, you know how I felt about the last time when we killed Frenchie."

Paco's face changed two shades in no time. He was now a blackish purple.

"Look, Imani, we ain't got time to go back and forth about this shit. The police are probably on their way right now. They'll be here any minute."

"The *police*?" she asked, her face now covered in fear. "What do you mean the police?" She started trembling like she was about to cry.

"Bitch, you shot a hole through the fucking wall. Muthafuckas around here aren't deaf. Somebody probably called them by now."

"Damn it, Keema, I knew I shouldn't' have let you talk me into this shit."

Before I could say another word Imani dropped the gun on the bed and headed for the door.

"Where the fuck are you going?" I asked, as my eyes followed her to the door. I turned back around just in time to see Paco quickly reaching for the gun. Immediately, I snatched the 9mm from the bed, making him grab nothing but air. "Freeze, you son of a bitch!"

He stopped.

Quickly I turned and darted in front of Imani just as she was opening the door. I slammed it shut. "Where the fuck do you think you're going?"

She shook her head repeatedly. "Uh-uh, I'm getting my ass the fuck up out of here while I can. I'm not going to jail for this shit."

"Ain't nobody going to jail," I replied.

"Yes, we are. For murder! We'll *never* get out!" She began to cry. "I don't want any more parts of this shit."

Click-Click

The sound silenced the both of us. We both recognized it. It was the sound of a gun's hammer cocking. Me myself, I knew exactly where it had come from. *Damn*, I thought to myself as I realized I'd forgotten Paco's gun was in the top drawer of the nightstand. The both of us turned to see him sitting on the bed with the gun pointed directly at us.

"Uh-oh," Imani said as she stared at the gun with eyes as big as paper plates.

It was either his life or ours.

As if by reflex and without thinking, I fired, causing him to duck. Seconds later, he fired back with bullets flying everywhere.

"Run!" I screamed at Imani.

She opened the door and darted out into the night. I never realized she could move so fast in heels. I darted out behind her, but struggled to keep up with the gun in one hand, along with the money and jewels in the other.

"You scandalous bitches!" Paco screamed as he ran out the door behind us.

Shots kept blasting off from behind.

"I'ma kill yo' ass Keema!" he shouted for anyone in a two mile radius to hear.

The shooting sounds made both me and Imani cover our heads and duck as we ran. By the time we reached the end of the parking lot we parted ways.

EIGHT

The heels of my flip-flops smacked the bottoms of my feet loudly as I paced the carpet of my living room back and forth more times than I could count. Shit, I wasn't even aware that I was doing it. My body was controlling itself, I guess. Pacing was the best way it could think of to deal with the nerve racking situation I'd gotten myself in.

"Bitch," I said into my I-phone speaking to Imani's voicemail. "Where the fuck are you? I've been calling your scary ass for the past couple of days. I've been leaving voice messages on your voice mail. I've sent your ass a million fucking text messages. I even came by your house today but no one answered." I paused for a second. "Imani, real talk. You need to get at me. I know you're fucked up about what went down the other day. Shit, I am, too. That's why we need to talk. We need to make sure we're on the same damn page. Call me as *soon* as you get this message. I'm serious, hit me back as soon as you get this. As a matter of fact, fuck calling. Just bring your ass over here, alright?"

With those words said I hit the end button and stuffed the phone into the back pocket of my tight fitting jeans. I took a puff of my Newport and totally flooded my lungs with smoke, still pacing the floor from wall to wall, unable to stop. In just the past several hours I'd smoked up an entire pack of cigarettes. This shit definitely had me on edge.

My mind kept seeing flashes of Imani bending that corner in her heels. The fear filled words she'd spoken during the robbery also kept playing in my head. Damn, I hoped she hadn't done something stupid and gone to the police. Each time I called and got no answer, I wondered if she was sitting in one of those interrogation rooms you see on *The First 48* spilling her guts. The thought of the possibility always made my heart drop to my feet.

When I'd rolled by Imani's apartment a few hours ago and knocked on the door, I got no answer. That seemed odd. I didn't even hear any sort of noise coming from inside. Imani lived with her mother, aunt, and her grandmother. Her brother, who constantly went in and out of jail, also crashed there on a regular so there was always some action and noise going on. Not this morning though. I heard nothing. I even called her mother's cell phone, but got no answer. The shit had me more than nervous. It had me paranoid.

All of the shades and curtains in my apartment, including the ones in the kids' rooms, were closed. It was broad daylight outside. The mid afternoon sun was beaming from the sky, but I wasn't allowing any of it to penetrate the apartment. The lack of sunshine left the apartment dimmed and creepy. Occasionally I peeked out of the curtains at the parking lot downstairs making sure there was no sign of Paco. Luckily the nigga didn't know where I lived, but since the streets talked it wasn't like he couldn't find out.

My television was off, and there was no music playing. Usually I always had one or the other blasting. Without either now, the entire apartment was utterly silent and still. That was just the way I wanted it. That was just the way I *needed* it rather. My ears needed to hear everything around me. I couldn't take a chance on getting crept up on. That could quite possibly cost me my life.

It had been two days since the Paco robbery. That shit still had me shook up just as badly as Imani not answering her phone. The muthafucka was supposed to be dead. That was why I'd tried to talk Imani into pulling the trigger on his fat ass. If he was dead, I wouldn't have to watch my back right now. But as it stood, since Imani was too damn scared to murk him, I was most likely on the nigga's shit list.

I didn't know if he was the type to kill a bitch or if he was the type to just whoop a bitch's ass. Whichever he was, I wasn't taking a chance. Bullets killed and I *definitely* knew how a good ass whippin' felt. I wanted no parts of either one. That's why as I paced the apartment and occasionally peeked through my curtains, my hand stayed locked around the handle of my gun. If it came down to it, although I didn't have the heart to kill his ass in the motel room, I was ready and willing to pull the trigger now.

Over the past couple of days I'd been laying low at my cousin Raven's house in Randallstown. Coming back to the apartment was way too risky, but I was hoping shit had cooled down a little. Hopefully, Paco had gotten busy selling dope.

When I first got back to my side of town, I circled the block like ten times with the gun in my lap to be sure I didn't see Paco or his car anywhere around. There was no way I was going to let the nigga get the drop on me. When I finally parked the car two blocks over like I always do, my heart ran like a race horse as I made my way through the projects with the gun stuffed in my purse. My eyes watched every face. My ears heard every sound. If anything looked or sounded suspicious, it was going to be on out there. I was going to light shit up like the muthafuckin' 4th of July.

I had no idea if Paco had spread word around the hood about what happened. With the type of cheese he had, he could've easily put a ransom on my head. If he did, the crack heads and goons around this hood would love to collect. Eventually I reached my building and my apartment with no problem. Once inside I turned every single lock; all four of them bitches. Since then, I hadn't been outside.

My fingers were shaking as I placed the cigarette to my lips again.

"Damn," I said to myself, suddenly realizing I needed to

call Tia out in D.C. She worked at the Motor Vehicle out there, and was the perfect connect for me to get welfare benefits out there.

Just like I had a plan A and a plan B. I also had a plan C. If shit didn't work out with the Dupree set up or the Peppi venture, I was planning on having monthly disbursements coming in from several different states. D.C. was one of them. Tia was going to hook me up with a driver's license out there. She also had connects in several different states, each employed at DMVs. But her best asset was the hook up with people in each state who would help me work my magic. As long as I paid them each a fee every month they would allow me to use their addresses to apply for welfare in their states. It would be raining money every fucking where.

Exhaling the cigarette smoke I snatched the phone from my jeans and called Tia.

"What's good, guuurrlll?" Tia answered, smacking her lips between words as usual. I had no idea why she stretched out some of her words.

"You," I returned. "How shit looking?"

"Everything's good. You'll have your license by the end of the week. My girls up in New York and Philly are also ready for you to holla at them, too. As long as you got the money, it's on."

"I nodded, pleased at the news. "Good, good," I told her. "I'm sending your money out by Western Union tonight."

"Alright."

BOOM-BOOM!

The surprising pounding at the door scared me so bad I immediately dropped the phone. "Shit," I uttered, kneeling to pick it up while keeping my eyes directly on the door, wondering who the hell it was.

"You alright?" Tia asked as I placed the phone back to my ear nervously and with shaking hands.

"Yeah, I'm fine. Look, I'll call you back." I pressed the end button, darted across the room to the cocktail table, and snatched up the gun as the knocks continued.

The pounding made me jump. My body tensed as Paco's angry face appeared in my mind. My ears could still hear the bullets shot from his gun the other night. The memory made me entertain the thought of bussing several shots through the door. If it was him on the other side, obviously I didn't want to give him a single chance to get *near* me, let alone shoot me.

My feet were stuck in one place. It occurred to me that I'd told Imani during my last message to come directly over. Maybe it was her on the other side of the door. I wasn't sure.

I cocked the gun as the knocks grew louder.

The 9mm was now parallel with my chest as my finger locked around the trigger.

"Keema!" Rick's voice came loudly from the other side of the door. "Open the door!"

My breaths quickened at the sound of Rick's voice. It felt like the entire world had just been removed from my shoulders. I uncocked the gun, slipped it underneath the pillows of the couch, and headed across the room to the front door. Just to be sure it was him I placed an eye to the peephole. What I saw sent a wave of surprise and fear through my entire body.

Rick was looking directly at the peephole with an angry look on his face. Beside him stood Shane.

"Shit," I grunted as I immediately backed away from the door nervously.

Without telling them to, my feet began to pace the floor again. My hands then began wringing each other out like wet rags.

"Shit, shit," I said, staring at the floor as I paced.

All types of thoughts raced through my head. How did Rick know Shane was in jail? Had Shane told him I'd set him up to take the case? Had Rick spoken to Dupree about the money I'd taken from the club? Had word possibly gotten to Rick about what went down with Paco? Each thought and question tugged at me relentlessly. They wouldn't stop.

"Keema, I saw you look through the peephole. Open the

door. I got Shane out here!"

Quickly I darted to the couch and grabbed the gun from beneath the cushions again.

"Keema, open the door!" Rick yelled then knocked once again.

The roar of his voice made me juggle the gun. After getting control of it I didn't know what to do. How in the hell did I get my ass into this shit? What the fuck made me think all of this shit would work? What was I thinking? Rick was probably out there wanting to kill me. All I could do was keep pacing.

"Keema!"

"Shit," I said, realizing he wasn't going to leave, knowing I was inside.

There was no sense in continuing to hide. Whatever was about to go down, I had to face. Fuck it. I tucked the gun into the back of my jeans, and pulled my long off the shoulder tunic over the pockets. I took a deep breath, and walked over to the door. Slowly my fingers twisted the locks one by one. Finally my hand grabbed the knob and turned it slowly. I stepped back.

"What the fuck?" Rick yelled as he walked into the apartment. He shot by me looking around like he thought I was hiding someone.

I turned to keep my body between him and my gun. My eyes were on him closely.

"What the fuck were you up in here doin'?"

"I just got out the shower," I lied, my eyes glancing at Shane. "I had to put some clothes on."

"It took *that* long?"

"Why are you worried about how long it takes me to get dressed?"

Rick shook his head. "You know what? Fuck all that. Why did I have to get a call from one of my homeboys 'bout Shane? His son is locked up down in juvee. He saw Shane down there and called me. What's up, Keema?"

I didn't know what to say.

"Them white folks talkin' 'bout they got his ass down

there on drug charges," Rick continued. "How some shit like that happen?"

Words still wouldn't leave my mouth. I had no idea what to say.

"I asked Shane what was goin' on, but he won't tell me shit. Keema, what's up?"

Those were the words I needed to hear. The fact that Shane hadn't told him anything gave me instant relief. Now, I could speak.

"Look, Rick," I began, putting on my act. "Shane's a good kid. He's a *great* kid as a matter of fact."

"Shane's a great kid," Shane repeated mimicking me.

I smiled at him. He smiled back.

"He just made a mistake. I've been letting him go outside lately, instead of keeping him cooped up in this damn apartment all day. He met a few friends. But I guess they haven't been good influences on him. One of them gave him some weed and the cops busted up in here meaning to hit the apartment next door. They found the weed in Shane's room."

"So, why didn't you tell me?"

"Because I didn't want anyone to know. I just wanted to handle it myself so people wouldn't be looking at Shane and thinking what *you're* probably thinking right now."

"Does Dupree know?" Rick questioned.

"Does Dupree know?" Shane interrupted.

"No, and he doesn't need to know, Rick. Please, don't tell him," I pleaded. "He's already stressed out enough trying to get his health back. He's going through hell right now. The last thing he needs to hear is that Shane is in trouble."

I stepped towards Rick and looked at him innocently. "Let me handle this my way," I begged. "If it becomes necessary to tell Dupree, I will. I promise. But until then, let me handle it, okay?"

Rick looked at me with hesitation.

"We gon' kill that muthafucka," Shane said unexpectedly as he took a seat on the couch.

67

Both me and Rick turned to look at him, taken totally off guard by what he'd just said or what he meant by it.

"With him gone, the money will be mine," Shane said, staring off into the distance.

His words sent shivers down my spine. I recognized them. They were *my* words. They were the words I'd spoken to Imani during several phone conversations concerning Dupree's set up.

"What are you talkin' 'bout, Shane?" Rick questioned. His face seemed totally puzzled by what he'd just heard. His voice roared scaring Shane half to death.

Shane didn't say anything else. He just continued to stare into space.

My eyes glanced from Rick to Shane, hoping Shane would remain silent.

Rick walked over to Shane and knelt in front of him. He looked up into his nephew's eyes. "Shane, who you talkin' 'bout? What money?"

I slowly reached behind my back and placed my hand on the handle of the gun just in case shit didn't go right.

"Shane, tell your uncle what's up? What's goin' on, big boy?" Rick continued to pry.

My heart started pounding.

Suddenly, Shane began to rock back and forth with his husky, solid body banging against the back of the couch.

"You can talk to me, Shane," Rick continued.

I raised the gun slightly from the back of my pants, just enough to get my finger around the trigger. I had no idea if Shane was about to say my name.

Rick turned and looked at me. "What the fuck is he talkin' 'bout, Keema?"

I shrugged my shoulders.

"Ain't no way in hell he supposed to be talkin' about killin' or robbin' niggas. What type of muthafuckas you been havin' up in here around my nephew? I know he only repeats what he hears."

"It's probably those niggas he's been seeing outside. It has

68

to be. That's where he's picking it up."

"Nah, fuck that," Rick said, not satisfied with my answer.

Panic filled me. I was ready to pull the gun from behind and blast Rick, but something held me from doing so.

"Come on, Shane," Rick told his nephew. "You comin' to stay wit' me."

"No!" Shane shouted directly into Rick's face leaping to his feet. He charged across the room and hugged me. "I stay with Keema!"

Rick looked at me suspiciously.

Surprised at Shane's decision I pushed the gun back and wrapped my arms around him, thankful that he'd kept our little secret quiet.

Rick stood up. Still not quite satisfied with things and taking a look around he asked, "Where the other kids at?"

"Huh?" I answered completely off guard. My nerves were rattled heavily. Shane finally let me go. He took my hand in his and stood beside me.

"Where the other kids, Keema?" Rick repeated.

"With Imani."

"Why Imani got 'em?"

"Damn, Rick, why you looking at me all crazy and shit? If the kids want to kick it with their Godmother, they can. She took them shopping if you must know."

The room was silent.

Rick eyed me.

Refusing to look like guilty, I eyed him back sassily.

"Alright," he finally said. "But from now on, keep them goon ass niggas Shane been associatin' wit' from around him before I have to murk one of them fools."

"I got you," I told him, relieved.

"I'm for real, Keema."

"I said I got you, damn."

Rick turned and headed for the door.

"Can I get some money, Rick?" I quickly blurted out.

He turned and glared at me like I was crazy. "What?"

"You heard me. I need some money. Since Dupree has been in the hospital, money has been tied up. I'm on my last couple of dollars."

He sighed and reached into his pocket to pull out a thick folded knot of hundreds. My eyes glistened at the sight. He counted out a thousand and handed it to me. I walked over to get it. However, as my hand grabbed the money, Rick jerked me suddenly towards him. Our bodies were pressed tightly together. He placed his lips directly to my ear.

"I don't know what the fuck is goin' on around here lately, but whatever it is, my nephew better not get caught in the middle of it, you hear me?" he whispered.

Rick squeezed my hand tightly, causing me to wince in pain as the money exchanged hands. "Nothing's going on, I swear," I said, staring over his shoulder.

"It better not be. If I find out you lyin' to me, that lil' gun you got tucked in your pants won't be able to help you."

He turned me lose, allowing the money to stay in my hand. He then glared in my eyes, making sure I got his message loud and clear. Satisfied that I had, Rick looked across the room to his nephew and smiled.

"Alright, big boy, I love you, man."

"I love you, man," Shane replied with a stupid grin.

Rick turned and opened the door. As he walked out, he turned to me and said, "And make sure you take him to see his father tomorrow."

NINE

Dupree was lying in his bed talking to Shane as the afternoon sun shined brightly through the large window. Shane was sitting in a chair beside the bed talking back and forth with his father as I sat beside him.

What Rick had said to me the day before just before he walked out of the door stuck with me. The way his eyes looked at me remained etched in my brain. I'd never heard him speak to me like that before and I'd never seen him look at me that way either. Both the words and the glare even played in my dreams. It was obvious he wasn't joking. I wasn't quite sure if he would actually kill me, but I wasn't going to test him, at least not yet. As soon as I woke up this morning, I got Shane up and told him to get dressed so we could go see his father just like Rick had ordered.

As I got dressed I called Imani again. She still hadn't returned any of my calls or stopped by the apartment. When I called her again on the way to the hospital, she still didn't answer. The shit had me highly suspicious. Imani had never missed my calls before the Paco episode. We were always on the phone with each other. Something obviously wasn't right. I'd even gone as far as to wonder if maybe Paco had somehow caught up with her. The shit had me puzzled, but I decided I'd worry about it later.

As Dupree lay in the bed, it was obvious he was losing

weight, at least ten pounds or more. His face appeared to be sunken in and his eyes were blood shot red. And as he spoke to Shane, his voice didn't have the same authority and confidence it used to convey. He didn't look or sound like the man I once knew. It was obvious the hospital stay and the attack on his life were affecting him terribly.

Between the two, Dupree led the conversation. Shane responded but as usual, he stared off into some strange distant place only his brain could take him to. Every now and then he would say something weird out of the blue, unrelated to anything else in life. Occasionally he smiled or rocked back and forth in his chair too. I could see from his eyes he had questions about all that was happening around him lately. I couldn't describe how they looked. It was just something I knew from being around Shane for so long. When his father spoke to him, something inside of them always seemed to glimmer and shift. That look, although distant, bothered me.

Dupree reached out from his bed and touched Shane's knee. Usually, Shane hated to be touched by anyone. Sometimes he would throw fits and tantrums if it even appeared like someone was going to even *try* to touch him. But with Dupree, it wasn't like that. Myself as well. He always seemed to welcome our touches. Even in the midst of a fit or tantrum, our touches or words always seemed to calm him down.

Dupree told Shane he loved him several times. He also told him he was proud of him and that no matter what, he would always be one of his favorite people in the world. Those words were usual. Although Dupree rarely got a chance to spend time with Shane, when he did, he always went out of his way to show his son how much he loved him. This time seemed different though. The shit kind of made me nervous. It was as if Dupree was laying on his death bed or something. It sounded odd. Before I could worry, my cell phone rang. Looking at the screen and recognizing my lawyer's number, I excused myself from the room and went out into the hallway.

"Hello?" I answered, pressing the phone to my ear.

"Ms. Newell?"

"Yeah?"

"Hey, guess what? I've got great news for you."

"What is it?"

"Children's Protective Services is going to let you have custody of the kids again."

I couldn't believe my ears. "What?" I was in total disbelief.

He laughed. "Yes, you heard correctly. They're going to let you get them back."

My welfare benefits would be straight, I realized. "Are you sure?" I asked enthusiastically.

"Yes, but you're still going to have to go to court. I'll keep you posted on the date. But they have agreed to let you have the kids until the court date."

"Wow, when can I go get them?"

"Today. Right now, actually. I'll call and have them transferred to Family Court immediately. You can pick them up from there."

I was so happy, I wanted to do cartwheels, back flips, handstands, and everything else. I wanted to scream to the top of my lungs, but held it in.

After thanking my lawyer, I hung up, darted into Dupree's room, and put an end to the little father and son bonding moment. I had more pressing issues. Before Shane knew what was up, I was dragging his big over grown dumb ass down the hospital hallway onto the elevator. Moments later, we were out in the parking lot and into the car. I sped up out of the parking lot so damn fast, I'm surprised that I hadn't left the tires back in my parking space.

"Daddy loves me," Shane said out of nowhere as he rocked back and forth in the passenger seat, looking like Baby Huey from those old cartoons I used to watch as a kid.

Taking a hit of a Newport, I said halfheartedly, "Yeah, nigga, daddy loves your ass."

Shane smiled. "My daddy loves me," he repeated. "He

73

loves me."

I knew he was going to repeat that shit at least a hundred more times before we reached Family Court. He was like that. Not only would he blurt out shit unexpectedly, he would repeat shit over and over again sometimes for ten minutes straight. It was nerve racking. But for the moment, I really didn't care. He could stand on his head and sing the muthafuckin' Star Spangled Banner for all I cared. My mind was on money.

Money could make a bitch like me cum faster than a piece of good dick could. My world revolved around it. As a matter of fact, it was why I'd named all my kids after its different slang names; Treasure, Cash and Dinero. If I ever had another child the name would surely be Paper.

Once we reached the Family Court building and parked, I hopped out of the car and jogged quickly around the hood to the passenger side.

"Come on, nigga," I told Shane as I snatched him up out of his seat. "We got shit to do."

"My daddy loves me," he said once again, as I shut the door and began to drag him through the parking lot so fast, his neck snapped back.

"Yeah, whatever," I told him. "Just hurry your big ass up."

"Daddy loves me."

"Tell your story while walking."

We were inside the building in no time. The kids were standing with a social worker, one I'd never seen. She was tall, sorta cute and seemed to have a permanent smile. When Cash saw me, he darted towards me and jumped into my arms. Dinero, who was in Treasure's arms, smiled as well.

"Mommy!" he screamed, reaching out for me.

As soon as Treasure put him down, he dashed his little bowlegged self down the hall. He still hadn't learned how to walk quickly without stumbling and falling. He tripped over his own feet and hit the floor, but was back up in no time and darted to me with happiness in his eyes.

I hugged both of them tightly. I truly did love them. And

in all actuality, I really did miss them. But it is what it is. Love couldn't play a part in my plans. There was no room for it. The kids were a means to an end. They were my ticket to welfare benefits.

Treasure remained standing by the social worker with her arms folded across her chest. She looked just like her father at that moment, and just as stubborn. Out of all of my children, Treasure had the prettiest pecan complexion along with beautiful jet black hair that would never need a perm. She also had the longest eyelashes that often made me jealous. She looked a lot like a young Tatyana Ali from *The Fresh Prince of Bel Air*.

"Come over here and hug your momma, girl," I told her.

She didn't budge.

Man, I hope this lil bitch don't call herself trying to show out for these white folks. I'd hate to have to kick her ass in front of them, I thought.

"Treasure, did you hear me talking to you. Come here."

This time she sucked her teeth and rolled her eyes.

Oh no that lil' skinny bitch didn't just do that white girl shit, I thought to myself as my face twisted up like I'd just smelled something terrible. I looked at my oldest child like she'd lost her mind.

Treasure had always invited confrontation with me. She'd been like that since the day she was born. She'd always been the courageous one of the bunch. I always considered her an old soul because she always seemed older than she really was.

While the boys always did what they were told with no problem, she could never be satisfied with the way things were or how I ran the household. My word was never good enough for her. If I told her to do something, it always had to be met with a bunch of "Whys." She always had a damn question for every answer and an answer for every question. She got on my nerves with that shit. She reminded me of myself when I was her age.

With a little urging from the case worker Treasure finally walked toward my direction. When she reached me, her arms were still folded and her eyes were off in another direction. It was as if the sight of me disgusted her. Oh, she was definitely going to get her ass whooped royally when we got home. I didn't play the showing out, 'making a scene' in public game.

I glanced at the caseworker. Her blue eyes were on us, studying carefully how we interacted with each other so she could write it down and go tell the head honkey in charge. I wanted to snatch the shit out of Treasure, but I knew I couldn't under the case worker's watchful eye. Instead, I smiled.

"Hey, baby, can I have a hug?"

After standing there for a few seconds, reluctantly Treasure hugged me. But there was no life to it at all. No love or caring. Nothing about it was genuine. And just as quickly as it began, it ended. She stepped back and folded her arms again with her lips twisted in a way that made me want to slap them off of her face.

"What's wrong?"

"Why can't we stay with the foster lady?" she asked boldly.

She was trying my patience, but I didn't bite. "Because that's not your home, sweetheart," I said, still smiling.

"But I liked it there. She treated us nice."

My eyes glanced at the case worker again. She was writing something in her notepad. I knelt down in front of Treasure, making sure the nosey caseworker couldn't see my face.

"Look here, you little stuck up bitch," I whispered. "Don't you *ever* in your damn life front on me like this again. I'll kick your lil narrow ass all up and down this building. Don't ever think that I'm a muthafuckin' game. You know my fucking pedigree." I glanced at the case worker again. "*I'm* the mother and *you're* the child," I told her, poking a finger into her boney little chest. "So you better respect me. You got that?"

She didn't answer.

With a look like an angry Rottweiler, I asked again, "Do…you…hear…me?"

Treasure was quiet. But the look on her face showed she got the message. She nodded eventually.

Standing up, I smiled at the case worker.

"Is everything okay?" she inquired.

"Splendid, ma'am."

"Okay, we'll be in touch with your court date. Here's my card."

We met each other half way, so I could take something I probably had plans on throwing away. "Thank you."

As me and the kids walked out of the building, Cash immediately bumrushed my ears with stories about the new friends he'd met while in the county's custody. He told me what they ate, what they drank, what games they played, etc, etc. I knew he had plans on talking my ears off. When we finally reached the car, I strapped the boys into their car seats which was normally Treasure's job. Moments later, my cell phone rang. It was Imani's ring tone. I couldn't pick up the phone fast enough.

"Bitch, where you at?" I asked hurriedly, shutting the door and taking a few steps away, not wanting to take a chance on Shane hearing any more of my conversations. "I've been trying to get with your ass for the past three days."

"Keema," she said. "I can't take this anymore."

I pressed the phone even tighter to my ear. I didn't like the way she sounded. I could hear her crying. "Imani, what are you talking about?"

She sobbed heavily. "Keema, you know what I'm talking about. I can't take it anymore. The shit won't let me rest. I can't sleep. It won't leave my conscience alone."

"Girl, just relax. Everything's gonna be okay."

"Mommy, can we have McDeweys?" Dinero asked form the car, still unable to pronounce McDonalds properly.

"It's not gonna be okay, Keema. I'm done with this shit. I'm going to the police. I'm telling them what I did."

"What?" Her words kicked me like a horse. "What do you mean?"

"I mean what I just said. I'm gonna turn myself in. I'm not going to hell. I've been looking that shit up on the internet. You should hear the stuff people who died on operating tables and mysteriously came back to life say about it. The place is horrible, Keema."

I had no idea what she was talking about. "Imani, look…"

"No, Keema. My mind is made up."

"Imani, I was just going to say I wanna come, too," I lied.

"Huh?"

"Yeah, the shit has been fucking with my conscience, too. That's why I've been trying to reach you. I want us to go to the police together. I'm too afraid to do it by myself."

Imani perked up. "We're doing the right thing, Keema."

"I know, Imani. Where are you?"

"At home."

"Alright, I'm on my way to pick you up."

"Okay."

My finger jabbed the end button and I headed to the car. There was no fucking way I was going to turn myself in. And little did Imani know, she wasn't either.

TEN

The hemi roared like a hungry monster each time the sole of my six hundred dollar Giuseppe sandals pressed down on it. The speedometer was up to fifty as its wheels screeched down street after street and bent corner after corner recklessly. Houses whizzed by my window blindingly. Children and teenagers who played ball in the streets jumped out of the way immediately. Some even jumped their asses back on the sidewalks, scared to death that I was going to hit them.

Along with thoughts of Paco, my eyes were peeled, especially at the approaching corners for police. Summer always brought niggas out like flies, and the murder rate increased. Because of that reality, cops stepped up patrols in the hood around this time. My license was suspended for numerous unpaid traffic tickets, so the last thing I needed was to get pulled over. Not to mention if they happened to pull me over and search my car, they'd find the gun tucked underneath the seat.

Imani's fear filled words had my head filled with millions of thoughts and visions. I couldn't believe how damn selfish she was being. Her decision to go to the cops about Frenchie's murder would affect the both of us. If she told, I would be going down with her. Most likely though, she would get off with a lighter sentence for cooperating.

Imani was my girl. I loved her to death. She was the closest thing I ever had to a sister other than my cousin Raven. But she definitely wasn't the sharpest knife in the drawer. She'd always been a little slow, gullible, and submissive. She could be talked into anything. Especially, if it was *me*, her best friend who was doing the talking. She could never tell me no. It had been like that ever since kindergarten.

I could see her in court now. The judge, jury, and prosecution would clearly see how gullible she was, and consider her an innocent girl who'd just allowed her friend to take advantage of her. They'd feel sorry for her ass and give her probation or something while they gave me life or the electric chair. Fuck that! There was no way I was going to prison for her ass or anyone else. There was no other choice left but to go to her apartment and murk her ass. It definitely hurt my heart to have those thoughts, but it is what it is. It was either her or me.

As soon as I got the kids home, it didn't take me any more than ten minutes to change into a sweat suit and some Air Max's. Seconds later, I was out the door and half way to Imani's within minutes.

"Damn it!" I screamed, slamming my fists on the steering wheel as I was forced to stop at a busy intersection. Cars darted across my path in both directions.

"Hurry the fuck up!" I screamed impatiently. A bitch had shit to do. I could see Imani sitting on the phone with the police in my mind. She was scary that way.

"Fuck!"

The thought made me ease the nose of the Charger closer and closer to the intersection. Before I knew it, I was poking out. Cars swerved to miss me. Their horns blew.

"Fuck you!" I screamed, throwing up my middle finger. "Hurry the fuck up!"

Glancing up at the light, it was obvious it wasn't going to change anytime soon. I took another look up and down the street at the crossing traffic and decided to shoot through the red light. My foot pressed down on the gas pedal so hard that the engine roared and the ass of the Charger dropped and jerked upwards like a rocket. The rubber on my tires squealed and smoked as I darted across traffic, making drivers stomp down on their brakes and blow their horns. Ignoring them, I kept right on going.

Within moments I was pulling up to Imani's apartment on Alson Drive. After finding a parking space in front of her building, I grabbed the gun from beneath the seat, placed it in my purse, and leapt out of the car. As I walked through the courtyard, as usual dope boys were in front of it making transactions and prostitutes were strolling looking for dicks to suck. I reached the building and headed up the piss stenched staircase to the second floor. I walked immediately to Imani's door and knocked, noticing that it was no where near as silent as it was when I'd come by the other morning. It sounded like her family was having a party inside. The door opened and Imani's three hundred pound mother appeared.

"What's up, Keema?" Diane said with a rotten toothed smile.

A burst of marijuana smoke accompanied her. Even though I hadn't stepped inside, I could see Imani's grandmother and brother sitting on the couch. Two other niggas were sitting on the love seat. The apartment was messy as usual; empty pizza boxes and Wendy's bags were tossed everywhere. Empty forty ounce bottles were all over the cocktail table and end tables.

"You are *not* the father." I was just in time to hear Maury Povich say those words from the television screen. As the family passed a blunt they watched the latest episode.

"Where y'all been?" I asked, as Diane blocked me from coming too far inside the house. I'd only taken three steps into the kitchen and could only see the living room and the long, narrow hall leading to Imani's room.

"Excuse me?"

"Where y'all been? I've been coming by and calling, but no one's been here," I said.

"I don't know what's been up with you and Imani, but she said not to answer the phone or door for you," Diane stated.

My ears couldn't have heard her correctly. "What do you mean by that?" I asked with a crazy expression.

"Exactly what I just said, child."

"So, you mean to tell me that y'all were in here hiding the other morning like I was a damn Jehova's Witness because Imani told y'all to?"

Diane's face frowned. "Girl, who is *you* to be hiding from? Wasn't nobody hiding. We was sleep."

The shit didn't sound right.

"Whatever," I said, shrugging it off. I had way more important things to worry about. "Tell Imani I'm here."

"She ain't here."

"What do you mean she ain't here, Diane. I just talked to her."

"Well, she's gone now."

I'd just spoken to Imani forty minutes ago. She had to be here.

"Come on, quit playing. This serious. Tell her I'm out here." I was on my tippy toes trying to see over Diane's burly ass shoulders for Imani. I wanted to get a good look down the hall-way. "Imani!" I shouted like that would help. My patience level had reached its breaking point.

Diane placed a hand on one of her oversized hips and gave me a no nonsense type of look. "I'm not playing. She's gone."

"But she told me to meet her here."

"Well, maybe she did. What I got to do with that. All I know is she ain't here now."

"Where she go?"

"I don't know. She ain't tell me nothing."

"How long ago did she leave?"

"Ten minutes ago. What else do you need to know? What color panties she had on?" Diane responded. Everyone in the living room laughed.

I didn't believe a word of it. Why would Imani tell me she was going to be here waiting on me if she wasn't? It didn't make sense. Besides, she'd told her entire family to ignore my calls before, so maybe she'd told her mother to tell me this nonsense

82

now.

"Look, I really need to see her," I said, getting fed up with her mother.

"And I told you she's not here. Damn it!"

I couldn't take it anymore. "Quit fucking playing with me, Diane!" I screamed.

She looked at me like I'd lost my mind.

The entire living room grew silent and turned to look at me.

"Tell Imani to come the fuck out here! This ain't a game! This shit is important!"

Diane placed her hand on both huge hips and walked toward me, backing me up in route to her front door like a football player. "Bitch, I don't know who the fuck you think you talking to. But you better get your narrow ass outta my house before I stomp a mud hole in your ass."

I thought about shooting her big ass in the temple, but then I'd have to shoot the whole family. I wasn't looking for a massacre, I just wanted to get at Imani. Before I could say another word, I'd stepped backwards on the opposite side of their threshold as the door slammed in my face. The entire hallway began to spin. I felt dizzy. Everything seemed to close in around me, causing me to also feel claustrophobic. Feeling my knees buckling, I leaned against the wall.

Where the fuck was Imani? What the fuck was she up to? Had she gone to the police? Suddenly, I could envision myself lying on the table while some red neck ass warden gave me a lethal injection. I snatched my phone from my purse and dialed Imani's number. But my call went directly to her voicemail. There had to be a mistake. Maybe she was on the phone. I pressed the end button and called back. Still, only the voicemail.

"That fucking dumb bitch!" I yelled. My words echoed off of the walls.

After waiting in the hall for another half hour to see if she would show up, I headed back home pissed off, unable to wrap my mind completely around the fact that she had possibly played me. I could always count on her to do what I told her to do or be where I told her to be. What the fuck was going on in her head now?

When I got home and reached my door, I could hear the kids playing in the living room. The noise infuriated me. Treasure knew that while I was gone, she and her brothers weren't supposed to come out of their damn rooms. Her hardheaded ass was really pressing her luck with me. Ready to tear into her I jabbed the key into the lock and turned it.

"Damnit, Treasure!" I yelled as I opened the door.

The room went silent.

Immediately my eyes landed on my mother sitting on the couch with Dinero in her arms playing in her conservative looking weave. Cash was sitting beside her and Shane just a few feet across from them.

"You finally made it back, huh?" she said sarcastically.

Her voice agitated the shit out of me as always. Closing the door I said, "I was only gone a minute."

"I've been sitting here for forty-five minutes, Keema. I *hardly* call that a minute. You know CPS frowns on those types of things. They won't think twice about taking my grandbabies. I've seen it happen."

Sighing in annoyance, I made my way across the room to the couch. She'd left me on my own countless times when I was a kid. Now, she had the nerve to say I'm wrong for doing it.

"Ma, I don't need a sermon right now."

"It's not a sermon. It's merely something you need to hear."

Sighing again, I sat down on the couch. "You did it to me when I was a kid."

"Yes, I made a lot of mistakes when you were a kid. But that's not an excuse for you to go make the same ones."

Not in the mood, I grabbed the remote from the table and turned the channel on the television. "Here goes Miss Goody Two Shoes," I said, resting my head lazily on my hand.

She looked at me like I was crazy. "First of all," she

84

snapped with attitude. "The name is Gina. Second of all, I'm your damn mother, so you need to watch your tone when you talk to me."

"Whatever," I whispered.

She rolled her eyes at me then went back to playing with Dinero. "A hard head makes a real soft ass. I don't know how many times I have to tell you that. Those white folks are not playing. They will come in here and snatch your kids fast enough to make your head spin."

She got on my damn nerves with that shit. She always wanted to judge me. Yes, she'd gotten off welfare and went back to school. Yes, she'd eventually graduated and went to college. Yes, she'd gotten herself a good job and moved out the hood. But shit, she always had to come off like she knew everything.

She stood up and began to walk around the room in her Dolce & Gabbana pantsuit as she smiled and made retarded look-ing goo goo eyes at Dinero. At thirty eight years old she looked great. I had to admit, even though I was only twenty-five, I hoped I still looked that good when I got to her age. The bitch still got on my nerves though.

At the moment I could see her eyes sneakily scouring the living room as she pretended like she was so caught up in playing with her grandbaby. She loved him, but I knew when she was try-ing to be slick. This was one of those moments. Her eyes were slyly checking things out. There's no telling what she'd been snooping in before I got home. She was nosey like that.

"You want some juice?" she asked Dinero then turned to ask Cash the same thing.

They both nodded quickly.

"I want some now grandma," Cash chimed in.

"Alright," she said. "Let's go get some juice."

My lips pursed to the side. The bitch thought she was slick. She just wanted an excuse to go look in my muthafuckin' refrigerator like always, possibly even my kitchen cabinets. She did it every time she came over, like I was starving my kids or something. I could only shake my head.

Hearing them in the kitchen laughing, I turned to Treasure, who was still sitting on the couch. "I thought I told your hard headed ass not to let anyone in my house."

"But it was grandma."

"I don't give a fuck who it is. When I say don't let nobody up in here, that's what I mean. Nobody. The next time you do it, I'm gonna whoop your ass."

Seconds later, my mother came prancing out of the kitchen. Dinero was still in her arms, but now he was sipping from his sippy cup. Cash followed with a cup bigger than his face, grabbing onto her left leg.

"Don't y'all spill that shit on my carpet," I told them.

My mother twisted her face distastefully. "Why do you always have to talk to them like that?"

"Because they're *my* kids."

"I know they're your kids, Keema. But it's not good to talk to them like that. If they hear you using such foul language, they'll feel it's appropriate for them also."

She had gotten deeply under my skin. She used to be the most foul mouthed and loudest bitch in the hood. Damn near every word that came out of her mouth was a curse word once upon a time.

"Look, Ma." I was anxious to get her the fuck out of my house. My mind was still on Imani's bullshit and of course Paco. That shit had me worried and nervous. The last thing I was in the mood for was my mother's bullshit on top of it all. "What do you want?"

She sat on the couch. "Have you thought about what we talked about?"

My finger began to press the search button on the remote causing channel after channel to zoom by. My foot tapped on the floor repeatedly. I just couldn't get Imani out of my head.

"Well, have you?" she asked again.

"Yeah, I thought about it. And I'm not interested."

The last several times she came over we discussed me and the kids moving into her townhouse out in Reisterstown. Well, *she* discussed it. I spent most of the time ignoring her.

"Keema, I don't think you've taken the offer seriously. I don't think you've given it enough careful thought. I would love to wake up every day to my grandbabies running around. It's not good for them to be cooped up in this apartment all day anyway. At my townhouse they would have plenty of room."

I sighed again. Here she goes sounding like muthafuckin' Ivanka Trump. That newfound accent always worked my damn nerves mercilessly. I hated it.

"Ma, I'm good."

"Well, have you at least thought about going back to school?"

She'd discussed that also.

Tossing the remote, I got up and headed towards the window. Paco's face filled my head again. "Not right now, Ma. I haven't had the time for it."

She shook her head. "Child, is this what you want for the rest of your life? Do you want to be on the system forever? What type of example are you setting for the kids? They're going to grow up thinking that it's okay to lay around and milk the system."

I looked at her from across the room with spite. She was the pot calling the kettle black.

"I know what you're thinking," she said, seeing the look in my eyes. "When I was on it, my situation was totally different from yours. I had no choice. Keema, I had you young. Your father left me when he found out I was pregnant with you, so I was left on my own. I had no help. Welfare was my only option."

"Ummmph." I shrugged my shoulders nonchalantly.

"But you don't have to settle for that, Keema. You've got my support. Get off welfare and go back to school. I'll help you in every way I can."

She was smoking crack if she thought I'd give that any thought what so ever. Welfare was my safety net, my life preserver. Even though I got plenty money from niggas regularly and sold my weed on the side, those good government checks were consistent. Besides, I'd never had a job.

Ever.

And I was hooked on the system. Not being on it would cause me to go into convulsions. So, asking me to leave it was like asking a drug dealer to stop selling drugs. The shit just wasn't going to happen. Besides, my mother was selling me a pipe dream. Just because she'd made it out the hood successfully didn't necessarily mean I would. What if school didn't work out for me? What if I couldn't find a job? What would I be left with? It seemed like too much of a gamble. A gamble I wasn't willing to take. Since welfare was what I knew, it was what I was going to stick with, at least until either Frenchie's will or the day spa paid off.

"Ma, I said I'm good," I told her again, peeking through the curtains.

"You're lying, Keema. You're not good."

"Why would I lie?" I asked, turning to look at her.

"Because if you were good, you wouldn't keep looking out of your window every few minutes. Are you looking for that Paco guy that everyone's talking about?"

My eyes ballooned in utter surprise. How the hell did she know about Paco?

"Didn't think I knew, huh?" She rocked Dinero in her arms. "Just because I don't live around here anymore, doesn't mean my friends don't tell me what's going on."

Looking at her closely I asked, "What do you know about Paco?" Just hearing or speaking his name sent chills down my spine.

"Enough."

"Ma, don't play with me. This is serious. What do you know about Paco?"

Her face was overcome with worry. "I don't know the details, but I know he has a bounty on your head."

"A bounty?" I asked fearfully. That meant that he'd basically sicked the entire hood on me. Every crack head, prostitute, or dope boy would be willing to make the phone call to collect.

88

The room grew small. My heart rate sped up. Immediately, I looked out the curtains again to see if someone was looking up at my window.

"That's why I'm here, Keema. That man wants you dead. You and my grandbabies are not safe here.

Although I couldn't see anyone looking up at my window I began to pace the room nervously. I didn't know which thoughts were worse; the ones of Paco or the ones of Imani. Both had me terrified. Either the police were possibly going to kick my door in at any minute to take me to jail for the rest of my life or Paco was going to kick it in and blow my head off.

ELEVEN

The moment was happening so fast. Quickly back and forth I rushed from the open dresser drawers to the open suitcase sitting on my bed tossing clothes inside with trembling hands. I'd never been so scared before in my life. Knowing that in the upcoming moments your life could end was a terrifying feeling.

Over and over I kept seeing Paco or the cops kicking my door in. I saw ski masked goons trying to kill me for the ransom money. The visions made my body shake so badly that as soon as I put my mother out, I dashed straight to the bathroom to throw up. The situation had my body unable to slow down or relax.

In the kids' rooms I instructed Treasure to move quickly packing a suitcase for her brothers. Staying in the apartment for even a second more was not an option. We were sitting ducks and sure to be murdered if we stayed.

After getting my suitcase packed in a little less than five minutes, I zipped it, snatched it from the bed and charged directly to Treasure's room. She had the nerve to be moving as slow as molasses. The suitcase was only halfway packed.

"Why are you moving so slow?" I asked, charging into the room. "Didn't I tell you to hurry the fuck up?"

She had an angry look on her face. "I don't want to leave."

"I didn't ask you what you wanted."

"Why we gotta leave anyway?" she asked, casually tossing a pair of panties in the suitcase like she didn't have a care in the world.

"We don't have time for questions, Treasure."

"Who is Paco?"

I couldn't take anymore of her ass. Here we were possibly about to become the top story on the Fox 5 news, and all she could do was sit here and ask stupid questions. Shoving her out of the way, I snatched her dresser drawers open and began throwing shit in the suitcase, not giving a fuck what the items were.

Treasure folded her arms across her chest with an attitude. "I wish you would've just left us with the social services lady."

Just like that, I slapped the shit out of her leaving her little face stinging. The little skinny bitch was really pressing my buttons. I zipped the bag, slammed it against her flat chest so hard she stumbled backwards. "Let's go. Fuck all them damn questions."

Oddly, she never winced or cried. Soon, the four of us were out the door, down the steps, and walking quickly across the courtyard in no time. With Dinero and a large duffle bag on one arm and my Louis Vuitton tote bag on the other, I wouldn't allow my pace to be slowed.

"Hurry up," I ordered to Treasure and Shane. Both were walking fast, but struggling to keep up. Treasure was practically dragging Cash in one hand as she strained to carry a suitcase as big as her body in the other.

As we walked my eyes were on everyone around us. Knowing there was a bounty on my head, they were all potential enemies. Not one of them could be trusted in the least. I didn't know exactly how much the bounty was. But I did know any one of these thirsty muthafuckas would be eager to get paid so a bitch had to keep her eyes on every single movement they made and her ears on every single sound.

Even while holding Dinero and the bag, I still managed to keep my hand tucked into my purse and wrapped around the handle of the gun. Hopefully I wouldn't have to use it. I'd never actually pulled the trigger of a gun before the night I robbed

Paco, let alone killed someone with one. The possibility had me on edge, but there were no doubts in my mind that I would do it if I had to. We were walking tremendously fast, but the courtyard seemed to stretch farther and farther with each step we took. I swear the walk had never seemed this long before.

"Keema!" someone shouted from behind at a distance.

Recognizing the voice as some off brand ass nigga named Gino, I kept it moving.

"Keema!" he shouted again.

"Mommy, that boy is calling you!" Treasure said.

Ignoring her, my feet kept their pace.

"Keema!"

"Mommy."

"Shit, Treasure, I hear him," I told her angrily, but refused to slow my pace or stop.

"Keema, hold up a minute!"

"I'm busy, Gino!" I screamed over my shoulder without looking back.

"It'll only take a minute!"

My suspicion was aroused immediately. He hadn't been desperate to catch up to me any time before. He knew I didn't fuck with broke niggas like him. Something wasn't right. But I wasn't going to stick around to find out what it was.

"Keema, slow down a minute!"

He was getting closer and he had now started to jog. My hand clutched the gun tighter and my finger wrapped around the trigger much more snuggly than before.

"Keema!"

My heart was pounding at the thought of having to shoot him if he kept approaching.

"Keema, hold up!" he said, getting even closer.

Everything around me began to spin.

"Keema!"

He'd gotten too close. That was it. Quickly I dropped the suitcase, knelt down to drop Dinero on the pavement, and spun around with the gun aimed at Gino.

"What the fuck?" he said with surprise. He froze in his tracks.

"Get your ass back, muthafucka!" I screamed.

He held his hands ahead of him in defense. "What the hell is wrong with you?"

"I said get back!"

The kids watched me closely in awe at what they were seeing.

Gino took two steps back with his hands still raised.

"Damn girl, I just wanted to holla at you!"

"And I said I'm busy!"

"You a crazy bitch," he said, backing further away.

I didn't like the look in his eyes. There was something sneaky in them, something I hadn't seen in them before this moment. He was definitely trying to set me up. I knew it.

"Whatever, just stay your ass back!"

Snatching Dinero back up in my arm and grabbing the suitcase, I told the kids, "Let's go!"

They did as they were told.

We all headed out of the courtyard. Quickly, I turned to see Gino on his cell phone. Knowing who he was most likely calling, I stepped up my pace and told the kids to do the exact same. Before I knew it we were a few blocks over and approaching the Charger. As we got closer and closer to it, my head was on a swivel. I was looking everywhere for any sight of Paco. After me and the kids finally reached the car, we hopped in, and sped away from the curb within minutes.

My heart was beating through my chest as we drove, headed to a hotel. From my purse I could hear my cell phone beeping, signaling me that I'd missed call or a message. Hoping it was from Imani, I snatched it from my purse and checked. There were three missed calls but none of them were from Imani. They were from Ms. Vines, Tia, and Peppi. Each had left a message. I placed the phone to my ear to play the messages. The first was from Ms. Vines. She said she'd gotten word the children were back in my custody. Before she could continue my benefits,

I would have to see her again. Not in the mood to hear the entire message, I skipped to the next one. It was from Tia.

"Hey, Keema," her voice said. "Everything's good on this end. The paperwork for your D.C and V.A. welfare applications are in. Call me ASAP."

The message ended.

That was good news, but there was no time to celebrate. As I listened to the phone, my eyes were searching my rearview mirror for anything suspicious, especially Paco's BMW.

The next message began to play.

"Keema, its Peppi. Just checking in to make sure we're still on tonight at midnight. Call me and let me know."

The message ended.

Damn, I had forgotten all about my meeting with Peppi tonight. Immediately I called him.

"Keema," he said cheerfully. He always sounded that way when I called. "How are you, princess?"

"I'm okay," I lied. "I can't talk right now, but we're still on for tonight."

"That's great to hear. I'm looking forward to seeing you."

"Alright, see you tonight."

After hanging up I called Tia.

"What's up, gurlllll?" she asked, answering on the first ring.

"You. So, everything's good?"

"Yup, you need to come down here and get your license as soon as possible. Bring that money with you also. The girl who pushed your application through is bugging me about when she's gonna get paid. When you coming?"

"Soon."

"How soon? I mean, I don't wanna rush you, but my car note needs to be paid this week. I could really use that money."

She was pissing me off. I told the bitch I would pay her soon for allowing me to use her address to get my welfare money every month. There was no need for her to tell me anything about her fucking car note. She'd get her money when she got it.

95

"Look, I said you'll get it. I gotta go."
My finger stabbed at the end button.

TWELVE

It was just a little before twelve a.m. when I pulled up in front of the Havana Club on Water Street. Underneath the golden lights of the overhead street lamps I searched for a space. The club was jumping so the parking was minimal, but eventually I found a spot not even a block away.

The kids were back at the hotel. This time I'd left *strict* orders with Treasure that she was *not* to let anyone in the room, no matter who they were. If she did, she was going to get her ass tore up when I got back. She rolled her eyes, but got the message.

As I shut off the car's engine, off my eyes scoured the lot. I couldn't help it. My nerves were on edge terribly. Imani still wasn't answering her phone or returning my calls, and obviously Paco still wanted a piece of my ass. I didn't know which one had me more worried.

Before climbing out of the car, I reached into my purse and placed my hand around my protection. Just the feel of it gave me a little security and piece of mind; not much, but enough to allow me to step out the car and make my way toward the club. My eyes watched every single car entering and leaving the lot until I was inside.

"Keema!" Peppi shouted over the loud playing Salsa music spilling from the club's speakers. He was at the bar. "Over here!"

Wall to wall Mexican's and Puerto Ricans were dancing

and talking. I never knew they had a spot on Water Street. That shit was new to me. I made my way through the crowded club over to him. When I reached Peppi, he gave me a hug like he hadn't seen me in ages. He was dressed in a white button down shirt, black pants, and immaculately polished black pointed toe dress shoes. I'd never seen a pair of shoes with a point so sharp. Normally he dressed nice, but he'd definitely missed the mark in the shoe area this time.

Giving me a huge smile, he said, "I'm so glad you could make it."

My lips curled into a forced smile.

Seeing the nervousness in my face his own turned into a frown. "You don't look good, my little princess."

"I'm okay," I lied.

"No, you don't look good. I see it all over your face. Something is troubling you."

Avoiding his eye contact, I said, "It's nothing."

Softly placing a hand on my cheek and turning my eyes to him he said, "You're too beautiful to let life's troubles make you sad. I need you to forget them tonight and smile for Peppi. You can do that, yes?"

I attempted, but stress wouldn't allow it to come out fully.

"No, not good enough. Give Peppi a smile big as the world."

I attempted again.

Not satisfied, he began to make funny faces while crossing his eyes and stretching his ears. I couldn't hold it in. I was forced to smile and laugh.

He smiled immediately. "That's what Peppi is talking about. A big smile. Peppi likes big smiles."

Peppi always knew how to make me laugh. He was one of those people who was just full of life. It was as if just breathing the air made him high. He loved living and always wanted the people round him to love it, too. Whenever in his presence he made people feel good. That was a trait I wished I had sometimes.

98

"Here, sit, my little precious flower," he said, pulling a stool from the bar.

I sat down and he ordered drinks for us. As the bartender began to pour them, Peppi said, "I have wonderful surprise for you; one you will love."

I hoped so. I could use something uplifting right now.

He opened a bag sitting on the chair beside him and pulled out several colorful brochures. He handed them to me. My eyes brightened at what was on them. They were brochures of the day spa. I loved them.

Seeing my joy, he said, "You like, yes?"

"Peppi, I love them," I said joyously, unable to take my eyes away. My dream was ever so close to becoming reality. Thoughts of Paco and Imani left my mind.

He laughed enthusiastically. "I knew you would."

"Peppi, they're gorgeous."

"It is never too early to promote and advertise. Clientele is already setting up appointments."

"Are you serious?" I asked in disbelief.

"Peppi is serious as heart attack," he answered with a huge smile. "He never lies about business."

God, he was a life saver. I could picture myself cutting the red ribbon in front of the doors the day of the Grand Opening.

"Each of them are already begging me to allow them to be our very first customer," he said with excitement." Our first day open will be a very busy one. I know it."

He was immensely hyped as he spoke.

Dollar signs appeared in my mind. I could see decimals and averages repeatedly. It was going to be raining money.

"Did you bring the money for the contractor?" he inquired.

Damn it, I thought. I'd forgotten about the contractor's money. My pockets were strapped right now. I had nowhere near what I owed them.

"I only have fifteen hundred," I said, the disappointment clear in my voice.

Peppi placed a hand on my knee, seeing the change in my attitude. "No, princess," he said with a big smile. "No worry. Peppi will double your fifteen hundred."

"Are you serious?"

He laughed. "As I said before, Peppi never lies about business."

"I really appreciate it."

"It's my pleasure. As a matter of fact, Peppi will match every penny from now on, no matter how much."

I couldn't believe my ears.

"You are a great woman, Keema. You're smart and business minded. I like that. There's no way I will allow you to come this far to fail. Peppi can not allow that."

I hugged him. What he'd just told me was the best news I'd heard all day. As long as I got out here and grinded like crazy, my dream would come true.

"Now," he said, releasing me and sliding off of his stool. "No more talk of business. Let us step out on the floor and dance to our success. We must celebrate."

As I slid off of my stool to happily join him, my cell phone rang. Recognizing it as Dupree's ring tone, I told Peppi I would join him soon.

"Don't make me wait long, my princess," he said, softly kissing my hand. "We must dance the night away without a single second to waste."

As he headed to the dance floor I answered the phone.

There was heavy coughing coming from the other end of the line.

"Dupree?" I asked, plugging my other ear with a finger to block out the music.

Heavy coughing again.

The sound was creepy. "Dupree?"

"Keema," he answered in a low raspy voice. "I…I…I need you here."

"Baby, what's wrong?"

"I don't…think…I'm going to make it too much longer."

100

"Dupree, what's going on? Why are you talking like this? Has the doctor told you something?"

He coughed again.

"Dupree?"

"Please come tonight, Keema. I…I…I need you here."

"Dupree?"

The line went dead.

As hundreds of people danced happily around me I could only stare blankly at my phone.

THIRTEEN

The morning sun poured brightly through the window of the Days Inn despite the fact that the curtains were closed. I lay on my back in one of the two beds staring up at the ceiling silently thinking about everything that had led me here. My mind was getting absolutely no rest. My body hadn't truly gotten any either. Sleeping had been impossible. Throughout the night if I wasn't lying down, I was flipping over and over again through the television's cable channels or walking back and forth to the window peeking through the curtains. Paranoia wouldn't let me sleep. The few times my eyes closed and my body attempted to sleep nightmares of Paco finding me and blowing my head off woke me up.

Despite Dupree practically begging me to come see him last night, I didn't go. He'd even called several times more, but his calls went unanswered. I just didn't have it in me to talk to him or see him. I just wanted the nigga dead so shit could start going a lot easier and smoother. I was tired. With that money from the will, I could just leave all the damn headaches behind me and finally rest. There wouldn't have to be no more sneaking and cheating. I'd have my spa, my money and the stress could finally be over. I could finally have the life I'd been dreaming of.

As I lay silently the kids were sitting on the other bed watching cartoons and laughing like they didn't have a care in the world. Looney Tunes was on. Shane was even sitting there staring at the screen laughing and holding his stomach. I wasn't sure if he was laughing at the show or not. With that nigga you could never tell. Treasure was also sitting there with an evil look on her face. I guess she was still pissed off about having to leave home. Oh well, she might as well get over it because until I could figure out our next move, this tiny ass hotel room was home whether she liked it or not.

Looking at the clock, I realized it was time to call Hype. We'd spoken last night on the phone because my pockets were hurting and in need of a quick fix. Fast food and hotel rooms were going to get really expensive, really fast. He was on the highway, making an out of town run when we spoke. He told me he would be back in B-more by nine o'clock. We could hook up then. Overnight, I'd come up with a much more profitable idea. Instead of getting just a few hundred out of his ass, I was going to get *everything* in his pockets. The nigga just didn't know it yet.

Hype always kept a few thousand in his pocket. That type of money was like spare change to a hustla like him. He was always good for it like clockwork. He was also one of them low key type of niggas; a pretty boy, soft spoken, didn't believe in stuntin' too hard. He preferred to let his S550 Benz, clothes, and his jewels do all the speaking for him. And believe me, they spoke volumes.

I rolled out of the bed and went into the bathroom to call him so my kids wouldn't hear my conversation. He answered the phone on the second ring.

"What's up, Keema?"

"What's up, nigga? You still gonna let me get some of that dick? My pussy is wet as shit."

"Yeah, I got you. I'm just getting off the highway. Where you wanna meet up at?"

"Let's do Motel 6 on Bloomfield Avenue."

That motel was about five miles from where I was at. There was no way I was going to attempt what I had planned for his ass at the same spot me and my kids would be forced to lay our heads at for the time being.

"It's on," he said.

I could picture him rubbing his hands together in eager anticipation. Not only was he a balla, but he also *loved* to eat pussy. He'd eaten mine for hours like it was sea food.

"I'll be waiting in the parking lot for you, baby," I told him.

"I got you. See you in about twenty minutes."

We hung up.

I then called Rayquan's dumb ass to see what was up with the damn job. I needed to know when it would be done. Obviously I wanted this shit to be over with as soon as possible. The phone rang several times with no answer, so I called back. He finally answered.

"Hello?"

"Rayquan, what's going on with that?" I asked, not wanting to mention specifics on the phone. I never knew who might be listening. I definitely didn't want a repeat performance of what Shane had pulled the other day.

"Who dis?"

What the fuck? This nigga had heard my voice a million different times.

"Nigga, stop playing with me. You know who this is."

"Oh, what's up?"

"You *know* what's up. You know what I'm calling for, too."

Silence.

"Rayquan?"

"I'm here. What's up?"

He was pissing me the fuck off.

"Stop playing stupid. Is the shit ready to go down or what?"

"Uh-huh."

It sounded like he was talking in codes, like someone was near him. I knew that way of talking because I'd done it a million times while laying in the bed with Dupree or being somewhere close to him when another nigga called me. This dude had me

105

paranoid. Since I'd seen him in Dupree's club that night, I just didn't trust him anymore.

"When?" I questioned.

"Soon."

"How soon?"

"Just soon. I gotta go."

Rayquan hung up, making me extremely skeptical about whether or not he was going to come through on our deal. I had paid him six stacks. That shit was an investment. Just as I was getting ready to call him back my phone rang. Rick's name and number appeared on the screen. He, along with my mother, had called me several times last night. I never answered either of their calls.

After pressing the decline button to get rid of him, I jumped up from the bed and took a quick shower so I could get ready to meet Hype's fine ass. After climbing out the shower, drying off and getting dressed, I tossed Treasure a twenty dollar bill and told her to run over to McDonalds to get her and her brothers breakfast while I was gone. I also told her to make sure she brought herself straight back to the hotel room after she got the food. Seconds later I was out the door and hopping in my car, headed over to meet Hype. When I pulled into the lot, he hadn't got there yet. As I waited, he finally pulled into the lot with the newest Lil Wayne banga playing loudly from the Benz's speakers. Seeing my car, he parked beside me.

"What's good, sexy?" he asked, climbing out of his car dressed in grey Hugo Boss sweatpants and a Boss shirt that matched perfectly.

"You," I said, climbing out of my car with a huge smile.

After giving each other a hug, we walked inside the hotel and up to the front desk where Hype paid for a room with a king sized bed. Once the desk clerk handed him a key card, I started hugging his slender frame, squeezing his dick, and loving up on him as we walked away.

"Damn, girl," he managed to say between my kisses and my tongue repeatedly shoving its way down his throat. He palmed my ass tightly in his hands as he returned as many of my kisses as he could.

When we reached the door, Hype laughed. "Let me at least get the key in the door."

"I want this dick," I told him, feeling it grow into full hardness as I squeezed it.

My hand unzipped him, reached into his boxers, and took it in my hand aggressively. He moaned as I stroked it. My free hand then eased slyly around his waist to check for a gun. With what I had planned, I didn't need another near death incident like the one with Paco. Thankfully there wasn't one.

As soon as Hype opened the door, I shoved him inside backwardly, making sure not to allow him to turn on the light. Closing the door, I began to undress him while kissing his entire hundred something pound body from head to toe. Within seconds he was totally naked. All his clothes were on the floor. I hadn't even allowed him to wear his socks or underwear. I then pushed him onto the bed.

"I'm gonna fuck you good, girl," he said, lying on his back with his dick poking towards the ceiling. His arms were stretched out wide as he eyed my hips and curves, anxious to shove something inside of me.

He was right where I wanted him. It was more than perfect. Smiling, I reached inside my purse, pulled out my gun, and pointed it at him. I then turned the light on.

His smile turned into disbelief. "What the fuck you doing?"

"Shut your damn mouth."

"Keema, I ain't playing with…"

Cocking the gun, I ordered loudly, "Shut the fuck up!"

Hype reluctantly did as he was told, but the look on his face was beyond furious. He wanted to kill my ass. I could see it in his eyes. Nothing in the world would have meant more to him at the moment than to see me take my last breath.

Immediately, I started rambling through his pockets while keeping my eyes on him. They were locked on me, refusing to blink. I knew he was hoping that I'd slip up just once; just enough for him to get the gun from me. I left him disappointed though. My eyes stayed glued on him and I kept myself at a safe distance until I found his money. Pulling out a thick stack of hundreds, my eyes glimmered like diamonds but only briefly. My pussy grew wet at the sight of so many benjamins, but I knew I couldn't stay and gloat. There was no time. I stuffed the money in my purse, snatched up all Hype's clothes, and headed to the door.

"This is fucked up, Keema," he said angrily. His erection was gone. "You a scandalous bitch."

"Whatever," I said while opening the door with his clothes underneath my arm.

"You should've killed me. When I catch you, I'm gon' fuck your ass up. That's a promise, bitch. I swear on my life I'm gon' kill you!"

Shutting the door, there wasn't a single doubt in my mind that he was serious. But I couldn't sit there and ponder on that shit. Within one minute flat, I'd dashed from the room while stuffing the gun back into my purse. Luckily, the desk clerk had given us a room on the opposite side of where we'd parked. When I finally approached my car, my head was down in search of my keys. When I finally found them I raised my head. What my eyes saw sent a bolt of fear through me. I stopped in one spot at the sight of who was leaning against my trunk with their arms crossed across their chest. My heart dropped to the ground.

It was Rick. For several moments neither of us spoke. We only stared. I myself had no idea what to say.

"You don't know how to answer your phone?" he finally asked angrily.

"Huh?" I knew damn well I'd heard his question.

"You heard me," he said, taking a step in my direction.

I didn't know what to say as I quickly turned to look at Hype's car knowing I needed to get ghost.

"Uhhh," was all I could say.

"Whose clothes are you carrying?"

"Uhhh," escaped my lips again.

Lies had always been my specialty. I always had plenty of them in my repertoire and ready to go at any second. But at the moment, my mind was blank. My catalog was empty as my head rotated back toward the motel room. It wouldn't be long before Hype snatched the curtains or something to cover his body and ended up in the parking lot with us.

"So, your ass was up in a motel room wit' some nigga. Where's my muthafuckin' nephews?"

I knew I couldn't tell him I'd left them alone, especially so I could go out to rob somebody. All I could do was stand there all jittery like a scared child who'd just gotten caught with their hand stuck deep in the cookie jar.

Rick shook his head. "I knew all this foul shit I've been hearin' in the street about you was true. You a triflin' bitch. My nephews are comin' wit' me. Where the fuck they at?"

I quickly turned around to see Hype running my way with a pillow covering his nuts and balls.

"Shit!"

"You skank ass bitch!" Hype screamed as he got closer.

Rick looked over my shoulder at him. "Who the fuck is that, nigga?" he asked me.

"Nobody," I said, pushing him towards his car. I wanted to get the hell away as soon as possible. "I'm gonna take you to the kids."

"I'ma kill your ass!" Hype spewed.

"What the fuck did you do to that nigga?" Rick questioned.

I couldn't tell him.

He looked at me even more angrily than before. "What the fuck did you do to that nigga?" he asked again. The expression on his face demanded an answer.

Shame wouldn't allow me to speak. My eyes could only give him a pitiful stare, wishing the moment would just go away. At that moment Rick knew exactly what I'd done. He knew definitely that the rumors he'd heard were true. Shaking his head at me, he said, "Get your ass in your car!"

109

I stumbled as he pushed me towards my driver's door and Hype quickly drew closer.

"Oh, so this nigga wit' you, huh?" Hype shouted.

Without hesitation Rick reached underneath his Ravens jersey, pulled out a gun, and aimed at Hype.

"Rick, don't…"

Before the entire sentence could escape my lips three loud shots caused my ears to ring. All three bullets hit Hype directly in the chest, dropping him to the concrete immediately. Rick then quickly walked up on Hype, stood over his already lifeless body and sent another bullet through the center of his forehead just to assure he was dead.

My body was frozen. And my eyes were locked on Hype as blood poured from his chest and began to pool around him.

"Didn't I say get in the car?" Rick yelled at me as he jogged away from the dead body headed towards his Jag. "We gotta get the fuck out of here!"

I gave Hype one last look and hopped into my car. After dropping his clothes on the ground, I cranked up the car and sped out of the parking lot directly behind Rick.

FOURTEEN

Our cars pulled into the parking lot of The Days Inn and parked side by side. Hopping out of mine first, I told Rick as he was climbing out of his car, "I'm so sorry. I swear on my mother I am."

With a dead serious look on his face he said, "I don't want to hear it, Keema."

"But, Rick," I attempted, hoping he would give me just a moment to run some game on him. My mouth had always been my greatest weapon. All I needed was a willing pair of ears.

"Go get my nephews," he said, refusing to listen.

"Rick, please…"

"Now, Keema!"

"Rick, just give me one second to…"

In the blink of an eye Rick snapped. He grabbed me by the neck and wrapped his big burly hand around my throat so tight I couldn't breathe. Immediately my eyes began to go glossy.

Slamming me by the neck backwards to the hood of my car and pressing his face directly into mine, he said through gritted teeth, "Bitch, *fuck* what you got to say. I don't want to hear none of it. I'm not like my brother. Your words don't mean shit to me. They don't work."

No air could get to my lungs; not a single solitary bit. My eyes were beginning to bulge from my skull.

"Muthafuckas out here got a damn ransom on your head.

They want to kill you. The triflin' shit you out here doin' to nig-gas is puttin' my nephews' lives in danger. You playin' games wit' their lives like you have that right."

My knees were growing weak. My brain needed oxygen. I felt like I was going to black out any second as my fingers grabbed at his hands, which seemed to be tightening more and more with every passing second. I honestly thought he was going to kill me right in the middle of the parking lot.

"This ain't no game. Fuck your excuses. I don't want to hear none of 'em. Now, go get my muthafuckin' nephews before I snap the shit out of your sneaky ass."

He shoved me toward the door by the throat. Coughing as I stumbled along the way, the two of us headed to the room. When we reached it and walked inside, Dinero's eyes lit up when he saw his uncle. He immediately ran to Rick's arms.

Picking up Dinero, Rick said, "They don't need any bags. I'll buy everything they need."

He was so angry. All he wanted to do was get the kids and leave. He wanted no conversation of any sort. Treasure watched everything quietly as she sat on the edge of the bed next to Shane and Cash.

"Shane needs his medication," Treasure told Rick.

"Well, go get it, Keema. Now!" he belted.

"It's back at the apartment," I responded shamefully. "I was going to go back later this afternoon and get it," I lied.

I'd realized it the night before while lying in the bed. Apparently I was so scared and moving so fast when trying to get up out of that apartment his meds had totally skipped my mind. He had several prescriptions, including Prozac and Haldol, which had to be taken every day.

Rick's fist balled and his face grew into a sneer. He wanted to erupt all over me. It was obvious. Out of fright for what I now knew he was capable of, my feet took a step back on their own.

"Not only do you leave him and the kids here by them-selves while you out here robbin' niggas, but you got Shane out here without his damn medication?"

My body tensed. I thought he was going to hit me.

"What the fuck is wrong wit' you?"

His chest began to heave back and forth heavily and he looked at me with spite. I could tell Rick wanted to fuck me up, but somehow regained his composure. He just shook his head and said, "Let's go get his shit before you fuck around and make me kill your ass, Keema."

Seconds later we were in our cars headed back to the projects. I hadn't planned on returning, but I guess in this case I didn't have much of a choice. Treasure and Cash were with me while Dinero and Shane were with Rick. Shane didn't want to go with Rick, and he definitely didn't want to leave me permanently. He threw a fit in the motel room. I had to talk him into it by telling him it was only temporary.

There were tears in my eyes as I drove and every single inch of my body was shaking. I'd gotten myself in a world of trouble and staying in Baltimore any longer was out of the question. With Paco now looking for me, and with the type of money he had, he wouldn't have too much of a problem spreading it around enough to make the streets talk. Knowing I was marked for death was the most terrifying feeling in the world. There was nothing left to do but leave, at least until the heat blew over.

As I drove, I quickly sifted through the money I'd stolen from Hype. It looked like a little over three stacks. With the three thousand, I was going to take Treasure and hit the highway to D.C. I was even going to leave Cash behind over my mother's house. A four year old would only slow me down. I had plans for Treasure though. Once down there, I'd get with Tia about my welfare benefits and figure out what direction I needed to head.

The day spa was still on my mind. It was so close. And with Peppi promising to match everything I invested from this point forward, in all actuality, I could put Baltimore in my rearview for good. I just needed to hit D.C and hustle. Dupree's set up was also still on my mind. It was already set in motion. But without Shane and Dinero, everything was for nothing. It

113

was definitely best for me to get as far away as possible. If it was discovered that I had anything to do with Frenchie's murder and Dupree's potential murder, Rick would kill me for sure. I *had* to go. There was no other choice.

When I pulled into the parking lot of my building, Rick was already there waiting. The kids were in his car and he was posted against the hood with the handle of his Glock poking out from underneath his jersey. Obviously after hearing about Paco, he wasn't going to allow himself to get caught slipping in the middle of the situation. He didn't know Paco personally since they ran in totally different circles on different side of towns, but killers killed the same way in every hood.

I pulled up beside him, climbed out of the car, and headed towards my building's entrance through the courtyard with Cash and Treasure. Rick followed with Dinero in his arms and Shane beside him. As we walked numerous sets of eyes were on me from windows, stoops, and the nearby playground. People whispered to each other. Evidently the whole hood now knew about Paco. Soon they'd also know about Hype. I sped up my pace and kept my hand stuffed in my purse clutching the handle of my gun. When we finally reached the hallway, and headed up the iron staircase, we all walked down the narrow hall to my apartment. In my mind I kept expecting to see Paco leap out from nowhere. The thought had my nerves rattling. Not even knowing that Rick was behind me with his strap could ease my fears and nervousness.

When we walked into the apartment, Shane rushed by everyone into the living room, sat on the couch, and turned on the television with the remote. He then leaned back into the pillows with a scowl on his face and folded his arms over his chest. Everyone knew it was going to take a lot to get him out of that spot. He didn't want to go and his face and body language showed it clearly.

"Hurry up," Rick told me.

He didn't have to tell me twice. Moving quickly was already my intentions. I didn't want to be here no longer than I needed to be. I headed to my room to get Shane's meds. While in there, Treasure went to Shane's room and got his favorite blanket, his PS3 and his collection of games. We both came back out into the living room at the same time.

Treasure handed Rick the blanket, the system and games. "He likes to play Madden mostly," she told him. "He also won't sleep unless he has his blanket."

Rick nodded.

She got on my nerves trying to be grown. I hadn't asked her to go get no damn games or blanket. All she had to do was stay in a child's place. Why did she always have to stick her nose into grown folk's shit?

As I approached Rick with the meds, he snatched them away from me and gave me a seething stare. "Let's go, Shane."

Shane ignored him.

Rick sighed with annoyance. He wasn't in the mood. "Shane, I said lets go." His voice was much more stern than before.

Still Shane didn't say anything or move. He simply stared at the television.

"Shane."

Shane began to rock back and forth, his face growing angry. In his own way, he was refusing to leave.

"Damn it, Shane!" Rick blared.

"Damn it, Shane," Shane repeated.

Treasure walked over to Rick, slipped her hand into his, and squeezed. With a sympathetic look, she said, "He doesn't like to be yelled at. That only makes him drift farther away from you."

With Rick looking at her she let go of his hand and slowly walked over to Shane. She knelt in front of him as he continued to rock back and forth with his arms folded. "Hey," she whispered.

He continued to ignore her.

Besides the television the room was completely silent.

She placed a hand on his knee and said, "Hey," once

again. This time much more softly.

Shane stopped rocking and looked down into his sister's eyes.

"It's okay," she told him with a smile. "Your uncle loves you. He wouldn't let anything happen to you."

Her words were beyond soft and caring. They were motherly.

"I know you don't want to go," she continued. "But it's only temporary." With those words she glanced at me with a look in her eyes that let me know she didn't like having to lie to him.

"You'll be coming back real soon," she continued.

"I'll be coming back real soon. You promise?" Shane asked. It was the first set of original words he'd said today.

Treasure glanced at me again then dropped her eyes to the floor for a brief second to muster up the strength to do what she knew she had to do. She raised her head and said, "Yeah, Shane," with a smile. "I promise."

He returned her smile and looked at his uncle, then looked at Treasure again. It was almost as if he was unsure.

"It's okay," she assured him. She then stood, kissed him on the cheek, and helped him up. She took him by the hand and walked him over to Rick.

Suddenly, my cell phone rang. The ring tone was Dupree's. Of all the times for him to call, damn it.

As Rick stood at the door with Dinero and Shane he looked at me, expecting me to answer. He knew Dupree's ring tone.

With no other choice I answered. "Hello?"

"Hey, Keema," Dupree said weakly.

My eyes dropped to the floor, too ashamed to look at Rick.

"They're letting me out today."

The news seemed bizarre. He'd just called me last night saying he wasn't going to make it. Now, he was calling to tell me he was coming home. I didn't know what to say. Something wasn't right.

"Hello?" Dupree said."Hello."

"Yeah, baby, I'm here."

"Damn, ain't…you…happy?" he asked with way too many pauses between each word.

"Of course," I returned with fake enthusiasm.

"Alright, well come get me."

"Okay."

The line went dead.

The room was silent.

Rick finally spoke. He saw my worries and doubts clearly. "He wants you to come pick him up, doesn't he?"

Evidently the two brothers had spoken to each other some time earlier. I didn't trust it. It could possibly be a set up. There was no telling what all had been said or what all they may have had planned for me. I wasn't sure if Rick had told Dupree about Paco and Hype. I wasn't even sure if Rayquan was or wasn't possibly involved. Taking that trip to the hospital could possibly turn out to be my very last trip on earth.

"Yeah," I said, answering Rick's question.

Rick shook his head disappointedly. He could see in my face that I wasn't going. No matter how hard I tried to fake it, the shit was obvious. "All he ever wanted was for you to be that one he could trust," he said. "But just like most bitches, you just out for yourself."

He turned, opened the door, and headed out with the kids. "I'm going to pick him up."

"I'll be behind you," I shouted, wondering why I even attempted that lie.

"Yeah, whatever." He shut the door.

At the closing of the door Treasure rolled her eyes at me and plopped down on the couch. Her entire world looked shattered at the sight of seeing two of her brothers walk out. She and Dinero had never been separated since he was born. This was the very first time.

There was no time to feel sorry for her. There was no doubt in my mind that someone had called Paco by now. He was probably on his way at that very moment. It was time to roll out, drop Cash off at my mother's and hit the highway.

"Let's go," I told Treasure as I grabbed the remote from the table.

Just as my finger was about to press the power button Imani's face appeared on the screen. "What the hell?" I gasped and clutched at my chest.

Underneath Imani's photo read: **WOMAN'S BODY DISCOVERED MUTILATED.**

I couldn't believe my eyes. My heart sunk as the newscaster stood by an alley I recognized. Imani's family appeared briefly. They were crying and holding each other as the newscaster said that Imani's body had been discovered a few hours ago. She'd been stabbed over thirty times and gutted. Her throat had also been slit so badly that it had nearly taken her head off. A homicide detective appeared and said that it was the most gruesome murder he'd come in contact with during his entire fifteen years on the force.

Everything around me disappeared.

My ears couldn't even hear the television anymore.

Only visions and sounds of Imani pleading for her life were all my mind could manufacture. Along with her face came Paco's. My knees grew weak and my stomach turned until it jerked. I could feel myself feeling like I had to throw up. I dashed to the bathroom, dropped to the toilet, and let loose everything in my stomach.

For several moments I stayed on my knees weeping. Tears streamed from my eyes as memories of Imani came rushing back. Guilt enveloped me. I'd gotten her into this.

Treasure walked into the bathroom, grabbed a wash cloth, and turned on the sink. After wetting the rag she knelt beside me, took my chin into her hand, and began to wipe my face clean. When she was finished, the two of us could only stare at each other. This time though, our stare was much different than any ones before.

She could see my pain.

She sympathized with it.

She also, for the first time in days, realized just how serious the situation was. She now understood what we were running from.

"Momma," she said in a voice just as soft as the one she'd spoken to Shane in. "We can't stay. We gotta go."

FIFTEEN

Besides a few meaningless words from Cash, the entire drive over to my mother's house was completely quiet, the atmosphere depressing and gloom filled. Neither Treasure nor I said a single word to each other. We both could only watch the passing houses and moving traffic as we placed street after street behind us. Knowing Imani would never call or visit again was one of the most difficult things I'd ever been forced to accept. My heart didn't want to. Several times during the drive my hand had to wipe away tears that fell uncontrollably. A constant lump remained lodged in my throat. Imani was my best friend, the closest thing in this entire world I had to a sister. And now she was gone. My heart was shattered.

Several minutes later, the Charger pulled into my mother's neighborhood. The suburban streets were clean and quiet. Each of its houses and townhouses were perfectly sized; driveways and curbs were laced with fairly nice cars, most not too expensive.

My mom had pretty much come a long way from the projects. Although her neighborhood was a black suburb and some of its residents had gotten in by Section 8, it was still an extremely far cry from where she'd come from. Crime was rare. There were no drug dealers posted on corners and winos standing in front of stores. The city demanded the properties be kept up or the owners were harshly fined. Cars didn't swerve up and down the street with music blasting and were only allowed to park on the curb during certain times of the day. The schools were respectable and the police tolerated no bullshit.

"Ewwww, we're at grandma's house!" Cash screamed excitedly from the backseat.

He couldn't wait to get out of the car. Every time he saw his grandmother he reacted like he was on an amusement park ride. He knew she would spoil him, let him run wild, and buy him pretty much anything he asked her for.

My mother could never seem to tell her grandkids 'no', although she never seemed to have any problem telling it to me when I was a kid. With her they could have all the candy and ice cream they wanted. They could stay up as late as they wanted. And if they did something they had no damn business doing, she refused to whip them. In their eyes she never wanted to be the bad guy. All she wanted was to see smiles on their faces.

As I pulled to the curb in front of my mother's home, a lady who looked to be somewhere in her early fifties was quietly working in a front yard garden of her own home. Turning off the engine I could see that my mother's silver Cadillac SRX wasn't in the driveway. Looking in my rearview at Cash as he anxiously pressed his face to the window, my heart felt remorse for him. Yet, I knew this had to be done. Quickly looking away from him, unable to take the guilt, I looked over at Treasure.

"Take your brother up there," I ordered.

"Yaaaaayyyy!" Cash yelled happily, too young to know or even suspect what I was doing. He began hopping up and down in his seat anxiously.

"But grandma isn't home," Treasure said, leaning forward in her seat in an attempt to see if her grandmother's car was somewhere further up the driveway.

I knew it wasn't. My mother never parked her car in the garage or behind the house. The Cadillac, besides her home, was her baby and her prized possession. She kept it fully detailed and was proud of it. Parking it where it couldn't be seen was not an option for her. She *always* kept it in the driveway, intentionally showcasing it to her neighbors.

"Just take him up there," I said, turning away from her.

She looked at me and frowned. "But grandma isn't…"

"I know she's not home!" I yelled, sick and tired of Treasure always having to give me some sort of back talk anytime I told her to do something instead of just staying in a child's place. "Just do what I told your ass to do!"

"Yeah, Treasure," Cash said. "Do what she told your ass to do. And take me so we can see grandma."

I sighed at the realization that my child knew how to curse because of me. I couldn't face either of my children.

"But after what happened to aunt Imani, we should stick…"

"Look, Treasure," I said, trying to put a lid on my temper and blood pressure. She was truly getting on my nerves. "That old lady up there next door will watch him."

Treasure turned and looked at the old lady tending to her garden. She turned back to me. "But we don't even know her," she said. "I don't think…"

"Treasure, I don't give a damn what you think."

She looked at me speechless.

"Now, just do what I told you to do. We ain't got time to go back and forth."

"No," she said, sitting back in her seat and folding her arms defiantly as if she wasn't going to budge.

I looked at her like she'd blown a damn fuse. "What did you just say to me?"

"I said no." Her face was full of defiance.

That was it. That was *muthafuckin'* it! Treasure had been trying her damn luck with me ever since she got back from CPS. She'd forgotten what her role in our mother and daughter relationship was. And it was far past time for me to remind her ass. Unable to hold my temper or keep my composure with her any longer, my hand grabbed a hold of her shirt and jerked her little narrow frame towards me like a rag doll. I had such a tight grip on her shirt that it was wrapped totally around my hand, and my knuckles were jammed deeply into her chest causing her to wince in pain.

"Listen here, you little fucka. Ever since you brought your little hard headed ass home from CPS, you've been trying me. And I'm sick of it."

Something beyond fear was obvious in her big brown eyes. She couldn't even blink them. They were locked on me, too scared to even move side to side or leave my face.

Snatching her even closer to my face and getting an even tighter grip of her shirt, I said, "What the fuck I say goes around here. Do you understand me?"

She didn't answer.

Snatching her again, I repeated even more angrily than before, "Do you fuckin' understand me?"She nodded quickly.

"Make sure you do. Because the next time you try me, I'm gonna fuck you up." Her eyes were wide.

"You got that?"

"Yes," she sniffled as she spoke.

"Now, take your brother up there on the porch, leave him, and get back in the car. We got somewhere we need to be. And hurry the fuck up."

I released Treasure's shirt and shoved her forcefully back against her seat. With tears in her eyes, she opened the door, climbed out and got her brother. The two walked up the walkway to the front porch. I watched as Treasure sat her brother down on a little stool my mother kept outside. He looked behind him to the front door attempting to see his grandmother. Treasure whispered something to him and slowly headed back to the car with her eyes to the ground. As she climbed in the car I turned the key in the ignition.

The old lady next door looked up from her garden. She looked at Cash sitting alone on the porch and then at my car. With no hesitation we pulled away from the curb. As we headed up the street further and further away from the house Treasure could only stare at the floor with a mixture of both sadness and anger. It hurt me like hell to leave Cash behind. He was my flesh

WELFARE GRIND BY: KENDALL BANKS

and blood. Maybe I'd come back for him later on some time. But for now I needed to be free to stick and move. Since Treasure was older and would be eleven soon, I could maneuver with her. Cash would be extra baggage. He would only slow me down. I had no time for that.

My conscience weighed on me heavily, but oddly enough it wasn't because of Cash or even Imani. It was Dupree that was bothering me. Leaving him behind knowing he had a death warrant tugged at my heart more than anything right now. I didn't know why exactly. I just felt that way. Wanting to see him one more time before I left, I grabbed my cell phone and called his hospital room. A nurse answered and told me that he'd just been released a few seconds ago. Without giving her a chance to say anything else, I pressed the gas and headed to the freeway.

We hit the entrance ramp in less than three minutes. Fifteen minutes later we were exiting and headed down the street of the hospital. My eyes were scouring the parking lot. As we pulled into the turning lane they landed on Dupree. He and Rick were standing beside Rick's car at the hospital's entrance/exit doors. Dinero was in Dupree's arms. Shane was standing there as well. I also noticed a black Cadillac Seville in front of me quickly turned just as the traffic light was turning red.

"Damn," I said," as I was forced to stop and wait.

Treasure was still looking down toward the floor. Her face immersed in pain; a look I'd never seen before. Her heart was obviously broken in countless pieces.

Finding myself feeling sorry for her I said, "We're gonna come back for him. All of them," I added.

She tightened her lips sideways, refusing to believe me or look at me.

I wasn't going to kiss her ass. If she didn't believe me, oh well. I turned my eyes back towards the parking lot. As I watched Dupree open the passenger door of the Jag with Dinero still in his arms, I wondered what Rick had told him. Fearing that Dupree might hate me, I realized it was definitely best that I remain out of sight. Besides, I'd only come to see his face one last time before I hit the highway.

As my eyes stared at him from the distance, they noticed the black Cadillac that had left me at the light. It was slowly pulling alongside the Jag. Suddenly gunfire erupted from its passenger side. My eyes grew wide as bullets poured loudly from its open window at Dupree, Dinero, Rick, and Shane. Everyone standing at the hospital doorway began to scream and drop to the ground as shots shattered windows and put bullet holes in everything in sight. Others dashed behind cars or back inside the hospital for cover. Even Treasure screamed as she quickly pulled her eyes from the floor to see her family in the line of merciless fire. I could only sit speechless, my hand totally covering my mouth, knowing that I myself had set the scene in motion.

Rayquan had come through after all.

There was nothing I could say or do. I didn't know how I felt watching Dupree become the main target. Obviously I hadn't expected to actually witness him dying or blood spilling into the air from his body. I'd expected to be far away when it happened. Being a witness to it was like having an outer body experience. It seemed unbelievable. Everything seemed to be happening in slow motion. But in a brief moment the entire area had emptied. As the Cadillac finally stopped spitting bullets, no one was standing or even in sight. Everyone was either lying on the ground or somewhere inside the hospital. I had no idea if they were dead or just scared to show themselves too soon. I prayed like crazy that Shane and Dinero had gotten on the ground and were still alive.

The tires of the Cadillac wailed loudly as they burned long black stretches into the pavement and sped off. Within only seconds the car had made its way to the far end of the parking lot and recklessly whipped out into traffic, causing cars to swerve out of its way. A brief moment later it disappeared.

Rick's Jag was completely riddled with bullets. All of its windows were gone. My heart raced as my eyes searched for any sign of him, Dupree, Dinero, or Shane. They searched frantically. The search came up useless.

There was no sign of any of them. *Damn!*

SIXTEEN

"Damn, gurllllllll, you okay?" Tia asked as she placed sheets and pillows on the couch, making it up for me to sleep on. "You haven't said too much since you got here. What's up?"

My mind was in an inescapable daze as I sat at her dining room table. I could barely hear anything around me. I was wrapped up in my own world and definitely didn't feel like hearing Tia drag out her damn words. Treasure was lying in the lounge chair underneath a flowered looking sheet staring at the ceiling. Only total silence came from her mouth also. It was obvious she was lost in her own world, too.

"Keema?" Tia asked.

I didn't hear her. My ears had blocked out everything around me.

"Keema?" she asked a little louder.

Finally hearing her voice, I jolted from my daze. "Huh?" I responded, forgetting where I was for a brief moment.

Tia looked at me strangely as she continued to make up the couch. "Gurlllll, I asked you if you alright. You haven't said much since you got here."

"I'm good," I lied somberly while fiddling with my fingers.

"You sure? It don't look like it."

I nodded. I hadn't told her about the shooting. And I'd told Treasure's wanna-be grown ass not to mention a single word about it either. "I'm good."

"You don't look like you gooooooood."

"I just got some things on my mind. That's all."

"Wanna talk about it?"

I definitely didn't want that. "Nah, it's nothing serious," I pretended to carelessly shrug it off. In reality serious wasn't the word. Getting over what Treasure and I had witnessed was impossible.

The sounds of gunfire, the sight of blood, and the visions of bodies dropping to the ground had me gone. I couldn't see, hear, or think of anything else. My ears could even still hear the loud screeching of the Cadillac's tires as it sped away from the hospital. My stomach felt heavily nauseous as I kept my phone clutched in the palm of my hand, subconsciously expecting some sort of news from someone about Dinero or Dupree. It rang several times with friends from the projects just trying to be nosey. None of them could tell me anything. They had simply heard about the shooting and wanted to see if they could get some information from me about it. All they wanted was ammunition to gossip with.

Shannon, a girl from my hood was the first to call. She'd called just as I was exiting the highway into downtown D.C. We weren't all that close. We'd gone to the same high school and ran in the same circle of friends, but we didn't talk regularly. Seeing her number on the screen of my phone, I knew exactly what she was calling for.

"Girl, did you hear?" she questioned as soon as I answered.

Knowing what she was calling for, I played stupid, hoping to get some information out of her. "Hear what?"

"About Dupree and Rick?"

"What about them?"

"Girl, some niggas shot 'em up today."

"Oh, God," I gasped.

"Damn, girl, I thought you would've heard by now."

"Nah, I didn't." I attempted to play like the news was new

and shocking. "Are they okay?"

"I don't know. The news is saying that someone died, but they're not releasing the name yet. They keep saying something about an investigation and details being sketchy."

"Oh my God!" I shouted then thought to myself how disappointed I was with the little bit of info I got from her. She was no fucking help. She had nothing to tell me, although I now knew someone had definitely died. But *who?* I hung up on her immediately.

I wasn't sure if my baby, Dinero was dead. I wasn't sure *who* was dead period. Immediately after seeing the four bodies sprawled out on the ground as blood pooled around them, both fear and common sense kicked in. I realized that since it was me who had set the shooting up, it was best for me to get as far away from the scene as possible. Regretting having to leave Dinero behind without being sure if he was safe or alive, I hopped in the car, hit the highway, and headed straight to D.C. just like I had originally planned.

Ironically a syndicated episode of *The Wire* was playing on the television as me and Treasure now sat in Tia's living room, reminding us both of the brutal Baltimore violence and murder we'd called ourselves fleeing away from.

Tia's apartment was in a small, four story building and smack dead in the middle of the Southeast. It was a two bedroom. She'd gotten it with Section 8 and lived there with her disabled uncle. Although the apartment was a decent size, the furniture was outdated and sheets hung from the windows, instead of curtains. The dark colored carpet was stained with everything from coffee and Kool Aid, to liquor and piss. Clothes were strewn about, a wheel chair sat by the door, old fast food bags were everywhere, the stench of weed smoke radiated from the furniture and walls, and the sink was filled with dishes. Countless cigarette burns were also branded into the furniture. It reminded me of Imani's grandmother's apartment. Usually, I'd be nervous about lying underneath the sheets she was preparing for me. Usually, in a place like this I'd be scared something might crawl on

WELFARE GRIND BY: KENDALL BANKS

me while I was sleep, possibly crawl in my mouth. But right now my mind and heart was a hundred miles away back in Baltimore. Besides, I wasn't in the position to be choosey.

"Sooooooooo, how long do you think y'all will have to stay?" Tia asked.

"About two weeks," I replied.

Her demeanor changed slightly. I could see that two weeks wasn't something she was happy with.

"Damn, why so long?"

Her bluntness pissed me off, but I kept it under wraps. I had to bite my tongue and hold my temper if I wanted a place to stay.

"Gurlllllllll, I be having niggas coming over here and we snort coke!"

Oh, boy, here she goes, I thought to myself. *She's talking like somebody is gonna cramp her style even though she don't have a style to cramp. The bitch don't even know how to keep her house clean. She was practically living in filth, but talking like she was the shit.*

"We won't be here that much," I assured her. I'll make sure we're not in your way."

"Two weeks is a long time. Are you sure it has to be that longgggggg?"

Shit, I could sense that she wanted to say no. But as long as I had Treasure with me, she couldn't see us out on the street. I didn't want to stay in this pig sty any longer than I had to. But since my pockets were hurting, I had no other choice or options for the moment. To keep her from tripping, instead of answering her question, I reached into my purse and pulled out a thousand dollars. There was nothing like money to take a bitch's mind off *anything*. Besides, I knew that's exactly what she'd been waiting for ever since I knocked on the door.

"This is for the D.C. and V.A. licenses," I said.

She quickly stopped fixing the couch and headed to her purse to get the licenses. She handed them to me and grabbed the money, but looked at me weirdly.

"What about my homegirls who pushed both welfare applications through?"

I twisted up my face. "What about them?"

"I told you they're both bugging me about the money, especially my friend in D.C. The one in Virginia hasn't called as much, but I'm sure I'll be hearing from her ass today. They both want a thousand."

"A thousand?" I said like she was crazy.

"Yes, we all asked for a thousand. I told you that before."

"That's ridiculous."

"Keema, do you know how much time they could get, if they get caught, let alone losing their jobs?"

I sighed in annoyance. Damn, I hated coming up off of money, especially money I didn't have to give away. I only had two thousand left now, and needed to keep that just in case an emergency popped off.

"It is what it is. The services they offer don't come cheap. Plus both of your cards should arrive tomorrow at the addresses we used. So, you need to give up the loot."

"I'll give it to you in the morning," I said aggravated. Little did she know, I only had plans on giving her some sob story to buy me more time.

Tia looked at me suspiciously. "Keema, I'm serious. They both need their money. They looked out so they're expecting a payoff."

"I said I'll hit you off in the morning, Tia, *damn.*"

The last thing I wanted to discuss at the moment was emptying my pockets even more than they already were. I needed every penny I had. But it was good to know that the girl could get my shit approved and money would be on my card tomorrow.

"Well, make sure you do. Fair is fair. You keep it one hundred with them and they'll keep it one hundred with you. Don't put no bullshit in the game, Keema."

I sighed again.

"I'm just saying."

My eyes rolled.

After saying some other shit I wasn't paying attention to, Tia finally headed to her bedroom for the night. As she disappeared my phone rang. It was my mother. She'd called several times over the past few hours. Each time she did I ignored her call, knowing she was going to get on me about leaving Cash. Right now I wasn't in the mood to hear that shit. I had enough problems. She was always talking about how much she wanted her grandbaby there with her. Well, now she'd gotten her wish.

The *Wire's* most notorious killers, Snoop and Chris, were on television murking a nigga on the corner of a neighborhood just blocks from my projects when the phone rang again. This time it was Raven. I answered quickly, knowing she was most likely calling for the same reason everyone else had. I just hoped she had more information than any of them.

"Keema, are you alright?" she asked.

"Yeah, I'm fine."

"Shit, I just heard about the shooting."

"What all did you hear?"

"That some niggas rode up on them and just started bussing off. I heard it might've been drug related or that Dupree might've owed some niggas some money. It's a whole lot of shit being said."

"Who got hit?"

"I don't know. The police ain't saying any names yet. They're just saying that it was heartless because some kids were out there, too."

Damn, I thought to myself. Dinero's face flashed in my mind. I felt so guilty. Tears started to form in my eyes. My hand trembled as I held the phone.

"Where you at?" she inquired.

Ignoring her question, I said, "What else are they saying?"

"That's all right now."

"You sure?"

"Yeah," Raven responded.

"You mean they haven't said anything about the kids being shot?" I asked desperately.

"Nope, they're just saying the kids were there when the shooting started. But they're not saying whether they had been shot or not."

The tears grew heavier. How could I have been selfish enough to jeopardize my son's life? I wished everything could just go away.

"Did they see who did it?"

"Nope."

Even though I was a nervous wreck over wondering if my baby had been shot, I still also wanted to be sure nothing could connect me to the shooting.

"Girl, you heard about Paco?"

The mention of his name sent chills down my spine. I'd forgotten about him for a moment. Now, he was all over thoughts just as freshly as he was the night me and Imani robbed him.

"Nah, what about him?"

"I hope you watching your back. That nigga got ten stacks on you, Keema."

I rested my head in the palm of my hand, knowing I could *definitely* not go back to Baltimore any time soon now.

"He really wants you bad. He's saying he'll hit any nigga off with ten thousand if they bring you to him dead or alive."

"Shit," I whispered to myself.

"And you know how damn thirsty these niggas out here are," she continued. "For ten stacks they'll turn in their own momma."

"You ain't never lied."

"Hey, I know this is off the subject, but my friend, Dedra wants to know if you're still gonna let her use your EBT card next month for food."

"She knows there's a fee involved with that, right?"

"Of course. She knows you wouldn't be doing that shit for free," Raven responded.

"As long as she got my money then we should be straight. Luckily for her, I don't have anybody else lined up right now."

"Cool. I'll let her know."

133

"Look, I gotta go."

"Keema, wait. Where you at?"

"I'll tell you later. Gotta go."

"Wait."

CLICK!

After hanging up I leaned back into my chair. I was absolutely lost. My mind had no idea where to turn or what to do. I looked over at Treasure. She was still quiet and staring at the ceiling. I knew her mind was filled with just as much uncertainty and worry as mine. The two of us were all we had. Standing from my chair I walked across the room and sat beside her on the couch. For a moment the two of us just stared into each other's eyes. Tears began to fall from mine.

"It's gonna be alright, Momma," she said, reaching up and softly wiping them away. "Have you heard anything?"

I shook my head. The two of us sat silently for another moment.

All of our arguments and disagreements seemed decades behind us. All of our bad blood, although recent, seemed lost somewhere in the past. We were now just a mother and daughter trapped in heartbreak. She had a mature understanding and compassion in her eyes as she said, "Why don't you just call the hospitals in Baltimore and see if they're there?"

With so much on my mind, it never occurred to me to do that. Her intelligence usually got on my nerves. This time it was what I needed. My mind was too damn stressed to think clearly. Her help was welcomed. I nodded, smiled weakly, and hugged her. The feel of her body in my arms was something I couldn't describe.

I looked into her eyes after we embraced. "How'd you get so smart?"

She smiled softly. "I got it from my mommy."

After kissing her on the forehead, I pulled out my phone and began to call the hospitals, hoping to find something out.

SEVENTEEN

With absolutely no time to react, I could barely breathe while being pressed into the couch. The weight was so heavy both my breasts hurt horribly. My eyes widened at the sight of the stranger in a ski mask straddling my chest. He scared me so bad I wanted to scream my head off but couldn't. His hand roughly covered my entire mouth completely. My vocal chords couldn't utter a sound.

I could feel the blade of the butcher knife in his hand pressed tightly against my throat. The slightest movement would get me sliced wide open. The thought had me shaken beyond words.

My heart raced as I stared up into the eyes staring angrily down at me from behind the mask. I recognized them at first sight. The mask did no good to conceal the man's identity. What terrified me most about those eyes was that they were the eyes of a ghost. They had to be.

He was supposed to be dead!

Seeing that I recognized him, Frenchie took off the mask and tossed it to the floor turning to say a few words to Rick and Dupree who stood nearby. My eyes widened farther hearing Dupree say, "Gut her!"

How was he breathing, I wondered? *He was real flesh and blood. He was alive. How? I watched him die. How was he here?*

"You thought you killed me! Didn't you, bitch," he whispered, refusing to uncover my mouth.

I was frozen in horror.

"I've been waiting for this moment so badly my dick is hard," he said, his eyes as rabid as a pit bull's.

I knew he deserved his revenge, but I still wanted to beg for my life. I wanted him to uncover my mouth so I could plead. I'd do anything. I wanted to at least talk to Dupree who stood back letting his brother do this to me.

"I'm going to enjoy cutting you open like a pig, you sneaky tramp."

Tears fell from my eyes and began to roll down the sides of my face, dissolving in the cushions of the couch.

He gave a sick twisted smile.

The smile was the evilest one I'd ever imagined.

He took the knife from my throat and raised it over his head like Jason in one of those *Friday the 13th* movies.

My wide eyes followed it. Muffled whimpers came from my mouth and underneath his hand. I wanted to scream for help. My heart rate tripled and sent me into cardiac arrest.

"Say goodnight, bitch," he said.

My eyes raced back and forth from his face to the knife.

Like a sack of potatoes the knife's razor sharp tip came down towards my face, causing me to scream underneath his hand.

"Mommy!" Treasure screamed. "Mommy, wake up!"

Feeling her shaking me, I awoke from the nightmare and immediately jumped up, sweat dripping from my forehead. The darkness had vanished. It had been replaced by graying daylight flowing through the living room windows. My head turned around, expecting to see Frenchie, but he was nowhere around.

"Mommy, are you okay?" Treasure asked.

I looked at her, still trying to focus on reality. "Baby, was Rick or Dupree here?"

"No, Mommy. You were tossing and turning in your sleep. Then you started screaming. Are you okay?"

Realizing the nightmare was over and that I was safe, I nodded. "I'm okay, baby," I told her.

"Are you sure?"

"Yeah."

"You want some water or something?"

My throat was dry. "Yeah."

She headed to the kitchen.

I couldn't believe I'd had another nightmare. My mind, imagination, and dreams last night were devoted exclusively to thoughts just like the one I'd just been awakened from. Some involved Dinero. My mind had never thought about him more than now. I'd called every hospital in Baltimore last night and couldn't get any information at all. They each said that they didn't have Rick, Dupree, Dinero, or Shane as patients. Obviously that was a lie. One of them had been shot. But I remembered both Shannon and Raven telling me that the cops weren't releasing any names. Most likely they'd told the hospital to keep it on the hush-hush also. Each conversation with the hospitals ended with me slamming the phone down in frustration.

Besides Dinero, my dreams, rather nightmares, were also devoted to Imani. I felt so guilty and I missed her more than words could explain. She really was my heart and best friend. But I'd gotten her killed.

I felt so guilty and sad that I called Imani's grandmother's apartment several times this morning to find out where and when her funeral services were going to be. Knowing showing my face there was a no-no, something inside me still wanted to at least know. No one answered. I called from the house phone several times just in case they recognized my number on caller ID and were refusing to pick up for some reason. They still weren't answering. I finally gave up.

Peppi also called me. Not really in the mood to speak and knowing he was most likely trying to find out what was up with my next payment, I ignored his call. After calling a second time and receiving no answer he finally left a message saying he needed at least five to ten thousand from me by the end of the week. The spa was still a dream of mine, but right now I was too depressed to think about it. Worrying about Dinero had knocked a bitch off her square, for real.

Still, the fact that I needed money and fast was always somewhere hidden in my mind. That couldn't be helped. Calculating money and conspiring ways to get money was a part of my chemical make up. Right now I knew me and Treasure had to get our asses up to Arizona. Next to the welfare grind, I was putting together down here in D.C., and the upstart of the spa, it was obvious I had to get back hard body about my shit. That was the only way I'd ever be able to rest. It was the only way I would be able to have a piece of mind again. But while knowing those things, Dinero's status was still eating away at my heart and emotions.

Treasure came out of the kitchen with a glass of ice water. After she handed it to me I took it directly to the head, quenching my thirst instantly.

The living room door opened. Tia sashayed in with her cell phone stuck to her ear. She was no where near as cute as me, but I had to admit she had a body that was bananas. She was only 5'5 with light brown skin, and had almond colored eyes. Her breasts were huge but well shaped, and her hips, thighs and ass were curved perfectly. Her body was thick. But not that sloppy type of thick. Her thickness was solid.

Dressed in a pair of leggings, and a long embellished t-shirt from H&M, Tia spoke into the phone as she shut the door, "A'ight, gurllllll, I'll see y'all hoes there tonight." She then pressed the end button and looked at me. "Bitch, you still laying down?"

"I don't feel too good," I moaned.

With no mercy she said, "Well, get over it. We going down to Ibiza tonight at eleven. It's a hot spot where all the niggas be at. We need to get your ass up and get your hair done. My girl Devon, at Salon Couture said to bring you by. She gonna hook your shit up. Fuck two weeks. We gotta get you down there so you can find you a paid nigga who can get you up out of here sooner."

Before I could say a single word she was pulling and tugging me off of the couch.

As we walked out of the door at a little after ten, Treasure was sitting at the living room table with Tia's uncle, who was sitting across from her in his wheelchair. The two of them were playing Chess, Treasure's favorite game. I never understood what she saw in the game personally. It was the most boring game I'd ever seen and took way too much time and concentration for someone like me. But something about it seemed to captivate her from the first moment she saw Dupree and Rick playing. Dupree taught her how to play. She'd been playing ever since. Sometimes she would play for hours by herself. Damn, I swear I didn't understand that girl sometimes.

We headed out the door, down the elevator, and out into the night. The rain had stopped but the streets were still wet. A light wind blew. In the surrounding distance barking dogs, police sirens, and shouting matches could be heard. Her D.C. hood was no different from my B-More hood.

The sharp tips of our heels clicked loudly against the street top as we crossed the street and climbed into her white Toyota Avalon. It wasn't brand new, but it was nice. And she damn sure kept it up much better than she did her apartment. She started the engine. Immediately the blaring vocals and bass of Tupac's classic song, *Hail Mary* flooded the interior. Instead of pulling off, she whipped out a blunt, slit it open, and began to fill it with weed as she nodded her head to the music. Once the blunt was filled and sealed she lit it and took a heavy pull. Satisfied and through slanted eyes she offered it to me.

"Here, bitch," Tia said, holding her breath at the same time. "Go ahead and hit that shit."

My stomach was still uneasy, but I could never turn down a blunt. Dick, money, and weed were my weaknesses. Wrapping my nude gloss covered lips around the wet tip, I took a pull and filled my lungs. The shit took effect immediately. It must've showed on my face because Tia smiled at me and said, "What you know about that right there?"

"This shit good," I told her, still holding my breath while taking the blunt from my lips and looking at it.

"That's that Cali weed. One of my home girls brought it down here from the west coast a couple days ago. I've been smoking it ever since."

After a few more puffs Tia finally pulled away from the curb and we headed to the club with Tupac's classic *Makaveli* CD blasting the entire way as we recited each and every word. By the time we arrived I was feeling good and high.

I strutted into the dimly lit spot dressed in six inch stiletto heels and a body hugging strapless dress. Tia was dressed in stilettos as well, but she chose to rock a pair of tight black jeggings, instead of a dress. Her body filled them out perfectly.

Young Jeezy's newest shit pounded from the club's speakers as we made our way through the bar. Since ladies got in free until twelve, I was expecting the spot to be filled with more women than men. That's the way clubs were back home. The dudes, at least the fine ones, usually didn't start piling in until after twelve. But I was surprised to find just as many men inside. Some were off brand with cheap looking knock off jeans, fake jewelry, and horrible shoes. They couldn't fool a bitch like me. But there were some others who were the real deal.

Some of Tia's friends were already at the bar sipping when we walked up. Tia introduced me to them and I began to make small talk. Usually it wasn't my style to talk to bitches for too long. Bitches were nothing more than back stabbing snakes. You couldn't trust them. But the weed, and the shot of Ciroc I'd consumed had me talkative as shit.

It felt good to get away from my problems for a while. It felt good to become the happy go lucky ass person I used to be if only for just a moment. Niggas approached me throughout the night offering me drinks and asking me to dance. The drinks, I accepted. The dances, I didn't. I wasn't going to turn down free liquor. Dudes were more than welcomed to get me drunk. But I had to draw the line at dancing. There was no way on God's green Earth you were going to catch me bumping and grinding on the dance floor against the some of the gruesome muthafuckas who had the nerve to approach me. That just wasn't going to happen no matter how drunk I was.

Each dude who approached me recognized immediately that my swagger and accent wasn't D.C. When I told them I was a B-More chick that made them want me more. They wanted to see how this Baltimore pussy felt, how wet it could get. I had nothing for them though. I needed a paid nigga. Fuck some dick and meaningless conversation. If I wanted that, I could get that from anywhere. The countless free drinks were welcomed. But all else I had no time for.

It was about a little after twelve when a small group of dudes walked into the club looking a whole lot different than what was already in there. Their jewels were shining hard. Some of them rocked Louis Vutton sneakers while others rocked the brand new two hundred fifty dollar Jordan's that had just come out two days ago. Everybody in the club seemed to know them as they were greeted with dap and shoulder hugs. All of them shined but one stood out particularly. All the bitches seemed to want a hug from him.

"Shit, girl, who is that?" I asked Tia as she exited the dance floor and walked up next to me to order another drink. My eyes peeped one of the guys out from head to toe.

She smiled when she saw who I was looking at. "Oh, that's Cee-Lo and his crew."

The nigga was past fine. He stood about six feet even. His hair was neatly cut and he had an athletic build. His eyes were an exotic shade of green that I'd never seen before.

"They're out of Clay Terrace," Tia continued.

"What's that?" I inquired.

"Some projects in Northeast."

I looked in amazement. "They getting money like that,

huh?"

"Hell yeah. I heard they got shit on lock on that side of town."

I shook my head. "Damn."

My mouth grew wet as my eyes studied him like a Thanksgiving turkey. It was on. He would be my next victim. For the next hour I watched, waiting for the right moment to press up on him. He sat at a table in the back of the club surrounded by his crew while bitch after bitch approached. I hoped to catch him on the dance floor, but he obviously didn't dance. I then hoped to catch him at the bar, but his drinks were always brought to him. Muthafuckas were treating him like royalty so I knew I couldn't just approach him like the other broads. He'd probably look right through me. I had to catch him by himself.

From the dance floor I watched him as me and Tia danced together to one of Jay-Z and Kanye's joints from *Watch The Throne*. My eyes wouldn't let him out of their sight. Finally he stood from his table and headed through the club to the bathroom with a thugged out swagger that turned me all the way on. Now was my chance. I left Tia alone on the dance floor and followed Cee-Lo to the bathroom. When he walked inside, I waited outside for him. After several minutes he finally came out looking even sexier up close than he did from afar. His head was down as he checked his I-Phone. Immediately I walked into his path purposely making him bump into me. He looked up immediately.

"Damn, shorty," he said with both surprise and genuine worry on his face. "My fault. I wasn't payin' attention."

"It's okay," I said with a smile.

"Nah, it's not okay," he responded. "I should've been payin' more attention. I'm sorry about that."

"I'm good, really."

"You sure?"

"Yeah, I'm a big girl. I don't break."

He smiled at my answer and looked at me quizzically. "You not from around here, are you?"

"Nah."

"B-More?"

I looked at him just as quizzically as he'd just done. "Yeah, how did you know?"

"I hear it in your voice. You got that B-More accent."

I cocked my head to the side. "What do you know about B-More?"

"Enough. I go back and forth up there on business from time to time. What you doin' in D.C?"

"Just chilling for a minute."

"Oh, yeah, how long you gon' be down here?"

I gave him a flirtatious grin. "Why you wanna know?"

"Cuz you cute."

"I'm pretty sure that's what you tell all those girls who've been around your table all night."

He laughed. "Oh, so you've been watchin' me, huh?"

"Couldn't help but notice you. The whole club gave you a ruler's welcome when you walked in."

He dropped his head and looked up at me slyly with those sexy green eyes. "Shit, I ain't nobody."

"Yeah right. Just tell me anything," I said, letting him know that it was obvious I didn't believe him.

He chuckled. "I like you, shorty."

Placing my hands on my hips and placing my weight on one foot I said, "What do you like about me? You don't even know me."

"You don't have to know somebody to like 'em."

"So, you still like me even though I ain't one of them girls you can just take home on the first night?"

"Even more so."

Quickly his eyes scoured my body checking me out, taking me all in within just a second. It was obvious he was digging my hourglass shape.

"What's your name?" he asked.

"Keema."

"Cute name. I'm Cee-Lo." He extended his hand.

As I accepted it, I couldn't help but notice his manicured

143

nails. His hand looked as if he hadn't ever done an honest day's worth of work in his life.

"Nice to meet you," I told him.

From that moment it was on. I had his ass hook, line, and sinker. Me, Tia, and her friends chilled with Cee-Lo and his Clay Terrace Crew until closing time. As Tia and her girls chopped it up and drunk top shelf with Cee-Lo's crew, me and him sat at another table a distance away having our own private conversation. When the DJ shouted last call, neither one of us wanted to part with each other's company so he offered to take me and my girls to Ben's Chili Bowl. We all walked out to the parking lot.

Moments later, my phone began to ring. Recognizing my mother's ring tone, I ignored it. It rang twice more, which made me put it on vibrate.

Tia and her friends hopped in the Avalon while I headed across the bustling lot towards Cee-Lo's brand new F-150. I'd expected something much more big boy from him, but I understood that some dope boys on his level understood that expensive cars and rims brought unnecessary attention from the police. His crew also hopped in trucks that consisited of Escalades, Suburban's and Avalanches.

My phone started vibrating in my hand. I looked at the screen and saw Raven's number.

"Your boyfriend?" Cee-Lo questioned with a slight grin.

"I don't have one of those."

As we neared the SUV my phone wouldn't stop vibrating. It was obvious something was up. I looked at the screen again and saw Shannon's number. Instead of answering, I rejected the call and hit Raven back.

"Keema?" She was immediately hyper.

"Yeah, what's up?"

"Did you hear?"

"Nah, hear what?"

"Rick survived the shooting but Dupree didn't. Dupree's dead."

I stopped dead in my tracks.

144

EIGHTEEN

It was a little after nine o'clock in the morning and once again I found myself on the couch with my eyes focused on the ceiling overhead. I hadn't slept most of the night. That was slowly becoming the story of my life.

My phone rang. Recognizing my mother's ring tone, I finally decided to answer her call. "Yeah," I said, placing the phone to my ear.

"Yeah?" she asked in disbelief. "That's how you answer my call?"

I sighed. "Ma, I don't feel like arguing right now."

"Where are you?"

"Somewhere."

"Well, somewhere is not *here* where you *should* be. Why aren't you here?"

I sighed again. Here she goes with another damn sermon. I was already feeling bad enough right now. I didn't need her to compound it. If it was about Cash, I knew he was in good hands.

Hearing my aggravation, she asked, "Have you spoken to CPS yet?"

"No, why?" Oh shit! Had she gotten rid of Cash?

"What do you mean, why?"

"Why? Did you call them?"

"Because Shane and Dinero are in their custody. There was a fucking shooting, Keema! They were with Dupree and

Rick, but the boys survived the shooting. Thank God!" She paused for several seconds. "But Dupree's dead. And his brother is laying in the hospital with four bullet holes in him."

"Damn," was the only word that managed to slip from my mouth.

"I went to the hospital as soon as I heard. His doctor says he's going to make it. You'd know all of that if you were here where you're supposed to be. Don't you even care, child?"

Damn, I wasn't as cold hearted of a bitch as she was making me out to be. Offended by her questioning the love for my son, I said, "Of course I care. Why would you ask me some shit like that?"

"Because I can't tell. A real mother would be here with her damn children. Bullets were flying around my grandbaby like UFOs, and your ass is off somewhere gallivanting."

"Oh, like you were always there for me," I said sarcastically, speaking of all the times she left me on my own."Besides, they were under Rick's supervision so how would I have known?"

Recognizing my sarcasm and knowing exactly what I was speaking of, she returned, "Keema, this has nothing to do with me. You really need to let go of that resentment you have for the mistakes I made when I was younger. You need to stop using them as excuses not to be a good mother to your own children."

"You've got your nerve."

"I sure do. I'm not the one who left my child on a damn doorstep. I'm not the one who doesn't even call to check on him."

She had a point.

"Look, Keema, I didn't call to argue. I just called so we could go get Dinero out of CPS' custody. You need to get here immediately."

She hadn't even mentioned Shane's name. Even though he wasn't legally my son, I couldn't just leave him in there, especially not with his condition.

"Alright," I said halfheartedly, in an attempt to shut her

146

up. I knew going back to Baltimore wasn't a good idea, at least not right now. Everything was still too fresh and hot. But at the same time, leaving my baby in county's custody wasn't an option. My conscience wouldn't allow me to live with myself if I did.

"When will you be here?"

"Ma, I said I'll be there, alright?"

"Keema, you *say* a whole lot of things. But your *actions* always mean something else. Are you going to be here today, tonight, tomorrow, *when*?"

"Tomorrow."

"I'm serious, Keema. Be here. Do you know what goes on in some of those damn foster and group homes? Do you?"

My eyes rolled at the ceiling.

"They molest kids, smack them around, and abuse them. I don't want my grandbaby in a place like that. I want him out of there pronto. I mean it, Keema. Get your ass here now."

I knew she was right. I'd heard myself a million horrible stories of what goes on in the system.

"How's Treasure?"

My eyes looked around the room. For the first time this morning, it dawned on me how quiet the living room was. I realized Treasure wasn't lying on the love seat.

"She's alright," I said.

"Let me speak to her."

"Ma, I gotta go."

"Why?"

Shit, because I was tired of the nagging. Knowing that Dinero had survived brightened my world, but only slightly. There was still tons of other bullshit going on in my life that had me stressed. I didn't have it in me to continue listening to her question my parenting skills.

"I just gotta go," I said.

"Well, we really need to…"

My thumb quickly pressed the end button before she could finish her sentence. She would've continued to talk my damn ear off if I'd let her. As soon as I tossed the phone beside me and closed my eyes for a moment, it rang again. This time the ring tone was Peppi's.

"Yeah?" I answered, after grabbing the phone and pressing it to my ear again. I really wasn't in the mood to talk to anyone.

"My precious little flower," he said perkily. "How are you?"

"I'm alright," I told him halfheartedly. "What's up?"

"It's very important that we meet this week. The contractors need their money. They're growing very antsy. We've come too close to begin making things complicated. The last thing we want is for them to start thinking they may have to abandon the project, due to money issues."

"There won't be any issues. I'm getting the money together as we speak."

Actually, I had a date with Cee-Lo already set up for tonight at eleven. He had no idea that he was about to become my latest investor.

"That's my girl. That's what Peppi likes to hear."

We spoke a little while longer and hung up. The living room door opened and Treasure walked in. She came over to the couch and handed me two cards. One was blue with the words Capital Access displayed across it, while the other said the word SNAP.

"What are these?" I asked.

"Before Tia left for work, she told me to go downstairs at nine o'clock to get these out of the mailbox. She said some girl left them for you. It's just like our EBT card from Maryland. She told me that the D.C. Capital Access card has thirteen hundred dollars on it, and the Virginia SNAP card has eleven hundred."

My face lit up like Christmas. Tia had come through, just like we planned. Thinking about my money from Maryland, I picked up my cell phone and dialed the 1-800 number that I knew by heart to check the balance. With Dinero back in the custody of CPS, I hoped that wouldn't affect my loot as I entered my ac-

count number, then said a silent prayer. After waiting a few uncomfortable seconds, a smile suddenly spread across my face
when the automated machine said that my account balance was
exactly sixteen hundred dollars. Everything had worked out.

"She also said you need to leave both of her friends'
money on the kitchen table."

Ignoring Treasure's last comment, I jumped up from the
couch and headed to the bathroom. In my excitement I told her,
"We're going back to B-More tonight, so be ready."

It was eleven o'clock on the dot as I pulled the car to the
curb of the dark side street. After shutting the car off I looked
around quickly to make sure no one was looking out of their window. Treasure was in the passenger seat. She stretched her neck
to look around, wondering where we were and why we were
here. In a sexy pair of heels and short skirt, I looked up into the
overhead mirror to check my make up. My eyeshadow had been
applied perfectly.

It was show time!

"Don't get out of the car for *any* reason," I told Treasure.
"Not any reason at all, you hear me?"

"Yeah, but where are you going?" she questioned.

"Don't worry about all that. It may take me an hour or so,
but just do what I said, alright?"

She nodded, although the look on her face showed she
wasn't too happy about it.

Throwing the strap of my purse over my shoulder, I
hopped out of the car, closed the door, and quickly began to trot
to the I-Hop only two blocks away. I was extra anxious to get the
upcoming shit cracking. From what I'd seen the other night, Cee-
Lo was one of them type of niggas who liked to walk around
with stacks in his pocket. Hopefully tonight was no different. I
wanted and needed all of that bread.

In all honesty, it always puzzled me as to why a dude

would be stupid enough to walk around with that kind of loot in his pocket. I mean, for a stick up kid like myself, it was a great lick. But never the less, why would a nigga want to make himself a target like that? The shit never made sense to me.

Oh, well.

For what I had planned for Cee-Lo, my car couldn't be parked where he could see it that's why I left it where I did. I reached the parking lot in less than five minutes. Cee-Lo's truck was parked facing the street. Finally slowing my pace, I walked up to his driver's side window.

"Damn, girl," he said, startled as Jim Jones' *Certified Gangstas* played at a low, but throbbing volume. "Where the fuck did you come from?" he asked, looking around behind me.

"At the gas station across the street," I lied then leaned against the door of his truck, purposely poking my ass out for everyone to see. "I had to stop and get some cigarettes."

"Where's your car?"

"Had to put it in the shop this morning. The transmission is acting up. I had to take a cab to get here."

"Why didn't you just call me? I woulda came and got you."

"I'm good. I don't like having to ask anyone for anything."

He smiled. "Shorty, quit actin' like that. The next time you need a ride, call me. I got you."

I gave him a flirtatious smile. "Alright."

"So, you wanna grab something to eat before we hit the club?"

"Nah, I'm cool."

"A'ight, hop in."

My heels headed around the hood of the truck without me having to tell them to. I hopped inside and leaned back into the leather seat. The truck was nearly fresh off the lot so the interior still smelled fresh.

Cee-Lo threw the truck in reverse, backed up, and headed for the lot's exit. As he pulled out into the street I went to work on him. "Can I make a confession?" I asked, looking at him seductively.

"Yeah, what's up?" he said while driving.

"My homegirl gave me an Ecstasy pill."

He smiled, knowing exactly what that meant. "For real?"

"Yeah," I moaned, leaning towards him and placing my elbow on the center console.

"So, what you sayin', shorty?"

"I'm horny."

He smiled again. "So, you wanna go to a hotel?"

Giving him an even bigger smile, I said, "You don't understand."

He looked at me with calm surprise as my body made its way over the center console onto his lap as he drove. "Damn, shorty, it's like that?" he asked while trying to watch me and the road at the same time.

"I told you I was horny."

My face began to bury itself in his neck. My lips began to kiss him slowly, sensually, and softly while one of my hands began to stroke and squeeze the growing bulge in his pants.

"Shit, girl."

"You ever fucked while driving before?"

"Nah, but there's a first for everything. I'ma pull down this street right here though," he said, turning down a side residential street.

My hands traveled all over his body feeling for a gun. With the type of money he carried and the type of level he was on, I knew he had to have one somewhere. As long as it wasn't on his body, I could work with it. The more my hand traveled his body, the more he enjoyed it. He was now thinking with his dick, instead of his brain. I could hear it in his soft moans.

His ass was mine!

Slyly I reached into my purse, pulled out the gun, and stuffed it underneath his chin so hard his head raised slightly.

"What the fuck?" he asked in surprise.

"You know what it is, nigga?" I said, with all the seduction gone from my voice. All traces of the Keema he'd met at the night club had vanished into thin air just that quickly. I was about business. Both my facial expression and the sound of my voice showed it. "Where that money at?"

"Keema, what the…"

"Shut the fuck up and put the car in park!"

"Keema, I'm not playin' with your ass."

"Do you think *I'm* playing muthafucka?!"

He didn't answer.

"Do you think this gun is a play toy or something?"

He still didn't answer.

"I didn't think so. This gun has a hair trigger. Pull anything and it will tear your head all the way off. Now, park this bitch now!"

Reluctantly Cee-Lo did as he was told. He slowly pulled into what seemed like three empty spaces, even running one of his tires up on the curb. As soon as he put the truck in park, while still watching him and all his movements closely, I climbed off his lap and sat in the passenger's seat.

Cee-Lo watched me as closely as I watched him, but he knew the gun was too close to him to try anything. His eyes expressed how badly he wanted to tear me apart, but he also knew the ball was totally in my court as long as the gun was on him.

"Empty those pockets, nigga," I ordered.

"Keema, you're not gonna get away with this shit. Me and my niggas are gonna hunt your ass down. I know mufuckas in Baltimore."

"Blah, blah, blah," I said dismissively. "Don't bore me to death. Just break them damn pockets."

He began to reach in his pocket.

"Do that shit slowly, muthafucka!" I yelled, not wanting any surprises. "And keep the other hand where I can see it!"

He slowly did as he was told. Just like the other night, his pockets were filled. My eyes glimmered and my pussy got wet but my attention remained dead on him. He sat the money on the center console.

"Now, get your ass out," I ordered.

"What?" he asked in disbelief.

"Nigga, you heard me. Get your punk ass out of the truck!"

He stared at me for a moment as if thinking about refusing.

"Don't make me catch a body up in this muthafucka. Get your ass *out* or get your ass *dead*!"

He sighed angrily.

"This shit ain't over," he promised while reaching for the handle. He opened the door, and climbed out. "I swear on my momma this shit ain't over."

"Whatever."

I climbed into the driver's seat, slammed the gear in drive, and sped off; leaving his dumb ass standing in the street looking stupid. Immediately I hit the very first side street I saw, sped down to the end of it and made a left. From there I bussed a couple more rights and lefts to be sure Cee-Lo wouldn't be able to find me if he came looking. After finally pulling to the curb I grabbed the money and began counting.

"Wow," I whispered, realizing there was nearly ten thousand dollars in my hand.

There was no time to rejoice though. Fuck that. With the ten stacks me and Treasure were going to do a nice hotel room tonight; possibly The Westin, and hit the highway first thing in the morning. We were going to get the fuck up out of here and hit Arizona. But first, I had to run back to Baltimore and get Dinero out of the county's custody. As I pulled away from the curb to go and get Treasure, I called my mother. Unfortunately I got her answering machine, but left a message anyway.

"Mama, I'm so sorry for all the shit I've been talking. I promise I'm gonna get my life together and do right. I'll see you in the morning."

NINETEEN

The next day rolled around way too fast. As usual my mother's street was quiet, empty and serene as my car pulled to the curb directly in front of her Reisterstown's home. If felt weird to have such a cool day in the middle of July, but the breeze felt good as me and Treasure stepped out of the car and into the sunlight.

My nerves had been twisting and turning ever since I laid my eyes on the Baltimore sign back on the side of the highway 295. Obviously I didn't want to be here and was looking forward to putting it as far in my rear view as possible as soon as I got Dinero and Shane from CPS. But until I hopped back on that highway, I knew my nerves were never going to ease up.

After grabbing my purse and closing the car door, I quickly looked around as me and Treasure began to make our way up the driveway. Most likely Paco had no idea where my mother lived, but I still couldn't help looking around, scared he'd jump out from behind a bush or tree ready to blow my damn head off.

My mother's prized Cadillac was parked in its usual spot and freshly detailed like always. The windows of her house were open. The breeze was causing her sheer curtains to sway. We climbed the steps of her porch, and knocked on the door. As soon as my knuckles made contact with the door it flew open immedi-

ately, which surprised me. She must've been watching us come
up the walk way.

"My baby," she said, brushing me to the side and taking
Treasure in her arms and smothering her with countless kisses
like she was scared she'd never see her again.

The shit looked overly dramatic to me. But that was how
my mother was these days. She was fresh up out of a soap opera.
She reminded me of Alexis on that old soap opera Dynasty. Of
course my mother was the low budget version, but the both of
them could still practically pass for twins.

"Mommy!" Cash screamed, appearing from a back room.
He darted towards me at full speed.

Holding Treasure by the hand my mother quickly turned
and blocked Cash's path. She then scooped him up in her arms
and carried him back towards the kitchen. "Finish eating your
food," she said before placing him back on the floor.

"But I want to see my mommy," Cash pleaded.

"You will. She isn't going anywhere. Now, finish eating."

The nerve of this bitch, I thought to myself. *Don't want to
let me touch my own child; like I got a disease or some shit.
Whatever*, I decided. There was no time for drama.

"You ought to be ashamed of yourself," she said as soon
as Cash walked away. She stood behind Treasure with her hands
on her shoulders. "You see how damn crazy that boy is about
you. How could you just leave him like that?"

"Ma, whatever. I don't have time for this."

"Well, make time, damn it."

I sighed. I knew she wasn't going to let me go without
buckets and buckets of earfuls.

"You hungry, child?" she asked Treasure.

"Yes," Treasure responded.

"It's some roast beef and potatoes in the oven. Go eat all
you want."

Treasure quickly disappeared.

"Ma, I thought we were going to CPS?" I questioned
growing aggravated and annoyed.

156

"Oh, we are."

She began to pace the floor.

"Child, you worry me so much," she said. "You worry me to the depths of my soul. You make it hard for me to breathe sometimes."

Oh boy, here she goes. She's headed into her damn Betty Davis mode.

"Keema, how did you get to the point where you had to put my grandbabies in harm's way? I mean, doing that to yourself is one thing. But the kids? That's another. You don't have that right."

All I did was listen. When she went into her *Mommy Dearest* mode, the best thing to do was just shut up and let her talk. That would make it go a whole lot faster. Trying to slip a word in edge wise would only prolong shit.

"Where were you at anyway?" she asked, now standing behind the couch. She only stood there for a brief moment then she was back on the move. Her eyes seem to be redder than normal. Maybe she'd been crying all night.

Sighing, I said, "Laying low. That's why I dropped Cash off with you. I had no choice. There are things going on that you don't understand."

"It's about this damn Paco nonsense, right?"

She wouldn't stop moving and pacing. That struck me as odd. I'd never seen her that way. Usually, nothing ever got her this emotional or antsy. *Damn, me leaving Cash with her really shook her up.*

"Child, I pray so hard for you every night. Do you know how hard it's been for me to sleep? When I call you don't answer. Keema, you had me worried sick. All this stuff going on about guns and people getting killed; it worries me. Then my grandbabies are all caught in the middle of it. I can't have their lives in jeopardy anymore."

"Ma, look, I would love to stay and enjoy this little moment with you, but I can't. There are things going on in my life that I can't discuss, things you wouldn't understand."

"You won't even give me a chance to try and understand. You don't tell me anything." She placed her hands over her face.

"Ma, let's get down to CPS. I've really got to move."

Arizona was the only thing I could think about.

For the first time since she opened the door my mother finally stopped moving. She finally stopped fidgeting. She stood at the entrance of the kitchen. But there was a look on her face I'd never seen before. There was something sad in her eyes.

"Keema, I love you, but you put me in a bad situation."

Something in her voice didn't sound right. It was the way a voice sounds just before it tells you something bad. I wasn't feeling it at all. I looked at her with an odd expression. Something was definitely wrong.

"You put me in a real bad position," she repeated.

Seeing that something about her, her voice, and her demeanor was off, I said, "Ma, what's going on?"

"You did this to yourself," she returned.

"Did what?"

Damn, this didn't feel right. I backed towards the door. She didn't answer my question.

"Did *what*, Ma?" I inquired much more sternly this time.

"You made me do this."

"What the fuck are you talking about? Stop talking in riddles."

"He gave me fifty."

"Fifty *what*?" I asked, having absolutely no idea what she was talking about.

"Fifty thousand dollars."

"Who gave you fifty thousand dollars?"

"I had to do it." Water welled up in her eyes as she spoke.

"Ma, who gave you fifty thousand dollars?" She was scaring the shit out of me right now.

She didn't answer. The look on her face grew weirder than before. Then she began to shed countless tears and ran close to the children, wrapping her arms around the both of them.

"Who?" I asked again. "Who gave you fifty thousand dol-

158

lars and for what?"

To get the words out caused her pain, but eventually she did. Immediately I wished she hadn't.

"Paco," she said.

The sound of his name made time stop and everything around me spin. I couldn't speak. I couldn't move.

"Baby, I'm sorry," she continued. "I didn't want…"

As she continued to speak, her words didn't register. I couldn't hear them. I only heard Paco's name. I was in a trance. The only thing that broke me out of it was the sound of tires screeching to a halt outside the window. Something inside me already knew who they belonged to. As my mother continued to ramble on, I quickly looked out the window to see Paco and a few of his goons hopping out of two black Escalades.

"Shit!" I screamed.

With no hesitation I dashed by my mother, shoving her out of the way and onto the floor. My feet were moving in a blur as I hit the kitchen and burst through the back door with more power than I ever knew existed. By the time I made it to the back of my mother's yard I realized Treasure was behind me. I hadn't told her to come, but I guess she knew she was supposed to be with me, in good times and bad. We dashed across the lawn to a fence at the far end with gun shots sounding off behind us. With a quick glance I could see two guys scrambling trying to figure out how best to catch up with us. I tossed my purse over the fence and began to scale it, knowing my life depended on it. Treasure did the same. We hopped it and landed in someone else's yard. As soon as my feet touched the ground I snatched up my purse and ran like crazy.

"Come on!" I yelled to Treasure hoping she wouldn't slow me down.

There was absolutely no time or toleration for lagging. We had to get going quickly. Even though we couldn't see anyone trailing us, we knew we had to keep running. As we neared the back of someone's house a loud scream came from behind. I recognized it as my mother's.

Treasure yelled, "Mommy!" She then stopped to look back.

The sound of gunshots made me stop and look back with worry as well.

The screaming stopped.

"Oh, God," I whispered, fearing the worst. What if one shot was for my mother and the other for Cash? What if they were both now dead? The possibility terrified me beyond belief.

I finally realized that there was no turning back now. There was nothing I could do. What was done was done.

"Lets go!" I ordered.

"But Grandma and Cash," Treasure said with tears in her eyes.

"We gotta go!" I yelled snatching her by the hand so hard she tripped and fell.

I snatched her up from the ground and immediately began running again. My heart raced as we began to run from street to street. My adrenalin flowed wildly. We both knew getting caught would be like signing our own death certificates. We couldn't let it happen.

Everything whizzed by us in a blur as we ran as far as our feet could carry us. People looked at us strangely as we darted past them. Cars slammed on breaks and blew their horns as we shot out into the street in front of them. We were both out of breath in no time but refusing to stop. We finally reached a busy street just in time to see a bus coming. I flagged it down and we both hopped on. After quickly paying the fare we both headed straight to the back and sat down, breathing heavily and trying to catch our breaths.

As we sat in silence my mind immediately drifted to my mother. How could she tell me I was being a bad mother then turn around and do some shit like this to me? How could she? Never in a million years would I have expected her to do something this fucking grimy.

NEVER!

The thought of her handing me over to Paco for fifty thousand made me angry, but it also made me want to cry. And the fact that she kept saying I was putting them all in harms way infuriated me. Besides my kids, she was all I had in this world. She was all I could trust. I'd burned far too many bridges and crossed too many people to even *think* about trusting anyone else.

"Damn that bitch!" I shouted angrily, causing everyone to turn around and look at me.

The only thing that freed my mind from thinking about my mother was Cash. His face made me rest my head in the palm of my hand shamefully. What if he was dead? What if Paco had killed him?

"My baby," I whispered broken heartedly.

Treasure sat looking out of the window in total silence. Although her face was turned away from me I knew she was crying.

Why did I get us into this? I wondered. *How could I have been so stupid? How could I have been so narrow minded*?

Me and Treasure were truly on our own now. Even my car was left back at my mother's house so we had nothing to our name. The only thing left to do was hop on the Greyhound tonight and get as far away from Baltimore as possible. Arizona was now a definite.

At least I still had the ten thousand I'd robbed Cee-Lo for and the EBT cards. Me and Treasure were definitely going to need it.

TWENTY

The food court at the Harbor was packed with people and chattering with conversation. Couples and families sat at the scattered surrounding tables eating and enjoying each other's company. Unable to sit completely still both my head and my eyes repeatedly scoured my surroundings for Paco, or anyone who looked suspicious. I couldn't stop even if I wanted to. Yesterday had me shook like crazy. I'd calmed a little, but hadn't totally recovered. My hands couldn't even stop shaking.

I still had no idea what exactly had happened back at my mother's house. I had no idea if she was dead or even if she was okay. I had even watched the local news both last night and this morning. There was no mention of it. But the possibility of her getting killed saddened me somewhat.

Oh fucking well. I hated to see her go out like that. But when you cross, you *get* crossed. She shouldn't have tried to play her own daughter, her own flesh and blood. My prayers and worries were now with Cash. My heart ached for him. A darkness was over me that wouldn't be lifted until I found out if he was safe.

As my eyes kept a close look out for my enemies, they also watched for Peppi, anxious for the sight of him. He'd called me last night to ask about the money again. He said the contractors had received a contract for another job. If they didn't get their money from me ASAP, they were going to have to abandon finishing the spa and move onto their next job. Obviously I couldn't let that happen. I was too close to fail; especially when he told me the sign had been put out front that said, *Keema's Day Spa*. Damn, that shit felt good to hear. I told Peppi I had ten stacks so he agreed to meet me at the food court.

Absolutely no one around me could be trusted these days. Whatever friends I had back in the projects were most likely eager to get their hands on that bounty money Paco had on my ass. They'd turn me over to Paco in a heartbeat. And of course my mother was possibly pushing up daisies for crossing me so she was out of the question. Besides Treasure, all I had was Peppi. He didn't know Paco so it was safe to fuck with him.

It may sound corny, but Peppi was like my knight in shining armor. He could always be depended on to come through. Shit, he could have offered the spa investment to anyone. He fucked with bankers, lawyers, doctors, and business men. A hood bitch like me should've been the last person he'd decided to let get down with something that important. I was glad he'd decided to fuck with me though. He didn't know just how much of a life saver that investment was.

Treasure was sitting across the table from me not saying a single word as she just stared at her slice of pizza like she was expecting it to get up and walk away. She hadn't spoken a word since last night. I really couldn't blame her. I hadn't said much to her either.

"Treasure, what happened yesterday was fucked up. I know this honey. But we're gonna be okay."

She nodded.

"You're too young to understand. Just know that we can't trust anybody but Peppi right now."

"Okay," she finally said.

I realized the best thing to do was just leave her alone. There would be plenty of time to talk later. The both of us still had on the same clothes we had on the day before and my hair was all over my head. I looked terrible. Usually shopping could always put a smile on my face. It could always cheer me up. But today it couldn't. Depression was too great. I couldn't stop thinking about Cash. Dinero and Shane were heavy on my mind, too.

Damn, how did things get this bad?

The only thing that brightened my day was knowing my fortune was about to change for the better. Shit was about to look up. Although all me and Treasure had right now were the clothes on our backs, the money I took from Cee-Lo, and the EBT cards everything was about to change. I was about to give Peppi the ten grand to finish building our new and bright future.

Treasure and I had stayed at The InterContinental downtown the night before. Amazingly, despite what I'd endured, I got a decent night's rest. There were no nightmares. Subconsciously I felt ashamed of myself for it. Of all the nights for me to get a decent night's sleep, why was it the night I had possibly lost Cash and Dinero forever? Why was it the night my mother was possibly killed? That shit was eating at my conscience.

As my phone began to ring, I quickly hit the button to ignore the call when I saw Tia's name pop up on the screen. I knew what she was calling about. Hell, she'd been calling non stop all morning. I'm sure by now she was pissed that I hadn't left the money for the new EBT cards, but her ass would just have to get over it. I wasn't in the position to come up off two grand right now, especially after what had just happened. For now, she was gonna have to fall back until I got myself together.

Peppi finally strutted into the food court with his normal swag. The way he walked always amazed me. It wasn't a walk at all. It was something indescribable. The best way I could think to describe it was that he seemed to be floating or gliding in a rhythm no one could imitate. Not a care in the world. I'd never seen a walk like his. And was sure I'd never see one like it again.

As usual he was brimming with excitement and happiness. His smile was wide. His eyes were sparkling beautifully. His long jet black hair was razor straight and falling past his shoulders hanging to his chest. Dressed in a dark grey suit, the pants had creases in them sharp enough to cut some of that government cheese. He was also rocking a large diamond ring on his right pinky finger.

As Peppi approached us he began to do The Cha-Cha, although there was no music to dance to. He didn't care who was looking as he swayed his hips and arms like he was on an episode of *Dancing With The Stars*. There was no embarrassment, only pride. But that was just the way Peppi was. I'd never seen a human being like him.

"There's my little chocolate rose petal," he said, extending his arms for a hug when he finally reached the table.

I stood and hugged him, smelling his Armani cologne.

As we released he looked at my face and could see my stress. "No, no, no," he said disapprovingly as he softly took my face into his hands. "Peppi senses heartache. Peppi senses discomfort."

I forced a smile. "I'm okay."

He gave me the type of look an elementary school teacher gives a student when she knows their lying. He wagged his finger. "You're telling a fib to Peppi." He frowned. "Peppi can see it in your face. Talk to me. Tell me what's wrong."

"It's nothing important. It's gonna be okay."

He looked at me sideways. "Are you sure? You know Peppi always has an ear for your words and a shoulder for you to rest the side of your angelic face upon."

I chuckled. He always knew what to say.

"I'm good. But I do need to get out of Baltimore *now*."

He looked at me worriedly. "Are you in some sort of trouble?"

"Nah, just really want to put this city behind me. I can't take the stress anymore. It's definitely time for a change."

He nodded. "Peppi understands. Life places many of us in that position sometimes."

As I reached into my purse for the money, he looked at Treasure. "Is this your beautiful daughter?" he asked. "Is this your princess?

Before I could answer he walked over to her and said, "It

must be. She has the flawless facial features of an angel just like her mother. Her eyes sparkle like crystals and her skin is so beautiful. Her beauty exceeds that of a China Doll."

Treasure looked into Peppi's face. Then she looked him up and down. Her lips twisted to the side as if she felt he was trying to run some sort of game on her. She rolled her eyes and looked back down at her slice of pizza.

"Forgive her," I told Peppi, embarrassed by what she'd just done. "She's going through some things right now."

He laughed it off. "Peppi understands."

I handed him the ten thousand dollars.

"I'm going to fly out to Arizona this evening at six o'clock to give the contractors the money plus the ten I promised to match."

I hugged him, unable to hold back. He was truly a savior. "Thanks, Peppi," I told him as he returned my hug. "You don't know how much of a help you are."

"No need for thanks. It is an honor to be in a partnership with a woman such as yourself. We will grow much more successful together. You watch and see. Peppi guarantees it."

When we let each other go I asked him for the address to my spot. Me and Treasure were going to take the Greyhound out there. It would take a day or two. But once we got there, the first place we were going to stop was going to be the spa. I couldn't wait to see it in person. Peppi whipped out a gold plated pen and wrote the address on a piece of paper enthusiastically. He handed the paper to me.

"I can't wait for you to see it," he said. "It is breathtaking. I promise you will be so mesmerized."

"Did they send you pictures of the sign yet?"

"Absolutely. Your name is spread across the top of it in lights just as you wanted."

I visualized it in my head. It excited me.

"Oh, I almost forgot," he said, reaching into his pocket and pulling out a small piece of paper. He looked around, leaned towards me, and whispered, "This is the number to the marijuana

167

connect. He is expecting to hear from you."

I took the number and stuffed it in my purse.

"Well, I must go," he said. "I have business awaiting me before I take the flight out to Arizona in a few hours."

The two of us hugged again.

"If we don't see each other again before you go to see the spa," he said, backing away, "make sure you call me as soon as you get there. Peppi wants to hear the fresh excitement in your voice."

"I got you."

"Peppi loves you!" He blew me a kiss.

I laughed and said, "Thanks for everything, Peppi. I love you, too."

Me and Treasure would be back on top soon. Just as quickly as everything had fallen apart, the spa would put it all back together.

Suddenly, my phone rang. Taking it out of my purse and looking at the screen, I recognized the number. It immediately sent a jolt through me and made me stare at it for a second. The number was Moose's, the bouncer from Dupree's club. Not sure whether I should answer it or not I took a chance.

"Hello?" I answered.

"Keema?"

"Yeah?"

"This is Moose. Are you okay?"

I listened skeptically, unsure of why he was calling or what he wanted.

"Yeah, I'm alright." I attempted to sound sad.

"Rick told me to call you. He said to watch yourself out here. He also said to get out of town as soon as possible and lay low. Things are going on."

I really didn't quite know how to accept his words.

"He said to tell you not to trust anybody. He'll call you soon."

Those words made me realize Rick still didn't know I was the reason his brothers were dead. He still had no idea. The realization brought a smile to my face. Damn, the day was going great. Everything was turning around for me.

"Did you hear me?"

"Loud and clear."

"This is real serious, Keema. Rick wants you to watch yourself. Shit's real hectic out here right now. Be safe."

"I will."

"Alright."

He hung up.

Immediately the thought crossed my mind to get Dinero. I second guessed it though. Shit was still way too hot. The best thing to do was just stick to my plan. Hit Arizona, open my spa, and take everything as it comes.

TWENTY ONE

Treasure and I walked out of the Greyhound station into the blazing afternoon sun after a fifty-four hour bus ride. As mountains could be seen in the far distance the temperature was every bit of 106 degrees, but felt even hotter. I'd heard about how hot it got in Arizona but *damn*! It was absolutely miserable. The scoring temperatures Maryland got during the summer months didn't have shit on this. It was the most stifling humid heat I'd ever felt in my twenty-five years on earth. There wasn't a hint of a breeze anywhere. Immediately sweat began to form underneath my Love Pink T-shirt and my eyes were forced to squint heavily. I couldn't wait to hit the hotel and jump into a cool shower. But first, I had to check out my new place of business. Treasure and I quickly hopped into a cab.

As the cab traveled through Phoenix passing countless stores, restaurants, and people I looked over at my daughter. She was still silent as she stared out of the window. She'd even been that way the entire bus ride.

"Treasure, you're going to like it here," I uttered attempting to cheer her up.

"I doubt it,' she said plainly, still looking out of the window. "I hate it already."

"Really, you will. It's never cold so it never snows."

"I like the snow." Her voice was still plain.

"You'll make new friends, too. You'll even be in a new

school."

"There was nothing wrong with my old friends or my old school."

"I've got a lot planned for us out here. We'll have a much better life here than we did back in Baltimore," I kept trying to convince.

Treasure didn't say anything though. She just turned more toward the window and pressed herself closer to it.

"I've got a business out here, Treasure. We're gonna be important."

"Whoopi," she said sarcastically and with no emotion.

"Baby, we've got to let Baltimore go. We've got a new life here."

Although Treasure's back was turned to me, I could tell by her body language that she was rolling her eyes. She did that more often these days. The last thing she wanted to do right now was give Phoenix a chance. Shit, I seriously doubted she would give *any* city a chance besides Baltimore.

There was no use. She hated life right now. And one thing I never did was kiss a hater's ass. This was our new life. She had no choice but to accept it. Just like her, Baltimore was all I'd ever known, but today was a new day. An old saying my mother used to say to me when I was a kid crossed my mind. "You better scratch your ass and get glad." She always threw that line at me when I was mad about something. The memory made me chuckle and made me wonder about her and Cash.

During the entire bus trip I'd thought about them, and all I was leaving behind. Even though I was pissed at my mother, I definitely prayed that she and my son were okay. I thought about the memories I'd created. Some of them brought tears to my eyes. I realized that I was truly going to miss Baltimore despite just how badly I wanted to leave it behind. My heart broke the further and further we traveled, but there was no other choice but to suck it up and press forward. The future was much brighter in Phoenix. Besides I heard the niggas were caked up.

Realizing there was no use in trying to persuade Treasure

any longer, I pulled out my phone from my purse, took out the weed connect's number, and dialed his number. I wanted to introduce myself to him and let him know that I was in town. If everything worked out, me and him were going to do business together for a very long time. Once I got my clientele where I wanted it, I was going to buy big from him.

"Hello?" he answered.

"Is this Lucky?"

"Who this?" he asked in a suspicious tone.

"Keema," I told him. "Peppi gave me your number."

"Oh yeah," Lucky said a lot more enthusiastically. "You the girl in Baltimore, right?"

"Yeah, that's me. I just wanted to let you know I'm in Phoenix now."

His voice sounded like he was black. Sexy and black. I explained to him my plans for doing business and soon he was in agreement. As the minutes passed, it seemed as if he couldn't wait for us to move forward.

"Where you at right now?"

"On my way to see my day spa. It's called Keema's," I stated proudly.

"Well, how about I come pick you up from there and take you out to lunch. We can talk a lil' more."

"That's what's up."

"Let me get the address."

"4630 West Indian School Road."

"Indian School Road?"

"Yup."

"You sure?"

"Yeah," I responded.

There was a long pause. "Are you positive it's in Maryvale?"

"I'm not sure what the area is called, but that's the address Peppi gave me."

"Alright," Lucky said with hesitation. "I know the neighborhood well. I'll meet you there."

As soon as my finger pressed the end button my thoughts were filled with anticipation, expectations, and plans for the future. The first thing I had to do as soon as I got my pockets up was get me another car. I'd been peeping those new Camaros for a while. I would start off with a jet black one. Then I would upgrade to an X6 or a Porsche Panamera and show these country ass Arizona women how a hard bodied B-More bitch could do it. Right after copping a car I'd either get a single family house or a penthouse condo in some upscale building. Treasure and I would have to do a hotel to start off, but once my money was right, home ownership would be top priority.

As my eyes watched everything passing by my window it was impossible not to notice just how different Phoenix neighborhoods and houses looked from Baltimore. It was like a totally different world. I wondered what type of music they listened to, how they dressed, and what the clubs were like. But above all, I was wondering what the dick was like. My pussy was anxious to find out.

Twenty minutes later the cab made a left at a busy intersection and headed down a long street. This had to be their version of the hood. There was no doubt about it. I stared as several crack heads stumbled down the street looking so skinny that a heavy burst of wind would either tip them over or carry their asses away. I also noticed young boys standing in front of liquor stores probably making drug transactions along with different old school cars sitting along the curbs.

From what Peppi had told me about the safe, clean neighborhood where the spa was located, I was thankful the cab was just passing through this part of town to get to the next.

"My business could never make it around here," I said. I was so glad to be in a more upscale area.

Suddenly the cab began to slow down and pull towards the curb. Seconds later it came to a full stop.

"Alright, ma'am," the driver said as he put the car in park.

I looked around at my surroundings. "Where are we?"

"West Indian School Road."

174

"This ain't it!" I barked.

"Ma'am, this is it." He pointed. "This is the address you told me to bring you to 4630."

There was no fucking way this could be the address!

"There's got to be a mistake," I stated angrily.

"Ma'am, there's no mistake," he returned, growing agitated. "I know this neighborhood like the back of my hand. I grew up not too far from here. This is definitely the right address."

Looking at the building where the spa was supposed to be located had me frozen in disbelief.

The driver sighed. "Ma'am, I really need to go chase down some other fares. Can you please pay me so I can go?"

Still confused, I reluctantly paid him and climbed out of the car with my eyes locked on the structure. As the cab pulled away I could only stare as Treasure stood beside me. She looked around at the run down neighborhood and twisted her face. "Mom, where we at?"

My ears didn't hear her. My body couldn't feel her presence. All I could focus on was the building in front of me with 4630 West Indian School Road written across the front door. It was the correct address. But instead of my damn day spa, it was a boarded up gas station and convenience store with a huge CLOSED sign sitting on the edge of the lot. The lot it sat on was filled with garbage, broken glass, and a few abandoned cars sitting up on bricks.

"Damn, bitch," a guy shouted from a passing car as it played Tyga's *Rack City* loud enough to crack an ear drum. "You got a fat ass!"

I paid no attention. I was in a daze; hypnotized. Realizing there had to be a mistake I turned around to look for a sign that said KEEMA's. The sign Peppi had been bragging about. And where was the image he'd shown me in the brochure? My eyes looked up and down the street frantically. It had to be here somewhere. It had to be. But after several moments of desperate looking, I was forced to realize there was no sign with my name on it

175

anywhere in sight. Immediately I snatched my phone from my purse and called Peppi. The phone didn't ring. Instead, an operator's voice came on and said, "The number you're trying to reach is no longer in service."

I hung up and tried again.

"The number you are trying to reach…"

Pressing the end button I tried one last time. I was so angry and my fingers were trembling so badly I had to have dialed the wrong number. That *had* to be the explanation. Peppi's number was in service just two days ago. I placed the phone to my ear again.

"The number you are trying…"

"Fuck!" I screamed, realizing what I'd hoped wasn't true.

That son of a bitch had played me!

"You low down muthafucka!" I screamed referring to Peppi as I kicked a trash can so hard it tumbled over, spilling garbage on the already littered sidewalk. My pressure was sky high. My vision was candy apple red and my heart was now pumping tremendously.

"You Mexican piece of shit!" I spewed.

Treasure stepped back frightfully and stared at me, unable to recognize the angry woman in front of her.

I couldn't believe what had happened. That muthafucka had taken all of my money and ran off. Now me and my baby were in a unfamiliar city where we knew absolutely no one. Tears began to stream from my eyes. All I wanted to do at the moment was die.

The spa was my dream. It was my future. I'd sacrificed everything for it. Now, all of those sacrifices were for nothing. I had no car, no place to stay, no clothes, and very little money. What the fuck was I going to do? As everything around me spun I was scared. I had no idea of what to do or where to turn.

Suddenly, a dark blue Range Rover on twenty-six inch Giovannis pulled to the curb with smoked out windows. Moments later, the driver's door opened. A twenty something year old dude in a wife beater, True Religion shorts, and black, hi-top

Gucci sneakers hopped out. He was tall, like he could've played for the NBA with skin like a brown paper bag. He also had a low hair cut and rocked a nice trimmed goatee. He was slim but naturally cut. I couldn't stop staring at his body or the diamond studded earring in his ear that shined like a chandelier.

"You Keema, right?" the guy asked as he made his way towards me. "I'm Lucky."

Immediately I tore into him. "Y'all think this shit is funny!" I screamed, immediately thinking he had something to do with this.

He looked at me like I was crazy. "What you talking about, lil' boo."

"I ain't your damn lil' boo! I want my muthafuckin' money!"

The entire street stared at me.

"Whoa," Lucky said, extending his hands in defense. "Pump your brakes. I don't know what you're talking about. What money?"

"Don't play stupid! You know what money I'm talking about! All the money you and Peppi played me out of! I want my shit right now!"

"Look, I don't know nothing about no money. I don't even know Peppi all like that. What's going on?"

"I ain't the bitch to fuck with!"

"Huh?"

"You and that muthafucka are in cahoots. Ain't no since in lying!"

"Shorty, I don't do shady business. I'm in this game to *make* money, not run it off."

I looked at him like he was full of shit. I wasn't sure if he was lying or telling the truth.

Seeing my uncertainty he said, "Real talk, I don't get down like that. Now, I don't know what Peppi did to you. But I *do* know that I had nothing to do with it. Me and Peppi not even tight like that. He bought some weed from me once. And he brought a partner of his by my spot who bought a couple of pounds from me another time. That was when he told me about you."

I still didn't know if I should believe him or not.

"That's real talk, shorty. I had nothing to do with what Peppi did to you."

I was getting ready to say something else when my phone rang. Hoping it was Peppi I grabbed it from my purse so fast it almost slipped out of my hands. I finally got hold of it, pressed the answer button, and said, "Hello?"

"Keema, I just heard," she said with pain in her voice. "Girl, I'm so sorry."

"Sorry about what?" I asked Raven who was an emotional mess.

"Haven't you heard?"

"Heard what?"

The phone went silent.

Not in the mood for waiting, I said, "What is it? Haven't I heard what?"

I could hear her crying and sniffling.

"Keema, Cash and your mother are dead."

My world ended at that vey moment.

Everything around me went silent.

"Keema?" Raven said.

The phone fell from my hand.

My arms went limp and fell to my sides.

Treasure seemed worried. "Mom, what's wrong?"

"Shorty, you alright?" Lucky asked.

Unable to say a word, all I could do was cry. My knees grew weak and my body immediately dropped to the ground.

TWENTY TWO

That boring elevator sounding music played from hidden overhead speakers as hundreds of shoppers made their way through the Fashion Square mall in Scottsdale. Lucky, myself and Treasure were among them. Our hands were filled with bags, each full of new clothes and shoes; Armani Exchange, BCBG, Nordstrom's, Juicy Couture, Gap Kids. You name it, we had it. As we walked from store to store I felt like a zombie. I was empty inside just like a shell. The news from the day before about my mother had pretty much destroyed me.

The memory of Cash happily charging towards me and calling me mommy the last time I saw him wouldn't leave my mind. I wished so badly that I had hugged him. I wished so badly that I hadn't left him with my mother. If I hadn't, he would still be alive. Damn, there were so many regrets. The guilt was so terrible it took me several hours after hearing the news to get myself together. I was a total mess. Tears wouldn't stop falling from my eyes, snot wouldn't stop running, and sobs wouldn't stop coming. Treasure was the one who ultimately pulled me out of it. She was so motherly and I just couldn't figure out where she'd gotten the trait. Through her own tears and heartbreak she told me everything was going to be alright. Somehow I believed her.

Losing my mother hurt as well. But there was still a deep seeded anger inside of me for what she'd done. There was still tons of resentment. Her own selfishness had brought Paco and death to her door step. Even though she was gone, forgiving her for her betrayal would be something that would take time. Still, I wanted to give her and Cash a proper burial. I wasn't sure how, but never the less I wanted to.

Although my heart was broken, Lucky was turning out to be a Godsend. After I'd told him what happened to my family, despite me cursing him out for something he obviously had nothing to do with, he refused to see Treasure and I on the street. He ended up putting us up at the Homewood Suites Hotel and paid for an entire week.

Despite the fact that she was just as depressed as I was, he also seemed to really like Treasure. Lucky bought her a couple pairs of Jordans along with some cute costume jewelry from Claire's and several outfits. He said he always wanted a daughter but was waiting for the right woman and the right time before he made a decision that big. Lucky explained how all of his homeboys were constantly facing baby mama drama day in and day out, and he didn't want any parts of that. He also said his time was too devoted to hustling these days. Apparently Lucky didn't want to have a child that he couldn't give all of his time to. I respected him for that because there were already enough bad ass children running around terrorizing the streets because their fathers had no time for them. Lucky admitted that he himself had gotten into the game at an early age because he didn't have a father to teach him differently.

"So, how long are you gonna stay in town?" Lucky asked as we walked past the Betsey Johnson store.

"Don't know yet," I told him.

I really had no idea where to go from here. My pockets were shorter than a midget on his knees. Peppi had screwed me good; *real* fucking good. I had no idea exactly how I was going to recover. But what I did know was that if I ever saw that muthafucka again, he was going to get his ass put the fuck down.

That shit pissed me off and gave me a headache every time I thought about it. I couldn't believe I'd been so gullible. How could I have been so damn stupid? Shit, when Treasure sized him up the other day, I should've taken heed. If a child can see right through a muthafucka, he *has* to be crooked. But hindsight couldn't change anything. I had no choice now but to take the loss and move on. The only question was *how*.

"What are your plans?" Lucky asked as he took a sip from the straw of his soda. "Do you want to stay here or do you want to go back to Oxon Hill?"

I'd lied yesterday and told him I was from Oxon Hill, a section in P.G. County, where I'd gotten my hair done on a few occasions. I had no idea why. Maybe the word Baltimore just brought back too much pain. It reminded me of Imani, Cash, Dinero, and my mother. Then it dawned on me that maybe I'd lied because I didn't know what Paco was capable of or who he knew. As crazy as it sounded he might've known Lucky. Whatever the reason, I just wanted to erase the name Baltimore from my entire vocabulary.

Sighing, I said, "I honestly don't know. I don't know where to go from here. Peppi put me in a fucked up position."

"You could work for me," he said, giving me a sly look that was kind of sexy on him.

"Doing what?" I quickly asked.

"I got a couple trap houses. I'm always looking for workers to bag coke and weed."

Immediately visions of me standing at a table butt naked like that scene in *New Jack City* filled my head. I could see myself sweating like a slave in some broken down house with no air conditioning and wearing a doctor's mask as I put weed and coke in plastic sandwich bags while goons paced the room with guns. I could also see the Feds kicking in the door and putting me and every other naked broad on the floor face down ass up. The scene turned me all the way off.

"Nah, I don't think so." I waved him off with my hand as we walked casually.

"You've got to make some money somehow."

"I know. I'll figure something out."

I had no idea how I was going to get money. The thought

of setting up Lucky crossed my mind. He obviously had money to burn. In just one day he'd spent several hundred dollars on me and Treasure like it was nothing to him so he would definitely be a sweet lick. But I just couldn't do that to him. I was honestly feeling him. Besides, it was finally understood that every time I crossed someone, I got crossed. Karma was turning out to be a real bitch towards me lately. It had been turning on me like a snake. And right now I had enough problems to deal with. The last thing I wanted to do was complicate things in Arizona.

Lucky was cute and he seemed to be a thorough hustla. He seemed to have his head on straight. I liked that. It was obvious by the way he looked at me that he was feeling me too. It made me feel like if I decided to stay in Phoenix, there was a possibility me and him could have a chance at something special. It had to be taken slow though.

We passed by the Disney Store. "You want something out of here, baby girl?" he asked Treasure.

Before she could even shake her head yes, we headed inside.

Lucky's treatment of Treasure seemed genuine, which made me like him even more. I'd never had a man who liked any of my kids before. Niggas usually didn't want to accept that a woman and her children were a package deal, but Lucky seemed different.

While buying a Princess Tiana doll and a few board games, he asked Treasure when her birthday was. After she told him it would be in August, three weeks away and that she would be eleven, Lucky told her that if we were still in Phoenix, he would have something special for her. He looked at me slyly as he said it, hoping I would get the message that he wanted us to stay.

My cell phone rang. At first I thought it might've been Tia since she called at least twice a day, but it wasn't. Looking at the screen and seeing that it was Rick I didn't want to answer but did anyway. My heart started to beat like an African drum on steroids. I could barely get my word out as I walked away from

182

Lucky over by the escalator.

"Hello?"

"Keema?"

"Yeah."

"This is Rick. I'm out the hospital."

"I'm so glad you're okay."

I felt awkward talking to him. Although he didn't know that I was the one who'd gotten his brothers killed and him shot, a part of me still wondered if maybe he was just playing stupid. Rick had always been smart, so I wasn't sure if I should believe him or not. All I was sure of was that if Rick did know, he was going to want my head on a platter. The thought scared the shit out of me, had me sweating like prostitute in church actually.

"Look, I got Dinero and Shane."

My eyes closed at the sound of Shane's and Dinero's names. I missed them like crazy and wished I hadn't put them in the position they were in now.

"It was hell getting them from CPS, but I did. That family legal shit is crazy. My lawyer was able to get them to give me temporary custody since Dupree is dead and they couldn't find you."

"How are they?" I inquired.

"They're good."

I wanted to cry but held it in.

"How are you and Treasure?"

"We're alright," I lied.

"Are you sure? You need anything?"

"We're fine." I really didn't have the heart right now to ask him for anything, but later I would. Most definitely.

The line went silent.

After several moments he finally said, "Keema, I'm sorry about your mother and Cash."

My eyes dropped to the floor. Memories of their faces filled my head once again. My ears could still hear the gunshots like they were going off as we spoke. I could still hear my mother's screams just before the shots went off. The sounds sent shivers through my entire body.

Rick sighed heavily. A moment later I could hear him sniffing. I could tell he was crying. It shocked me. I didn't know how to react. Rick was a strong nigga, one of the toughest I'd come across. I'd never seen him cry before. He didn't even cry at Frenchie's funeral. He kept a stone face from the moment he walked into the church to the moment they put Frenchie in the ground. I'd found myself wondering how he could be so strong during that moment; especially when we all laid one rose on top of his casket at the burial. I remembered having to shed tons of tears to make myself feel like I was worthy of being there after what I'd done.

"Damn," he said with immense pain and sadness in his voice. "My whole fuckin' family is practically gone."

I felt so guilty.

"All I got is Shane and Dinero," he sobbed.

He paused. I knew memories were flowing through his thoughts just like mine. He was missing his family just as badly as I was missing mine.

"And you too, Keema," he added. "I got you."

That surprised me.

"I know we had our differences the last time we saw each other, but you're still family to me. That's real talk. If you need anything, all you have to do is call."

That felt good to hear, although I knew I didn't deserve it.

"You want to speak to Dinero?"

"Yes," I told him.

"Alright, hold on."

The phone went silent for a moment.

"Hi, mommy," Dinero said in his little pip squeak sounding voice.

My tears couldn't be contained. They flowed like crazy. They were causing my eyes to well up. I walked to the closet corner then covered my face with a hand.

"Hi, baby," I said.

"I got new sneakers, mommy. Uncle Rick got them for

184

me."

His little whiney voice shattered my heart into thousands of pieces. My knees wanted to give out. I wanted to just fall to the floor and cry my eyes out. I was such a terrible mother. Why had I done all of this and now didn't have my kids? Everything inside of me seemed to grow weak. I walked out of the store so Treasure couldn't ask me what was wrong.

"He got Shane some, too. He got us McDeweys too, mommy."

I chuckled at his pronunciation of McDonalds. He still hadn't learned how to say it.

"That's good, baby," I told him, still covering my face. "Are you being a good boy?"

"Yes."

I knew he was lying. He'd been hell on wheels from the moment I pushed him out of my stomach. He never knew how to sit still or be quiet. I'd be willing to bet he was terrorizing Rick just before he'd gotten on the phone. The thought made me grin.

"I miss you, mommy."

"I miss you too, baby." My voice shook with sadness. I wanted to hug him and never let him go. I wanted to look into his eyes. I wanted to touch him.

"I love you."

Shane's voice appeared from somewhere in the background. "I love her, too," he said. "Tell Keema Shane loves her, too."

Both voices killed me. They broke me down.

"Shane loves you too, mommy. He told me to tell you. Did you hear him?"

"Yes, I did. I love you guys, too," I returned. The tears were falling from my eyes so heavily my vision was now blurry.

"Uncle Rick wants to talk to you again, mommy."

"Okay." I really didn't want to let him go, but knew I had to.

I heard the phone changing hands.

"Well, I'm not gonna ask where you are," Rick said.

"There are all kinds of muthafuckin' investigations goin' on back here so the line might be tapped. Ain't no tellin' who might be listenin'. I just wanted to check on you."

I wiped the tears from my eyes, but they just kept on coming. They refused to stop or even slow up.

"Take care of yourself, alright. I'll call you again when shit cools down."

"Alright."

He hung up.

My heart was broken more now than it had ever been as I stuffed the phone back into my purse. My body convulsed with heavy sobs. I had so many regrets. I'd compromised so many lives. The thought made me cry even harder than before. With all of my heart I wished things hadn't come to this. When I walked back toward the store, Lucky was leaning over the railing looking down onto the lower level. My guess, he was probably surveying some bitch's ass.

"Where's Treasure?" I asked drying my face with my hand.

His brows crinkled along with his forehead. "I thought she was with you."

I didn't respond to him. Quickly, I turned to my right. Then my left. I called out her name, loudly. "Treasure!"

There was no answer.

Lucky did the same, running from store to store. "Treasure. Treasure!"

I placed my hand across my chest thinking the worse. I could no longer move my feet. Paco had come to Arizona and taken my baby!

TWENTY THREE

"I miss you, too," I told Raven, ending my call. It was crazy how I figured I'd never see my cousin again. She wanted to come out to Arizona to visit, but I told her to chill. The time would come.

I was sitting in the passenger seat of Lucky's truck as it pulled to the curb in front of an empty house. It had been a week since I'd gotten to Phoenix and I still had absolutely no idea what my plans were. My mind had been cloudy with thoughts of everything that had gone on in my life lately. It was like bad shit just avalanched down on me. And I had no idea exactly how I was going to climb out from underneath it all. Of course I was still having panic attacks, just like last week when I thought Paco had found us and kidnapped Treasure from the mall. All along Treasure had seen me crying and ran off to the bathroom to get me some tissue. I was a mess and just couldn't shake shit, or get back to the old Keema.

Usually plotting and scheming came easy to me. Usually it was never a problem. My skills had been shaken though. The fight had been knocked out of me, I guess. I was also homesick. I had no family out here and I didn't know my way around. Also, without a car I couldn't get around like I wanted to. I'd never been in a position like this before. I was used to being independent. I felt damn near helpless. That was a feeling I wasn't used to and knew had to be dismissed.

Me and Treasure were on the final day of our stay at the hotel. That meant some decisions had to be made immediately. It was crunch time. We needed a roof over our heads. My pockets were short. Paying for another night out of my own pockets would hurt terribly.

Lucky turned off the truck, opened the driver's door and said, "Come on. I want to show you something," he said, hopping out.

Hesitantly, I got out of the air conditioned vehicle and into the merciless Phoenix heat. The heat out here would definitely take some getting used to if I decided to stay. It was a miserable sort of heat. It was so damn hot from sun up to sun down that you could fry a fucking egg on the sidewalk.

As usual Lucky was dressed in all new Polo shit that looked as if he'd just popped the tags. I hadn't seen him wear anything old yet. However, I wasn't looking too bad myself in a coral Diane von Furstenburg maxi dress and Tory Burch Logo sandals. My freshly washed weave hung freely past my shoulders and my make-up was flawless. Despite how I felt, I at least looked good.

Since it was going to be a couple of hours before her braids were finished, I left Treasure at the hair salon along with my V.A. EBT card. I laughed thinking about Treasure's hair stylist. They were all borderline slow in Arizona. They'd never been turned onto the hook-up where they'd do our hair for free in exchange for me letting them go in the grocery store to get a hundred dollars worth of food off my card. Then I'd pick the card up later. It was a win-win situation for us all. Now, all the bitches who did hair at the salon were asking me when I was coming back.

"Where are we?" I asked Lucky looking around the residential neighborhood.

"You'll see," he said, grabbing my hand.

The two of us made our way up the walkway. Once we reached the door, he pulled a key from his pocket, slid it inside the lock, and turned it. As the two of us walked inside, the smell

188

of fresh paint filled my nostrils.

The house looked different from the ones back in Maryland with its stucco exterior and terracotta roof. Even though there was no furniture, it was a fairly decent size home and was located in a neighborhood that didn't look too bad.

Lucky stood in the center of the living room and folded his arms. "What do you think?"

I looked around. "It's nice. Is it yours?"

Lucky smiled. "Nah, it's my sister's spot. She's got several properties that she rents out. I was thinking that this one would be perfect for you and Treasure."

He caught me off guard with that one.

"Lucky, you know I can't afford anything right now. I don't have a job."

"Don't worry about none of that."

"What do you mean?" I blushed.

"I'll hold you down until you can get on your feet."

"Look, I don't get down like that. I prefer to pay my own way," I lied with a straight face.

I definitely wanted him to spend his money on me, but knew an offer like that came with a price tag. It always did. If I let him put me up in a place and pay my bills, he'd feel like I owed him something. Or he'd possibly start feeling like I belonged to him. I wasn't about to let that shit happen.

"I feel you," he said. "But for right now you need a little help."

Those words made me feel like a damn charity case.

"I haven't even decided if I'm even going to stay in Phoenix. I haven't made up my mind about it yet."

"Well, you and Treasure still need a place to stay while you're making up your mind. And that hotel isn't a good environment for Treasure. She needs her own space."

He had a point. A sigh escaped my lips. Damn, I hated being in the position of having to depend on a nigga. But for now I had no other choice.

"Look, just take the place temporarily, alright?" he said.

"What do you have to lose? If you decide to leave, cool. If you decide to stay, you've got yourself a place temporarily rent and bill free."

I had to admit, his offer was definitely tempting. It was a come up. While staying here I could stack my ends and get back on my feet. The goal was to get about twenty grand stacked up in my reserve. Immediately, my mind started thinking about my welfare hustle. It was all I knew. I was going to have to figure out a way to get it cracking in Phoenix. I needed to start asking around, finding all the chicks who were on the system and who they knew.

"Alright?" he pressed.

"Alright," I said.

"That's what's up. So, if you decide to stay in Phoenix, what are you going to do for money? Are you gonna get a job or something?"

A job? I don't do jobs. Obviously nine to five work schedules and punching time clocks had never been my thing. There wasn't even the slightest possibility. Shit, I'd never even considered being a slave to the white man or to the government. And I sure as hell wasn't going to start now.

"I'll probably get on welfare for a minute," I stated proudly.

He looked at me like I was crazy. "Welfare? Are you serious?"

"Yeah, just until I get something else going."

"Keema, you don't gotta do that. Just come work for me."

"Lucky, bagging work in some hot ass trap house ain't for me."

"You'll make a lot more doing that than you'll make on welfare."

"How you know?" I snapped. "I'm racking up." I stopped and looked at him. "But how much more are you talking?" I instantly became curious.

"I'll hit you off with a thousand a week."

"Whoa!" My mind spun like a windmill. *Lucky's money*

plus my welfare grind would bring me serious loot.

"You don't have to do the shit forever. Just until you get something else going."

He looked at me with those sexy brown eyes of his. I loved those eyes. There was something about them that couldn't be explained. He gave off a sexy ass vibe like Idris Elba. Lucky walked across the room and stood directly in front of me. He took both of my hands in his.

"You know I'm feeling you, right?"

I knew he was. I was feeling him, too. Over the past week we'd been talking about hooking up. But since I wasn't sure if staying in Phoenix was in the cards, I wasn't absolutely sure if I wanted to go there with him unless there was something big in it for me. I'd been down that committed road with Dupree before and didn't want to go there again. I had to be free.

But I'd be lying if I said I hadn't wondered what it would be like to be his girl. It turned me on to see myself pushing his Range Rover. He had money so I could see myself helping him spend it. Those things crossed my mind a lot. But they were always followed up with thoughts of something more, something I'd never really thought about before. Lucky had kind of stolen my heart.

The way he looked out for me and Treasure really touched me. No one had ever done that for me before, besides Dupree. But there was never truly any genuine love in my heart for Dupree. If there was, I wouldn't have set his ass up.

I tried picturing myself straightening up my act and leaving the scheming life alone. Lucky was heavy in these streets, so he needed a down ass ride or die type of bitch in his life. He needed the type of bitch who could hold him down. A part of me wanted to entertain that possibility, fill that position. But I wasn't sure.

"You hear what I said?" he asked, glaring into my eyes.

"I know," I told him.

"I'm serious, Keema. I'm feeling you and Treasure. I really want you to think about fucking with a nigga like me."

He looked seductively into my eyes in a way that made me drop mine to the floor. Refusing to let me off the hook, he placed a hand underneath my chin and raised my head. Looking into his face made my pussy moist. Damn, I wasn't sure if I liked this feeling. I'd never been in love before, but Lucky could possibly make me fall. The shit kind of scared me. I wasn't sure if I was ready.

"I could use a woman like you in my life."

His words made me melt. Plenty of niggas had run similar lines like that one on me, but it was always game. Lucky's words were sincere, or at least they *sounded* sincere. Everything inside of me desperately wanted me to trust in him.

Lucky slowly pressed his lips to mine. They tasted better than any I'd ever kissed before. My lips parted to allow his tongue entry into my mouth. He then wrapped his arms around me and began to push me backwards until my back was flat against the wall. Our hands began to rip and claw at each other's clothes.

Damn, my pussy was wet. No man had *ever* gotten my juices flowing like this. I'd quickly soaked my panties within seconds. My hands went for his belt buckle. I unbuckled it and reached inside for his dick. Immediately I was pleased at its thickness and length. The nigga was as long as a fucking freeway.

Moments later I was out of my dress. He stepped back away from me, reached into his pocket and pulled out a Magnum. As he placed it to his mouth to rip it open with his teeth, I said, "Wait, what are you doing?"

"I practice safe sex, Keema. I told you I'm not ready for no kids yet."

"I'm on the pill," I lied before I even realized it. "I can't get pregnant."

In all honesty I wanted his baby. The nigga was a bonafied hustla. If I could get pregnant with his child, no matter what happened between us from here on out, we'd always be connected. I'd be his baby mama for life. That meant a check for life. As always, my mind was calculating money. Even though I

192

was feeling him, it couldn't be helped.

If Phoenix was going to be my new home, my grind had to start somewhere. Why not this moment? I wasn't sure if me and Lucky would work out, so it was best to get some kind of insurance for my future. What better insurance than a baby? If I could get him to knock me up, that would work out perfectly for my welfare hustle. It was grimy, but I had to think about me first.

"Baby," I pleaded with him. "I want you inside me raw."

"Keema, I don't get down like that."

"What, you think I got something?"

"Nah, I just want us to be careful. There'll be plenty of time for us to do it without protection. I ain't the type of nigga who goes raw this early."

"I ain't the type of girl who does either," I lied with a straight face. "I ain't no hoe."

"I know that. But protection is something I feel strongly about. It is what it is." He shrugged his shoulders.

Seeing that he wasn't going to change his mind, I gave him a halfhearted, "Alright."

He bit open the gold colored wrapper and took out the condom. As he looked down and began to place the rubber on his dick, I tied my hair back into a ponytail, took off my hoop earrings, and placed one into my purse. The other I kept in the palm of my hand. What I was getting ready to do was grimy. A part of me felt bad about it.

Immediately after Lucky slipped the rubber on I began to kiss his chest. He moaned at the soft touch of my lips. He moaned harder as I took his nipple into my mouth and sucked it gently. Slowly, I began to work my way down his body. Eventually I was on my knees stuffing his rubber covered dick into my mouth greedily. The taste of the rubber was horrible, but I ignored it and worked his shaft back and forth.

I'd sucked enough dicks to know that there were two types of niggas when they're getting their shit sucked; those who liked to watch, and those who liked to lift their head and close their eyes. I was hoping Lucky was the latter.

After several minutes of working him slow and deep, I looked up at him. Just as I'd hoped his head was up toward the ceiling and his eyes were closed. Quickly with the earring in the palm of my hand, I slyly poked two holes in the tip of the rubber while never missing a stroke.

Moments later, I got up from my knees and escorted him to the kitchen. I hopped on top of the sink, opened my legs, and let him enter me. Lucky drilled me perfectly. For several minutes my thighs and hips matched the movement of his stroke for stroke. His thickness stretched me.

"Fuck me, baby," I urged him.

Our bodies began to sweat and our skin made loud slapping sounds as our thighs banged into each other over and over again. My moans began to turn into screams. I couldn't help it. I could damn near feel his dick in my chest.

"Shit!" I screamed. The nigga had me hitting notes even Prince couldn't reach.

He took my screams as an invitation to stroke faster and harder.

"Oh shit!" I yelled. "You're gonna make a bitch fall in love."

The nigga was beginning to beat the pussy like one of them damn Mixed Martial Arts fighters. I loved it. I liked to be kissed, caressed, and held just like any other woman. But other times I needed to be *fucked*. And now was one of those times.

Lucky pulled me off of the table and turned me around. He then bent me over, gripped my hips, and shoved himself into my nest again. The feeling made my eyes damn near roll up in my fucking head. Lucky smacked my ass hard enough with his hand to make it echo throughout the house. The sting of it made an orgasm build inside me. He began to pound me.

"Shit, Lucky, I'm about to cum!"

He smacked my ass again.

"Oh, God!" I screamed right before exploding all over his dick.

Lucky kept banging me like his life depended on it.

I worked my hips back against him with every stroke, trying to punish him as hard as he was punishing me. I felt him grip my hips tighter than before. He was going to cum, too. Immediately, my mind thought about what I'd done to the rubber. The thought made me throw the ass at him even harder. I wanted his nut to be hard and explosive.

"Damn, Keema!"

I reached back and grabbed a hold of him, forcing him to drill as far inside me as possible.

"Awww fuck!" Lucky shouted as he exploded like a volcanic eruption. His ass bust such a heavy nut, he instantly collapsed onto my back and held me tightly.

Turning to kiss him I smiled. "You okay? Should I call the paramedics?"

He let out an exhausted breath then laughed a little at my humor. "Damn, you got some good pussy," he said.

I chuckled. "I know. Trust me I know." *I guess it wasn't a good time to warn him that it was sometimes deadly, too.*

TWENTY FOUR

"What you got on?" he asked from the other end of the phone. His voice had become more and more sexier as the night went on.

"Just a t-shirt and panties," I said, lying in bed. The room was dark; perfect for masturbating if it came down to it.

"For real? What they look like?"

I snickered.

The sound of his voice had my pussy beginning to moisten.

"Who wit' you?" he questioned.

"I'm by myself."

"Whatever, I know you got a nigga over there bangin' that pussy out."

"Boy please, I don't just give my shit away like that."

"Well, make sure you keep it that way. I like the pussy tight."

"Why you all of a sudden so worried about how tight my shit is? You think you getting some?"

He just laughed.

"And while you talking about me having a nigga up in this pussy, what about you? You probably got a bitch over there? You probably got one lying right beside you as we speak."

"Nah, I don't fuck around too much since the shootin'.

Random bitches can't be trusted. I just need one woman. And that's you," Rick said like he meant it.

Those words made me turn over on my side and place a pillow between my thighs wishing it was him. Hearing that he wanted to make me his main girl turned me on.

"That's hard for me to believe," I replied. "I know those broads be at you. You paid and you fine."

"Yeah, but that doesn't mean I'm at them. Women out here are too damn scandalous nowadays. I can't trust 'em. Shit, these streets are stressful enough. I can't have some broad complicatin' shit even more. That's why I'm tryin' to fuck wit' you. You know what I been through."

"Yeah," I agreed. "You need a bottom bitch."

"Exactly."

I could picture myself waking up to him every morning. And even though he lived a modest life, nothing fancy, all that would change with me in the picture. *We would be spending all that cash*, I told myself. My mouth watered at the thought of waking him up every day with breakfast and head.

"I need one woman that's gonna hold me down," he continued, "make it all better for me."

I nodded in agreement.

We spoke for about twenty minutes more before finally hanging up. I hated having to let him go. I wanted to hear his voice all night if I could, but he had to hit the streets and check on his money. Rick grinded even harder than Dupree used to before he got killed.

As I laid in bed and stared up at the ceiling I couldn't help but think just how ironic and crazy life was. Who would've ever guessed that me and Rick would be talking about hooking up? The shit still didn't seem real to me. It was amazing what bad circumstances and a few weeks of phone sex could do.

Over the past two weeks the two of us had been talking a lot. When he first began to call me it was out of loneliness. He needed a shoulder to cry on, I guess. And he didn't trust anyone around him to be that shoulder. His defenses were up and he wasn't trying to let too many people get behind them.

After losing his family he was trying to pull closer to the surviving ones he still had, including me. Losing his brothers had made him see life a little differently. Rick felt as if he had to live it to the fullest now. He also wanted to make sure Dinero, Shane and Treasure stayed close. He wanted them to grow up together. That was important to him.

As the two of us spoke, he began to ask me if I'd met anyone new. Of course I didn't mention Lucky. With me and Rick forming a new bond and growing more intimate with each call, the last thing I wanted to do was fuck that up.

Rick had always been attractive to me. I'd always liked his swagger, but it never crossed my mind to get at him. Shit, honestly I didn't think he'd ever been interested in me or ever would be, especially after the last time we saw each other. So, it surprised me when he began to show interest during our nightly phone calls. I welcomed it and was definitely looking forward to seeing where it would lead and how far it could go. It wasn't clear to me if his newfound feelings for me were truly genuine or if they were merely a reaction to losing his family. Whatever they were, I wanted to explore and prayed he'd added me to his will.

Rick made it clear that although he was beginning to catch feelings for me, he felt bad for wanting his dead brother's woman. He said it made him feel like he was betraying Dupree. I assured him it wasn't like that. Dupree was never faithful to me. Besides, a person couldn't help who they caught feelings for. Shit happens. It was weird that it was us two though. I sure as hell would've never guessed it in a million years.

Obviously, I was looking at the big picture. It seemed selfish, but I had an agenda. With Dupree gone Rick was the sole beneficiary of his oldest brother's estate. He was now the owner of Frenchie's entire business empire. Fucking with him could have me set for life.

Lucky was getting paper. He was definitely doing his thing out here, but he was nowhere near Rick's level. Rick had money in corporate America and in the streets. Damn, I was anxious to find out just how much money he had in his bank account. I couldn't help wondering if it was in the millions. If so, how many.

I had also entertained the possibility of one day becoming his wife if things worked out. That meant if anything happened to him, those millions would become mine. Everything would revert to me. Shit, I could even speed up the process by just having him killed myself just like I'd done with Dupree. I could possibly use Rayquan for the job again.

Murdering him filled my thoughts just that quickly just as they had the past couple of nights. I imagined him dead on the ground, me crying over top of him, screaming for help. Then there were gunshots. The gunshots were always loud. The stench of blood was always fresh. But I would wake up and realize killing him was just too grimy. In all honesty I was trying to turn over a new leaf. Karma had kicked my ass enough. I realized the more bad I did the more my life got fucked up. I was sick of that. Right now things were becoming less complicated. And I wanted to keep it that way.

I even had a good thing going with Lucky. He was paying my bills and my rent just like he'd promised. It was obvious he was falling more and more in love with me every day. I had also talked him into hitting the pussy without a rubber.

Suddenly, the bedroom door burst open. Treasure bailed into my room dressed in a pair of her new tennis shoes, some white shorts and a cute graphic t-shirt with a metallic pink heart. Her braids however looked beyond tight from the way her skin was stretched near each temple.

"Damn, Treasure," I said with an aggravated tone. "What did I tell you about just coming in here without knocking?"

Rolling her eyes and ignoring my question, she said, "I thought you was supposed to be helping me bag up this weed."

"Girl, don't rush me."

She smacked her lips and gawked at me like *she* was the mother.

Over the past couple of weeks Treasure had definitely

changed. I didn't know if it was the loss of her brother and grand-mother or the move to a new city. Whatever it was, she seemed a little more hardened. The look in her eyes had even changed. She'd obviously always been smart for her age. But now she seemed to be much more mature.

I was still glad however that Treasure and Lucky seemed to get along really well. He seemed to treat her like a daughter; taking her places, buying her clothes, and keeping her stomach full. There used to be a time not so long ago that getting Treasure to comb her hair and wear an outfit that coordinated was impossible. She had no sense of style and didn't care. But now, Lucky had the little bitch looking and carrying herself like a young lady. She was actually getting some swagger about herself. She was becoming a mini me.

Just like he'd offered, Lucky had me bagging weed for him. It wasn't like the *New Jack City* scene I had originally imagined though. He would bring several pounds over to the house for me and Treasure to bag up. He also bought me a brand new chrome .45 for protection. I'd been taking Treasure up to some nearby railroad tracks to teach her how to shoot it. Even holding it with both hands couldn't stop her little narrow ass from stumbling backwards when she would blast shots off. But its power didn't scare or intimidate her in any way. She loved it. She was also making a little money. Lucky paid her fifty dollars a day to bag weed on top of all the clothes and sneakers he spoiled her with. I liked that. My little lady was finally getting a chance to learn the value of hustle.

"How many have you bagged up?" I asked Treasure, noticing her constant uncomfortable stare.

"You supposed to be helping me," she said, ignoring my question.

"How much shit have you bagged up, damn it?" I asked much more loudly than before.

She let out a loud sigh, placed her hands on her hips, and shifted her body weight to one leg. "About eighty bags," she replied. "We supposed to have way more than that done by now.

If you were helping me, we would. You know Lucky gonna be coming by first thing tomorrow morning to pick everything up."

I grabbed a blunt from the nightstand and lit it. As I placed it to my lips and let its smoke fill my lungs, I said, "Don't worry about that nigga. We good."

Lucky was pretty much wrapped around my finger these days. Just a whiff of this good pussy could practically make him stutter. But I had to admit he had me nearly gone as well. The dick was good. And the way he treated me was the best I'd ever experienced. He was different.

Treasure shook her head. "We got all that weed spread out on the living room table. And you laid up in here like some queen. Anybody could run up in here on us."

"Quit worrying, Treasure. Everybody around here knows Lucky. They ain't stupid enough to do no shit like that."

As I hit the blunt again, Treasure shook her head for the second time. "Whatever," she replied.

With Rick still fresh on my mind I asked her, "How would you feel if Rick, Shane, and Dinero came out here to visit?"

She stared at me.

"Why you looking at me like that?"

"You like Uncle Rick, don't you?"

She caught me off guard with that one. "What are you talking about?"

"I hear you guys on the phone all the time."

"That don't mean I like him."

She wasn't having it. Her facial expression told me she knew I was lying. The little bitch was so intuitive.

"Anyway, what about Lucky?" she wanted to know.

"What about him?"

"That wouldn't be right."

"How is having our family come out here to visit us not right?"

The little bitch got on my damn nerves being so smart.

"If he comes out here that's going to mess things up with

202

Lucky."

"No, its not."

"Yes it is. Besides, I like Lucky. He's nice. He spends time with me. He takes me places. And he buys me stuff. If Rick comes, everything's going to get messed up again."

She had a point, but that didn't make it any easier to hear. I got out of the bed and walked by her, toward the living room.

"Don't you like Lucky?" she asked following behind me.

"Yeah, I like him."

"Then why would you want to bring Uncle Rick out here to mess it up?"

"Look, Treasure, it's just some things you're too young to understand. I like Lucky a lot, but Rick has more to offer."

"Like what?"

"Just forget it," I told her as I sat at the table and started bagging up weed.

"But…"

"I said forget about it. I don't want to talk about it anymore!"

Treasure sat across the table from me visibly upset, but I could care less. She needed to understand that some conversations just weren't meant for her. Grabbing my new Ipad, I quickly hit the app for Pandora and went to the Chris Brown radio station. Lucky had bought the Ipad along with a dining room set, living room furniture, and bedroom sets for both my room and Treasure's.

As I smoked the blunt, bagged weed, and listened to music, my mind couldn't help but think about what my daughter had just told me. She was right. I'd thought about it all. But letting the chance to fuck with Rick get away wasn't an option. Niggas like him didn't come a dime a dozen. He was now super paid and interested in me. I would be a damn fool to pass that up.

However, I was falling for Lucky at the same time. That's why I'd entertained the thought of staying in Phoenix forever. But with Rick wanting me now, I guess my plans were gonna have to change. I wasn't going to jump ship yet though. I would see how the Rick situation worked out first. If it showed more than just promise, I would leave Lucky. If not, I would stay.

"Are you gonna apply for your benefits tomorrow at Social Services?" Treasure inquired. "You said you would do it yesterday."

Damn, she was on point. I had honestly forgotten about that. A knock came from the front door before I could answer her.

I glanced at the clock. It was a little after midnight. Who the hell would be knocking this late? I didn't associate with any one on this street, let alone this city. I was also sure it wasn't Lucky. He'd already told me about his run to Tempe tonight.

"Who is that?" Treasure asked, looking at both me and the door with a weird expression.

"I don't know."

Someone knocked again.

Turning the music down, I shouted towards the door, "Who is it?"

No one answered.

Pointing towards the bedroom was an instant signal for Treasure to go grab the .45 from the nightstand. While she was gone, the knocks continued; this time much harder than before.

"Who is it?" I shouted towards the door again.

Still no answer.

As soon as Treasure came back with the gun, I took it off the safety, cocked it back and walked to the front door. I then looked out of the peep hole, but still didn't see anyone. With the gun in my hand I opened the door slowly and peeked out. "Who the fuck is it?" I repeated. There was no one there.

"Who is it, mom?" Treasure asked from behind me.

Without answering her, I opened the door all the way and stepped outside. There was still no one in sight. As my eyes looked up and down the dark street, my heart rate began to increase. The shit definitely had me scared. Who was it? How did they disappear that quickly? Where did they go? I hadn't heard a car pull off. I began to wonder if Treasure might've been on point earlier when she mentioned us possibly getting robbed. The thought made me shut the door quickly and lock it.

"Mom, who was it?" Treasure asked again.

I didn't answer her. I developed a very weird feeling about that knock. The fact that the person disappeared so quickly bothered me. Who knocked on someone's door at twelve o'clock at night and just disappeared? I gripped the gun tightly as I stared at the door.

Something just wasn't right.

TWENTY FIVE

"Fuck y'all country muthufuckas!" I shouted.

It was a little after eleven in the morning as I walked out of the grocery store empty handed. As usual the Phoenix heat was stifling adding to the fucking attitude I already had. Being out in this shit for too long would make anyone pissed off.

"You don't ever have to worry about me shopping here again!" I roared then kicked a shopping cart that was right in the middle of my path.

I was pissed as I stormed across the parking lot to my rented Malibu. I'd done a bunch of shopping only to have to leave all my damn groceries at the counter. None of my EBT cards worked. After swiping the cards several times, not giving a fuck about holding up the long line behind me, the machine kept rejecting the cards, saying NOT ACCEPTED. I knew I had plenty of money on my cards. Convinced that something had to be wrong with the machine, I even made the manager come and check it, causing the little long head bitch behind the counter to catch an attitude. He assured me it worked. Nothing was wrong with the machine. "It's definitely the cards," he told me.

It annoyed me to have to look like a broke bitch in front of him and all those people in line. I rolled my eyes and walked out quickly without looking back.

"Damn cheap ass machine," I said, walking through the automatic doors and out into the parking lot. "Fuck!" I shouted after climbing into the car and slamming my fists against the steering wheel.

Wondering if maybe it was just the machines at the grocery store, I cranked the engine, drove across the street to the gas station, and tried the cards there. Still no luck. I even tried them at the next door beauty supply. They didn't work there either, causing the Chinese bitch behind the counter to look at me with a snobbish ass glare. Those damn Chinese muthafuckas got on my nerves thinking they ran shit. I was pissed off enough to slap the shit out of her slanted eye, short ass but just walked out of the store instead.

Sitting in the car seething, I wondered what was going on. Something was definitely wrong. How could all my muthafuckin' cards get rejected? That had never happened to me before.

"Damn," I whispered angrily.

I thought about the hair stylist Naomi, who I'd left the V.A. EBT card with. She was supposed to take a hundred and fifty off of that card for doing Treasure's hair then return it to me this week. But I had a feeling the card wouldn't work for her either. She was definitely going to be pissed at me. But that was the least of my problems. I needed my card to work, fast since I didn't have any cash. I'd run through the money Lucky paid me to bag up the weed this week, expecting the money from the EBT cards to be my safety net. This shit was totally unexpected. As all sorts of thoughts danced around in my head, I couldn't help but wonder if one of Tia's friends had found a way to get my shit cut off. Being that I'd left without paying them, it wasn't like my assumptions were way off base. At this point anything was possible.

Realizing the phone call I had to make, I dreaded it. Damn, I didn't want to have to call Ms. Vines back in Baltimore. But there was no other choice. She was the only one who could tell me what was wrong and fix the problem. I grabbed my cell from my purse and dialed her number.

"This is Ms. Vines," her voice sounded after three rings. "Hello?"

"Hi, Ms. Vines," I said perkily, sounding like everything was okay.

"Keema?" Ms. Vines asked like she couldn't believe I was calling.

"Yes."

"Keema, where are you?"

"Out of town visiting family."

"Really? Do you know the police are looking for you?"

"Really. For what?"

"You really need to get in contact with them. They've been calling me wanting to know if I've heard anything from you. As a matter of fact, they just called me again yesterday evening."

"I'm going to call them as soon as I get off the phone with you," I lied.

"Calling isn't acceptable, Keema. You should go to the police station. They really want to talk to you about what happened to your mother and son. And you should do it soon," she spoke. "And by the way, Keema, I'm sorry about their deaths. That was so terrible. I really do hope the authorities get whoever was responsible off the street."

I rolled my eyes. Obviously I wanted Paco's ass punished for what he did. But I'd be damned if I was going to walk up in a damn police station. There was no telling what the cops may already know. I wasn't taking that chance.

"Thank you," I said.

"Keema, I hate to ask you this. I know you're going through a lot right now, but I have no choice."

"Ask me what?"

"The system shows that you have recently started getting benefits in two other states. Why is that?"

"Huh?" I asked, unable to come up with a lie that quickly. Damn, I was busted.

"Do you realize that's fraud? It's a very serious offence."

"Someone must be using my name," I responded. "I heard there's a lot of that going on right now. These girls out here are thirsty. They'll do just about anything."

"I agree. But, Keema, you and I both know that's not the case in *your* situation."

"Shit," I whispered, taking the phone away from my mouth for a brief second. The bitch wasn't buying it.

"Keema, I had no choice but to notify the states the cards were issued in. The benefits in each of those states, including here in Maryland, have been cut off until further notice. You need to come into our investigative unit and talk to someone."

So, that's why my damn cards didn't work.

"I'm sorry. We can't allow the system to be taken advantage of like that. There's also a strong possibility that criminal charges may also be brought against you, Keema."

"Whatever," I said and poked the end button, terminating the conversation. My ears couldn't take any more.

That low down, player hating bitch. She'd never liked me. She couldn't wait to cut my benefits off. From the moment I first stepped into her office several years ago her fat ass had looked down on me like she was better than me.

I sat in the car angry and in silence for a moment. I had just applied for Arizona benefits before trying to go shopping. With the police looking for me back home, they'd possibly be able to track me down to Phoenix once my paperwork went into the Arizona welfare system. That kind of worried me.

Finally I started the car, turned on the air conditioning and pulled out of the lot. Damn, I shouldn't have let Treasure talk me into applying for assistance out here. I'd gotten greedy, and that could turn out to be my downfall. I should've just been satisfied with the money Lucky was paying me. It could've easily been stacked. After about six months I would've been good.

I wondered exactly what the Baltimore police knew. Obviously they wanted to question me about the murders. But I wondered if maybe someone had told them about Paco, or the bounty he had out for me. I also wondered if maybe my name had possibly come up in Imani's murder, too. If so, that would be too many coincidences. The last thing I needed was for them to

do some sort of bullshit investigation, getting all into my business and possibly revealing both Frenchie's and Dupree's deaths.
But I'm sure eventually the cops would figure it out. Sooner or
later they would put two and two together.

As I drove home, Lucky called and said he was on his
way to pick up the weed Treasure and I had bagged the night before. When I pulled into the driveway ten minutes later, Lucky's
truck was sitting out front, with its paint and rims shining hard
underneath the sun. Immediately, I remembered the strange
knock at the door. After we hugged I told him about it while we
walked up the stairs to the front door.

"You didn't see anybody?" Lucky questioned.

"Nope," I said, unlocking the front door and walking inside.

"No car or nothing?"

"Lucky, I didn't see anybody. That's why the shit was so
weird."

He shut the door.

"I was scared to death. I slept with the .45 in my hand all
night."

He finally shrugged it off. "It was probably nothing. It
might've been some bad ass kids running around knocking on
doors and running away like we used to do when we were kids.
Me and my niggas used to do it all the time."

I wasn't convinced. Stepping to him and placing my arms
around his waist, I looked into his eyes as he did the same.

"Baby, stay with us tonight."

"Keema, I'm telling you it was nothing."

"Maybe, but I'd still feel safer with you here."

"Alright, I got you."

"And bring your gun."

He laughed. "Damn, that shit really got you shook, huh?"

"I just don't want to take any chances."

He kissed me.

"Don't worry about it. These niggas around here know
me. That won't be necessary. But if it'll ease your mind, I'll

211

come after I wrap everything up. It'll be about midnight."

I smiled. "Thank you."

We headed up the steps to the bedroom to grab the weed that I'd stashed in the closet. As soon as I reached the top step I called out Treasure's name. "Treasure!" She was too damn quiet. "Treasure!" I shouted again.

"I'm trying to sleep!" she finally yelled from her room.

"Kids," I said to Lucky, then shook my head. "You sure your ass don't have any enemies that I should know about," I said as we entered the room. I couldn't stop thinking about that knock on the door.

Lucky closed the door behind us, placed his arms around me tightly, and began to kiss me around my neck. "Nah, Keema, and if I did, I'd never put you and Treasure in harm's way like that."

"I know. But something about it just doesn't seem right. I don't know what it is. Something about it just seems shady."

He squeezed me tightly. "Don't worry about it. Everything's good. I'll be here tonight."

I turned in his arms to face him and kissed his lips. What I'd gone through at the grocery store ran through my mind. I didn't want to tell him about the cards, but I did want to see if I could maybe get a raise for bagging up the weed and a little more.

"Baby," I said innocently.

"What's up?"

"I need a better job in your operation."

"What do you mean?"

"I mean how long do you expect me to be a bagger? I don't want to do that shit for the rest of my life. I appreciate you looking out. I really do. But I got plans. I want to open up a spa where I can do nails in the front and operate the spa in the back; maybe even sell heavy weed out the back."

He stared in my eyes intently.

"Baby, I'm an ambitious bitch. I want a lot out of life. But to get it I need to stack some real money."

"I feel you," Lucky responded. "We'll talk about it. That spa idea might be something I might want to invest in anyway."

We began to kiss again. A moment later he began to push me backwards towards the bed. I could feel his hardening dick against my thigh. My hand reached down, squeezed it, and un-zipped his jeans. I wanted it badly. But first I wanted to suck it. I guess Lucky knew those were my plans because he placed his hands on my shoulders and started to push me down to the floor. My mouth was watering for it. However, before I could even open my mouth, suddenly the door burst open, startling both of us.

"Mommy," Treasure said.

"Damn it, Treasure!" I straightened up quickly. "Didn't I tell your ass to knock before you come in here?"

Lucky hadn't turned around. He was fiddling with that long dick of his, trying to get it back into his pants without get-ting it caught in his zipper or Treasure seeing it. I stepped in front of him to block her view.

"Telephone," Treasure said with my cell phone to her ear.

"What you doing answering my damn phone?"

Ignoring my question she silently mouthed, "It's Rick."

Turning my head to make sure Lucky hadn't seen her, I looked back at her.

Treasure covered the phone and said, "It's the people at the summer camp. You promised me I could go if they had room for me. Mommy, you promised."

Damn, that little bitch was getting slick. I had no idea what had gotten into her, but she was learning how to lie just as good as me, if not better.

"Baby," I told Lucky, kissing him on the cheek. "I'm sorry. I gotta take this."

"Don't worry about it," he said, finally getting that big ass monster in its cage and heading to the closet to get the weed.

I walked out into the hallway with Treasure and closed the door.

"Why didn't you tell him I was busy?" I whispered to her

angrily when we were out of ear shot while quickly looking back to make sure Lucky wasn't coming out of the room.

Still holding the phone so the speaker was covered, she whispered, "Because Rick said that him, Shane, and Dinero need a ride."

"What you mean need a ride?"

"They need you to come pick them up. They're at the airport. He said they're coming to stay with us."

My eyes grew as wide as golf balls. How the hell was I going to explain Lucky to Rick, and Rick to Lucky?

How the fuck did I keep getting myself into this shit?

TWENTY SIX

I still didn't have the slightest idea of how I'd let him talk me into doing it. Before him, I hadn't let any nigga, including Dupree do it to me. Many had asked. Many had tried to sneak it in during our sessions. But despite their trying, I never once let it happen. Shit, before Rick I'd never even wanted to do it. I'd always thought it would hurt. I turned out to be wrong though.

Rick had me face down in the bed. My face was buried deeply in my pillow as he slowly and rhythmically shoved himself balls deep into my ass hole. The shit was sending convulsive shivers throughout my entire body. Surprisingly, it felt good.

"Damn, Rick," I moaned. "Work that shit, baby."

My words were more like pleading and begging. My ass wanted and needed the punishment.

"You like that?" Rick asked as he stroked deeply inside me over and over again, spreading my hole wider than I'd ever imagined it could be stretched.

"Hell yeah, don't stop. Please don't stop."

Rick did as I told him, stroking my ass artistically.

Up until this week Lucky, hands down, had been the best sex I'd ever had. His dick had been the biggest. However, since Rick had arrived in Phoenix all that had changed. Rick had taken the title...easily.

Since he'd gotten here we fucked almost three times a day

for the past few days. The nigga had the stamina of a beast. He could go for at least two hours with no problem. It was as if driving a woman to numerous orgasms was what he'd been placed on the earth to do. He made me squirt so many times during our sessions I'd be instantly worn out and ready to go to sleep. But instead of letting me off that easily, he would keep on beating the pussy up like a prize fighter, forcing me to prepare for another orgasm.

Rick was also pure fucking *fire* in the oral sex department. I mean the nigga's head game was mind blowing. He ate my pussy like Bill Cosby on one of those old chocolate pudding commercials. I'd lost count of how many times he'd made me cum in his mouth. Plus, his tongue was so long I could feel that muthafucka in my ovaries.

Today wasn't any different. He was putting it down as usual, making my ass his own as I squirmed and grinded back onto his dick. The bed springs were screaming for mercy as he repeatedly buried himself deep into my ass.

"Spread them cheeks for me," he ordered.

"Shiiiiit," I groaned into the pillow, feeling him all the way in my back.

The nigga had an amazing rhythm going. It felt like he was doing the Stanky Leg in my ass. It couldn't be described.

"Fuck it, baby. Fuck it."

He laid his body down onto me while still working his hips. "Is this ass mine?" he whispered into my ear.

"Yes," I moaned.

"Is this pussy mine?"

"Hell yeah."

Rick kissed me on the cheek, lifted his body, and grabbed a hand full of my hair; jerking me upwards and onto all fours. He then began to ram my ass nice and hard, causing our thighs to slap together.

"Shit!" I shouted.

"Take that dick!"

"I'm takin' it, baby. I'm takin' it!"

He pounded me for several minutes ultimately causing me to climax out my ass and onto his pipe. The shit felt incredible. I mean super *incredible*.

Seeing the sight of that white cream all over his pole made Rick fuck me like a damn pile driver. His dick rammed into me with no mercy. Finally he couldn't take any more. He exploded inside my ass with a nut that made his face look as if he was having a seizure. The nut was so heavy he instantly collapsed onto my back and laid there holding me in his arms with his dick still stuffed inside of me.

"Damn, girl," he whispered out of breath. "Shit."

I was out of breath, too.

We both laid still.

His thick arms felt good around my body. I felt safe inside them. But oddly they reminded me of how I felt each time I laid in Lucky's arms. Yeah, a bitch had developed a conscience.

Rick had been in town four days now, causing me to be extremely slick about the way I was doing things. I felt really bad about lying to Lucky, having told him that I had to rush out of town due to Raven's sudden illness. Of course he believed me. Lucky didn't deserve to be lied to though. From the very first moment he'd met us, Lucky had looked out for both me and Treasure. He'd been nothing but nice to us. Shit, the nigga had even gone as far as to put us in a house. I didn't know many dudes who would've done that. He'd definitely caused me to have feelings for him.

As I laid in Rick's arms, my feelings for him couldn't be ignored either. Not only did he fuck me the way I needed to be fucked, but I loved being around him. Everything about him turned me on; his voice, his smile, his smell, his walk, his touch. The nigga was like a natural aphrodisiac. I couldn't get enough of him.

Also, Rick had a toughness about him while Lucky was more laid back and calm. Both turned me on. But that thuggishness that oozed from Rick's pores drove me absolute crazy. Another thing going in Rick's favor was how he was talking. Last

217

night over dinner at Fleming's Steakhouse, he told me that he was *really* ready to settle down. He also said that he'd never known a woman to make him feel the way that I did. The nigga was talking like he was ready to wife me up.

Little did he know, anything short of wifey wouldn't be enough. The title of girlfriend definitely wouldn't be enough. I would either be wifey to him or nothing at all. As long as that happened, Lucky would be tossed.

Besides, I really wasn't feeling Phoenix the way I had hoped. Not only was it too damn hot, but the people seemed a little too uppity, and it just wasn't the type of atmosphere I could get comfortable with. I missed the speed of B-More. Although going back there was out of the question, I would consider maybe moving to New York or Philly.

Rick and I finally got up out of the bed, got cleaned up, dressed and went out into the living room. After sitting on the couch, Rick placed his arms around my waist and dropped his chin on my shoulder as we watched the children playing a game on the Nintendo Wii. They were shooting some zombie looking monsters in a haunted house.

It was great seeing Shane, Dinero, and Treasure back together again. The sight had made me realize how much I'd missed the days when it was an everyday thing. Shane was even much more talkative these days. He was playing the game with Dinero, while smiling and laughing. Before he'd moved in with Rick I'd never seen him that happy or playful. He was totally different from the Shane I was used to.

"You gonna lose, Shane!" Dinero said. "Ain't he, Treasure?"

Treasure didn't answer. She was sitting on the couch with her damn face twisted up about something as usual. I wasn't sure what had crawled up her ass this time, and didn't care. She'd been acting stuck up ever since our family arrived a few days ago.

"No, you gonna lose," Shane said. "Ain't he Treasure?"

Treasure rolled her eyes, got up and headed to the kitchen.

Today was Treasure's eleventh birthday. Rick had bought her a huge cake, plenty of gifts, and had even given her two hundred dollars. But that little spoiled bitch still didn't seem grateful. She even had the nerve to ask him if that was it?

Treasure spent the whole day with her damn ass up on her shoulders. She hadn't smiled, laughed or barely said more than a few sentences.

"What's up with her?" Rick questioned. "She been actin' funny since we got here."

"I don't know, but she'll get over it."

I suspected she was most likely still pissed off about me complicating things with Lucky. She liked him a lot. I couldn't blame her for that though. He was a nice guy, but Rick was still the better candidate. Although Treasure didn't like it, she would just have to get used to it.

"I got skills," Shane said to the TV.

I had to chuckle at that one. What the hell did he know about skills? He was just learning to join the real world. Now all of a sudden, he was talking like he had been one of us all along.

"Uh-uh, no you don't," Dinero replied.

Both of their eyes were locked on the screen.

"Yes, I do. Don't I, Uncle Rick?"

Rick chuckled himself. "Yeah, you got skills, Shane."

"I told you," Shane told Dinero. "Uncle Rick said I got skills."

After several minutes Shane finally beat Dinero and asked Rick to play with them. Rick grabbed a controller and joined in.

"You wanna get some of this?" he asked me.

"Nah, I'm good," I told him.

"Scared I'm gon' tap that ass, huh," Rick teased.

"Yeah, you scared he gon' tap that ass," Shane repeated.

I laughed.

"Boy, watch your mouth," Rick warned.

"Ewwww, Shane said a bad word," Dinero chimed in.

I couldn't help laughing. It felt so good to be a family again. It was also obvious that Rick felt good about the time spent, too. He'd been stressing over the past four days that he wanted the kids to be near each other and that he wanted to be near them. He also cried a few times whenever he thought of his brothers. I consoled him of course. "There's nothing in the world like family," he kept saying.

As I watched the game my cell rang. Rushing over to the kitchen counter I picked it up. "Hello."

"Girl, you're not gonna believe this!" Raven shouted into the phone.

"What? What is it?" I asked, watching Treasure roll her eyes, then made her way up the stairs to her room.

"That damn Peppi…"

Her words had me frozen.

"My dude, Jarrod saw him at the field yesterday. That nigga back in B-more. He was dropping his son off at a mini league football practice."

"Are you serious?"

"As a muthafucking heart attack."

"Payback is a bitch," I said, walking out of earshot from Rick. "Get the exact location of that football field," I whispered. "I'ma work some shit out where I get him and his son blasted. I'll call you tonight."

I hung up with my devious mind working overtime. Revenge filled my insides. Somehow I had to convince Rick that Peppi was the trigger man in Dupree's death and his shooting. Just as quickly as my mind twirled my cell rang again. This time Lucky's name and number appeared on the screen. Immediately sending it to voicemail, I stuffed the phone into the kitchen drawer. I felt bad. But for now, I had to do what I had to do.

When the game was finally over, Rick walked back over to me. He looked me in the eyes and gave me a kiss. His lips tasted so good. When our lips parted, he said, "I know this is supposed to be Treasure's day. But I got something for you, too."

I looked at him with complete surprise. "What is it?"

"I really want us to be a family, Keema," he said. "But I need to know you want the same."

"Of course I do."

Wondering what was going on, I watched as Rick reached into his pocket, pulled out a tiny velvet box, and dropped to one knee. My heart damn near stopped beating. My eyes widened. My mouth went absolutely silent.

Looking up at me he opened the box and smiled. "Keema, will you marry me?"

"Oh, God," I whispered, placing my hands over my mouth.

The moment didn't seem real. It couldn't be happening. I mean, of course this was what I wanted and was hoping for, but damn. It caught me by total surprise. The ring was big…real big. Placed in a platinum setting, the cushion cut diamond had to be at least four carats.

"Well?" he asked.

"Yes!" I yelled. "Yes, baby, I will!"

Rick stood up, placed the ring on my finger, took me into his arms and kissed me.

Shane and Dinero said, "Ughhhhh, they kissing."

My lips had never felt a kiss so precious, so sweet. When we finally came up for air, he just held me tightly in his arms. As my chin rested on his shoulder, I saw Treasure standing at the bottom of the steps. The look on her face was one I'd never seen from her before. It was a mixture of anger, spite, disapproval, and so much more. It was something evil. She looked like a real bitch. But instead of entertaining another one of her attitudes, I just closed my eyes and got lost in the moment and my new husband's arms. Finally, my dreams had come true. Finally, the world was going to be mine.

From the darkness behind my eyelids, I saw what my life would be. I saw the cars, the big house in the suburbs, the jewelry, the shopping sprees, the expensive clothes and so much more. Since Baltimore was off limits for me, there would be a new city in our future. It would all be mine.

There would be no more hustling. There would be no more welfare grinding. No more running from the police. There would be no more tricking with niggas for money or selling weed. My dream of having one spa would be replaced with the reality of having *dozens* of spas.

I would be the queen of Rick's empire. The devious side of me also realized I could even become the king of the empire. I could run it all if anything ever happened to him. Everything would fall into my hands. I felt guilty for thinking like that right now, but I couldn't help it. Being greedy was a part of me. The thought of a bullet flying through his head and scattering his brains everywhere even crossed my mind. Quickly, I disregarded it.

Suddenly, a knock came at the door breaking me out of the moment and dragging me out of my thoughts. The knock came again, this time louder. My eyes opened to see Treasure still standing near the steps. But now, instead of the indescribable spite filled stare she had a moment ago, it was replaced with a smirk; as if she knew something I didn't know. Her arms were folded across her chest.

The knock turned to a pounding.

"Who is that?" Rick questioned.

Giving Treasure one last glare, I turned to the door. Immediately Lucky had crossed my mind. Who else would be knocking? No one else knew us here in Phoenix.

It *had* to be Lucky. I had been parking my rental in the garage just in case he rode by, but I guess he'd seen it. Shit, how did I think I would ever be able to get away with this without him knowing?

The pounding at the door came again.

"You want me to answer it, Mommy?" Treasure asked.

Glancing back at her, I saw that the look on her face had gone from a smirk to a full blown smile.

TWENTY SEVEN

The little skinny bitch had set me up. Treasure was so pissed off and hate-filled about me getting with Rick she'd obviously called Lucky and told him that Rick was here. I would've never guessed she would do some foul shit like that. I also would've never guessed she even had it in her. But then again, I'd already realized that Treasure had changed since we got to Phoenix, so it shouldn't have been a surprise. She'd become a girl far different from the Treasure she'd been back in Baltimore. She was now standing somewhere behind me smiling, too immature and naive to understand just how detrimental the situation could turn out.

The moment had me tense. I had no idea how to react, what to say, what to do. My heart beat began to race. Dreaded anticipation of what was most likely coming soon had me scared to death.

"Are you gonna open the door, Keema?" Rick questioned.

I desperately wanted to say no, then go run and hide. How in the hell was I gonna get out of this shit?

"Keema, go open the fuckin' door!" Rick spoke with authority.

I knew I couldn't just stand there. I also knew that the person on the other end wasn't going away as the pounding continued. Walking over to the door, I held my head down trying to come up with the best excuse I could think of. But for some reason, my mind went blank.

Unlocking the door at a slow pace, I took a deep breath before turning the knob. As soon as I saw Lucky's face, I lowered my head once again. I couldn't even bear to give him eye contact.

Lucky and Rick immediately eyed each other up and down. Although they weren't saying anything it was obvious that all hell was about to break loose at any moment. I didn't know what to think. Obviously it was Rick that I wanted to be with. It was him who I wanted to spend the rest of my life with. He had the most to offer. But right now, I could lose him. My greed had once again come back to bite me in the ass.

"You need to start doing some talking, Keema," Lucky said. "Who the fuck is this nigga? I thought you went out of town to visit your cousin, Raven."

"Nah, nigga," Rick shot back. "Who the fuck are you?"

I turned around and grabbed Rick by the arm, trying to pull him back. "Baby, it ain't worth it. It's nothing."

"It's nothing," Lucky repeated in disbelief. "It ain't worth it? What the fuck do you mean by that shit?"

"It means she not feelin' your lame ass," Rick replied.

"Bitch, I put you in a house. I put money in your pocket," Lucky added.

Rick looked at me. "What the fuck is he talkin' about, Keema?"

"It's nothing," I tried to explain.

Rick snatched his arm away from me. "What does he mean he put you in a house and put money in your pocket? Is this his spot?"

Lucky quickly spoke up. "This is my family's spot, so yeah you could say it's mine."

"Rick baby, he just looked out. But that was all it was," I responded.

"What the fuck do you mean that's all it was?" Lucky looked at me in complete disbelief. "So, all that shit about us being in a relationship was all a lie?"

Rick looked at me even crazier. "A relationship? Bitch,

224

you told me you wasn't wit' nobody down here. You told me you were too depressed from Dupree's death to fuck wit' anybody."

"I...I...I...I," was all that could fall from my mouth.

"Get that shit out," Rick demanded. "That's what you said, right?" Anger was all over his face. His brows were frowned, and veins were popping out of his neck. Even his nostrils were flared. He scared the shit out of me.

"Did you fuck 'em?" I sensed in Rick's tone that he demanded an answer.

"Yes," I admitted. "But it didn't mean anything. Baby, I was just playing him."

Lucky's face twisted in disbelief at what I'd just said. He stepped further inside. "What?" he yelled. "You're a lying bitch. Everything that came out your mouth was a lie. You even told me that Treasure was your only child."

"What?" Rick asked. "You didn't tell 'em about Dinero and Cash?"

I didn't know what to say. I could feel everyone's eyes on me. I knew Shane, Dinero, and Treasure were staring at my back, wondering how I had allowed something like this to happen and why I had denied them. I felt horrible inside. Everyone was looking at me like the liar I was.

It was time for me to throw on the innocent damsel in distress act. It was the only thing that could possibly get me out of this. I manufactured some tears immediately and put a heavily pitiful look on my face. I was super desperate at this point, reaching for any lifeline in sight.

"Rick, baby, I...I...I only lied because me and Treasure didn't have anywhere else to go. I swear, baby, we didn't have any money or anything. All we had was the clothes on our backs. I had to do what I had to do."

The tears were falling from my eyes repeatedly. The more the fucking better. I had to look and be as convincing as possible.

"Besides, Rick, you were the one who told me to get out of Baltimore."

"Baltimore?" Lucky butted in. "You told me you were

from somewhere called Oxon Hill."

I completely ignored him. "Rick, I was just doing what you told me to do."

Suddenly, Treasure stepped in between Rick and Lucky.

"Move, Treasure," Rick demanded.

"No," she said defiantly.

"Get out the way, baby girl," Lucky told her.

"No, this is all *her* fault," she said, speaking of me. "She's lying."

"Treasure, stay your ass out of grown folks' business," I ordered. She'd already pissed me off so bad I couldn't wait to warm her ass up like a bowl of hot grits as soon as this shit was over.

"No!" she yelled. "You left Baltimore because of that Peppi guy."

"Damn it, Treasure!" I belted.

"Who is Peppi?" Rick questioned.

"The muthafucka who played her out on that spa deal," Lucky answered.

"Huh?" Rick was obviously confused.

"She gave him a whole lot of money and he took off with it," Treasure said spitefully.

"Shut the fuck up, Treasure!" I screamed at her.

"What is she talkin' about, Keema?" Rick asked.

"She gave Peppi money for a spa. They were supposed to be partners," Lucky added. "But Peppi turned out to be a crook. The shit was a scam. She got played out of her money. That's how I met her."

"Where the fuck did you get money for a spa?" Rick asked me. His eyes were full of suspicion. "And how long had you been investin' in it?"

I couldn't answer. If I did, he'd know that I had really been planning the Phoenix trip way before he told me to get out of town. He'd know that I'd left before he told me to leave.

"Well?" Rick repeated.

I could only stare. My mind was blank. I had no idea what

to tell him. The lies just wouldn't come. Shit, I had told so many already I was entangled in them.

"Answer the damn question, Keema!"

My body tensed even more than before. I thought for sure he was going to slap me to the floor.

"She's trying to think up a lie," Treasure said.

I looked at Treasure sadly. Tears were falling like a river. I felt so betrayed. "Treasure, why are you doing this to me?"

"You know why," she spewed with hatred. "Because all you ever do is lie. All you ever do is hurt people."

My eyes could only stare at her. It was like our roles had been reversed. It was like she was now the mother and I was now the child.

"You're always messing things up. It's because of you that Grandma and Cash are dead. You're the reason Aunt Imani is dead. That Paco guy wanted you, not them. You were the one who was supposed to be dead, not them." Treasure just wouldn't stop. "Uncle Rick, she was the one who told the police that Shane had the drugs when they kicked our door in. She was the one who had him locked up."

My heart was broken in millions of pieces. My own baby was sailing my ass up the river without a paddle. My own daughter was talking to me like she despised the ground I walked on.

"I wish you would've just left us with CPS," she continued. "At least then me and my brothers would've still been together."

Rick shook his head as he looked at me. His fists were balled at his sides. "You treacherous bitch," he finally spoke. "You low down, treacherous ass bitch."

I didn't know what to say.

The entire room went silent.

Everyone looked at me.

My head dropped.

The moment seemed like forever.

"We gon' smoke that bitch just like she did Frenchie," Shane said from the couch.

At first I thought my ears were playing tricks on me. I thought they were hearing things that weren't there.

"We gon' smoke that bitch just like she did Frenchie and Dupree," Shane carried on.

My eyes rose from the floor. I really had heard him correctly. I turned to see Shane sitting on the couch rocking back and fourth while staring off into the distance.

"She's not going to get away with that shit," he said.

The words were his but *not* his, I realized. They were coming from his mouth, but they belonged to someone else. He was merely repeating what he'd heard from somewhere just like he'd repeated my words that day back at the apartment in front of Rick.

The room began to spin. It hit me like a ton of bricks. I knew without a doubt who the words belonged to. I knew whose words Shane was repeating. I slowly looked from Shane back to Rick.

Rick stood silent. His face was stone. The ends of his lips were raised in a slight sneer. His eyes were staring deeply into my own and refusing to blink or look away.

"Oh, God," I whispered, realizing Rick knew that I'd murdered his brothers.

Petrified wasn't the word for how scared I was. My body began to shake and shiver like it was lying in a bathtub of ice cold water. I couldn't stop it if I wanted to. At that moment, Lucky made his way back toward the door.

"Lucky don't leave!" Treasure cried out. "Please."

He turned around to face her, then smiled. "I don't think there's anything else for me and your mother to talk about, baby girl." Lucky looked at me. "I do need you and your boyfriend to get the fuck out my sister's house though. Immediately."

All of a sudden, footsteps came from behind Lucky. Hearing them, my eyes made their way towards the door. They slowly widened as they caught sight of the one man I feared, even more than Satan himself.

Treasure's eyes widened, too. She'd never met the man

228

walking up behind Lucky. But from seeing the gun in his hand, she quickly realized who he was. It was Paco. And he wasn't empty handed. You couldn't help but see the gun he had at his side. Rick looked at him, wondering who he was.

Quickly jumping into survivor mode, Treasure dashed to her brothers and took them into the kitchen. I also wanted to run, but my feet seemed nailed to the floor. I couldn't move. And couldn't understand why. It was as if fear had me completely frozen.

Lucky turned just as Paco stepped inside.

"Who the fuck is…?" he asked.

Paco raised the gun and aimed.

The gunshot instantly ripped through the right side of Lucky's stomach. It hit him with such force that it violently tossed him back against the door like a rag doll. He had a wide eyed look of surprise on his face as his body slowly slid down the door to the floor, leaving a wide downward smear of blood to mark his trail. As soon as he sat onto the floor, he gripped his stomach and moaned like a wounded animal.

I wanted to scream but couldn't. All I could do was stare at Lucky. The shit had happened so quick it seemed unreal. The roar of the gun had left my ears ringing. Paco walked into the doorway and looked directly at me with a smile on his face. It was obvious he'd been anticipating this moment since the night in the motel room. Quickly, I turned to Rick. He was the only person who could save me right now.

Rick stared at Lucky's wounded body in disbelief. He appeared to be just as frozen as I'd been. He finally looked up and stared at Paco in shock.

Both men watched each other.

There was nothing but silence.

Finally Rick's lips slowly transformed into a smile.

What the fuck? I thought to myself.

Rick began to laugh.

Has this nigga lost his mind, I wondered. What the fuck was so damn funny?

Then Rick looked at me. "Now that's what I like. A nigga who's all about business. A nigga who don't freeze up when it's time to shoot a muthafucka."

Paco shoved Lucky out of the way, shut the door, and locked it. He then turned to me.

Taking a step back my blood ran cold as both men's eyes locked on me, both sets filled with blood thirsty vengeance.

TWENTY EIGHT

My heart raced like a thoroughbred. Something much more extreme and gripping than fear had a hold of me. I knew I was looking at the last moments of my life. I guess there's no fear on Earth like the fear of knowing you're about to die and there's absolutely nothing you can do about it. The dreaded anticipation made it even more unbearable. Suddenly, I remembered Imani talking about Heaven and hell. I knew which one I was headed for. Damn, I didn't want to go there. I could feel the flames.

Lucky was still sitting on the floor with his back against the wall. As he clutched his stomach and grunted in pain, blood gushed from underneath his hand like a water fountain. The bottom half of his shirt was soaked, turning it to the color of crimson.

Paco stood in the center of the living room with his eyes directly on me and my every movement. His gun was pointed at me, with his finger wrapped snugly around the hair trigger. He seemed anxious to pull it. The stare his eyes had on me was of a spite I never knew existed. I saw an undeniable evil and hatred behind them. Obviously killing me was going to be something he would savor.

Rick paced the living room floor with a mixture of happiness and anger on his face. I couldn't tell which one was more dominant as he rubbed his hands together like he was getting prepared to dig into a thick succulent T-bone steak.

"You a foul bitch," he finally said.

"Baby," I told him with a sad and pitiful look on my face. "Why are you doing this?"

My mouth had gotten me out of many traffic jams. I had to at least allow it to make an attempt at getting out of this one. My life depended on it.

"Baby, I'm sorry for lying about Lucky. I swear I am. But, sweetheart…"

Before my sentence could be completed, Rick sent a backhand towards my face that came so quick I didn't even see it coming. The sound of its contact with my jaw echoed throughout the entire house. The impact knocked me to the floor and made my eyes see stars, lights, and bright colors. The shit damn near knocked me senseless.

"Fuck Lucky! That nigga will be dead in a few more minutes!" Rick shouted as he stood over me. "This ain't got shit to do wit' that nigga! Do you think I honestly care about who your nasty ass fucks?"

My eyes were filled with tears as I stared up at him through a cloud of dizziness. Not only was my ear ringing, but the entire right side of my face felt like it was being eaten by hundreds of hungry fire ants.

"Did your triflin' ass really think I would marry a sneaky bitch like you?"

All I could do was cry.

Paco smirked. He was obviously enjoying every moment.

"Bitch, you know what the fuck this is all about!" Rick added.

Of course I knew. But I couldn't admit it to him. There had to be a way out of this. There just had to be.

"Rick, baby," I pleaded through my tears. "I'm sorry for the lies. I'm so sorry."

He knelt down in front of me and, grabbed a handful of my shirt and snatched me towards him. We were face to face.

"Fuck your damn lies!" he yelled, as specks of salvia sprayed my face. "You know what this is about! Go ahead and admit to it!"

"Rick, I swear I don't…"

Before I could get the entire lie out he punched me directly in the mouth. Blood started to spill from the blow immediately. I felt my teeth loosen.

"Stop lyin' to me, bitch!" Rick screamed as he yanked me towards him again so hard my brain felt like it had rattled against the inside of my skull. "I know about Frenchie and Dupree!"

The tears came flooding even heavier than before. I could only drop my head.

"I've known about it for a while! You think I'm stupid?"

"I didn't…"

"You callin' my damn nephew a liar, huh? You sayin' Shane is a liar?" Rick roared.

"You can't believe him, Rick. You know he's mental."

"Bitch, watch your fuckin' mouth when you talk about my nephew!"

"I'm just saying…"

"Fuck what you sayin'. You know he likes to repeat things he hears. He doesn't just pull shit out of thin air. He repeated your conversation wit' Imani. That's how I first found out."

"You and your boneheaded girlfriend also mentioned Frenchie's murder in front of me when y'all robbed me that night," Paco chimed in.

Damn, he was right. We did mention it.

FUCK!!!

"Not only that," Rick continued. "But your punk ass boy Rayquan also gave you up."

Hearing that, I could only gaze into his eyes through my countless tears in silence.

At that moment, Rick let go of me, reached into his pocket, and pulled out his Blackberry. He pressed a button and showed me the screen.

My blood ran cold.

The screen was a photo of Rayquan. He was dead and covered in blood. He stared lifelessly at the camera, his eyes dark but filled with horror. His dick had been cut off at the testicles and crammed into his mouth.

I wanted to throw up everything in my stomach.

"Yeah," Rick said. "He look familiar to you?"

I couldn't answer. I was too petrified to speak.

"Right after Dupree's murder I put a hundred stacks in the street. You know the streets don't keep secrets when money's involved. They gave Rayquan up. The nigga had been braggin' about what he'd done to my fuckin' brother. He was runnin' his mouth to his homeboys. When I caught up wit' him, just before I murked his ass, he told me you paid him to kill Dupree."

I was caught. Rick knew everything.

"Rick, please," I begged, snatching a hold of him. "I…"

"Bitch, get your muthafuckin' hands off me!" Rick demanded as he pulled away from me and stood up.

"But, Rick," I continued, crawling on my hands and knees to him and grabbing his leg. "I swear to God, I'm so sorry."

I was more than desperate.

Paco laughed. "That's exactly how your girl Imani sounded just before I sliced her ass a million times."

Those words made me drop my head.

"She cried and begged for her life, too. The bitch even offered to suck my dick for me if I would let her ass live. Didn't work though. It just made me shove the knife up in her ass even harder and deeper. You should've seen how much I had her squealing like a pig," Paco informed.

The pronunciation of each word and sentence seemed to give him a sick satisfaction. It was as if he was savoring the gruesome memory of what he'd done to my best friend.

"Yeah," he continued. "That bitch screamed good and loud for me. She begged me to stop all the way till the end."

My ears could hear Imani's screams. I could feel her fear. I could imagine the pain of a knife ripping through my flesh. Oh God, I didn't want to die that way.

"Please don't do this to me!" I begged Rick while tugging at his pants. "I'll do anything. I swear I will."

He slapped me so hard my teeth rattled.

"Bitch, you took my fuckin' family away from me!" he screamed. "You took my muthafuckin' brothers!"

I whimpered and cried uncontrollably from the floor.

"There's no way you can walk away from that! And there's only one way you can pay for it!"

I knew what that one way was.

"Rick, if you let me go, I promise you'll never see me again. I swear you won't. Please let me live."

The words were falling from my mouth at a rapid fire rate. I hoped at least one of them would be the one that would tempt him to take mercy on me.

"I'll do anything you want. Rick, I'll do anything you tell me."

Shit, I was so scared I would've sucked both Rick and Paco off like Vanessa Del Rio if I thought it would get me out of this. I would've given them the greatest blowjobs ever invented.

"Please!" I screamed.

Suddenly, Shane walked out of the kitchen with tears in his eyes. He was looking straight at me. It broke my heart to see him that way. I didn't want to die. But I definitely didn't want to die in front of him and my children.

"Go back in the kitchen!" Rick ordered him.

"Keema," Shane said.

"Baby, go back in the kitchen," I replied.

Treasure appeared beside him.

Oh God, please don't let this happen, I begged inside my head. I'd never really thought of my children before myself. I had always been too selfish. This time they were all I could think about. I didn't want them to see this. I prayed Dinero wouldn't walk out, too.

"Y'all get back in the kitchen now!" Rick demanded.

"Keema!" Shane shouted.

"Treasure, take him back in the kitchen now!" Rick yelled.

Treasure could only stand there silently. The look on her

face was of total shock. She'd wanted me to face punishment for playing Rick against Lucky. But she didn't want *this*. She didn't want to see me die. I could see it in her eyes.

"I said go back in the kitchen, damn it!" Rick belted.

All of a sudden Shane charged across the room and rushed Paco so hard he stumbled backwards and slammed against the wall. The entire room shook from the impact.

"Shane, what the fuck are you doin'?" Rick yelled.

Ignoring his uncle, Shane quickly grabbed Paco's wrist to keep the gun from being aimed at me.

At that point, Rick charged across the room to try and pull Shane away. The three of them wrestled.

"Get him off of me!" Paco hollered, surprised at how strong Shane was. "Get him off of me!"

It never dawned on me to run. All I could think about was Shane.

"Shane, stop!" I screamed as I got to my feet.

Ignoring me, he continued to fight and wrestle to get the gun away from Paco while Rick pulled at him from behind.

"Shane, stop!" Rick yelled.

Shane threw a strong right haymaker at Paco. It connected so hard I could've sworn I heard Paco's jaw break. But surprisingly, Paco kept hold of the gun despite the power of the punch.

"Get him off of me!" Paco yelled again.

"Stop, Shane!" I screamed. "Stop it!"

I'd never seen Shane fight before. Honestly, I'd never truly thought he had it in him. I'd never known he was so strong either. While battling with Paco for the gun, he was slinging Rick easily.

Suddenly, a familiar sound was heard.

A shot went off from the gun. The bullet tore through my shoulder and knocked me to the floor so hard it ripped the air right out of me. The pain was terrible. My shoulder and chest burned.

Rick, Shane, and Paco continued to wrestle.

As I glared up at the ceiling holding my shoulder, the gun

went off again. I looked in time to see Paco's body go limp as he held onto Shane. Somehow Shane had gotten him to turn the gun on himself. He slowly slid down Shane's body to the floor holding his neck. The gun dropped from his hand. Within moments, he began making a horrible gagging sound. He was drowning in his own blood. It wasn't long before the gagging stopped and his body stopped moving. He was lifeless. He was dead.

Rick shoved Shane backwards and quickly knelt to grab the gun.

Another shot went off.

I laid in a daze, wondering where the shot had come from.

Rick's body fell backwards against the door. He'd been hit in the chest. Blood poured from his body. He held his chest and groaned in pain as he fell to the floor.

I turned to see Treasure standing at the bottom of the steps holding the .45 that Lucky had bought me. She was clutching it with both her hands and still had it aimed.

Everything had gone silent, except for Rick's moans of pain.

Treasure stood silent, refusing to put the gun down.

I realized my baby had saved my life, as I lay on the floor and began to stare at the ceiling. Although I didn't deserve it, God had heard me calling out to him. I'd never felt so relieved.

Treasure slowly walked away from the steps towards all of the bloodshed. She passed me and walked over to Rick with the gun aimed. From the floor he stared into her eyes as he held his chest. Blood oozed from his wound.

Both could only stare at each other.

Shane stood at a distance.

The moment seemed like it would never end.

Treasure finally backed away from Rick slowly and grabbed Paco's gun from the floor. With a gun now in each hand she backed towards me. When Treasure reached me she turned.

Looking into her eyes, I whispered, "Baby, I love you."

I had never meant those words more than now. All I wanted to do was take my daughter into my arms and hold her as tightly as I did the moment she was born. I reached for her.

Treasure didn't say anything. She only stood with the guns at her sides.

"Baby, it's over," I assured her. My arms were still reaching for her.

Tears began to fall from her eyes.

"It's okay, baby," I assured.

"No it's not!"

"Yes, it is, sweetheart."

"You messed everything up," she told me. "It'll never be okay again."

Through her tears and with a broken heart she raised both guns from her sides and aimed them at my face.

To Be Continued…
Part 2 Still Grindin'
Comin Soon

V.I.P. is an explicit tale of two beautiful women both determined to become very important people 'by any means necessary'. After living in a world where you re only cool if you're the wife of an athlete, or a current T.V star they are both suddenly faced with jealousy and lies. Neither realize ...fame comes with a high, and sometimes deadly price tag. Meet India, the star struck, money hungry chick from Brooklyn, who's dead set on marrying someone well-known....even if she has to steal him from her good friend. In comes Royce, a tantalizing, sexy singer who's searching for fame in all the wrong places. Soon her past catches up with her and things spiral out of control. By hook, crook, or the good book, one of these ladies will fall hard.

LCB BOOK TITLES

See More Titles At
www.lifechangingbooks.net

ORDER FORM

MAIL TO:
PO Box 423
Brandywine, MD 20613
301-362-6508

FAX TO:
301-579-9913

Ship to:	
Address:	
City & State:	Zip:

Date: _____ Phone: _____

Email: _____

Make all money orders and cashiers checks payable to: **Life Changing Books**

Qty.	ISBN	Title	Release Date	Price
	0-9741394-2-4	Bruised by Azarel	Jul-05	$ 15.00
	0-9741394-7-5	Bruised 2: The Ultimate Revenge by Azarel	Oct-06	$ 15.00
	0-9741394-3-2	Secrets of a Housewife by J. Tremble	Feb-06	$ 15.00
	0-9741394-6-7	The Millionaire Mistress by Tiphani	Nov-06	$ 15.00
	1-934230-99-5	More Secrets More Lies by J. Tremble	Feb-07	$ 15.00
	1-934230-95-2	A Private Affair by Mike Warren	May-07	$ 15.00
	1-934230-96-0	Flexin & Sexin Volume 1	Jun-07	$ 15.00
	1-934230-89-8	Still a Mistress by Tiphani	Nov-07	$ 15.00
	1-934230-91-X	Daddy's House by Azarel	Nov-07	$ 15.00
	1-934230-88-X	Naughty Little Angel by J. Tremble	Feb-08	$ 15.00
	1-934230820	Rich Girls by Kendall Banks	Oct-08	$ 15.00
	1-934230839	Expensive Taste by Tiphani	Nov-08	$ 15.00
	1-934230782	Brooklyn Brothel by C. Stecko	Jan-09	$ 15.00
	1-934230669	Good Girl Gone bad by Danette Majette	Mar-09	$ 15.00
	1-934230804	From Hood to Hollywood by Sasha Raye	Mar-09	$ 15.00
	1-934230707	Sweet Swagger by Mike Warren	Jun-09	$ 15.00
	1-934230677	Carbon Copy by Azarel	Jul-09	$ 15.00
	1-934230723	Millionaire Mistress 3 by Tiphani	Nov-09	$ 15.00
	1-934230715	A Woman Scorned by Ericka Williams	Nov-09	$ 15.00
	1-934230685	My Man Her Son by J. Tremble	Feb-10	$ 15.00
	1-924230731	Love Heist by Jackie D.	Mar-10	$ 15.00
	1-934230812	Flexin & Sexin Volume 2	Apr-10	$ 15.00
	1-934230748	The Dirty Divorce by Miss KP	May-10	$ 15.00
	1-934230758	Chedda Boyz by CJ Hudson	Jul-10	$ 15.00
	1-934230766	Snitch by VegasClarke	Oct-10	$ 15.00
	1-934230693	Money Maker by Tonya Ridley	Oct-10	$ 15.00
	1-934230774	The Dirty Divorce Part 2 by Miss KP	Nov-10	$ 15.00
	1-934230170	The Available Wife by Carla Pennington	Jan-11	$ 15.00
	1-934230774	One Night Stand by Kendall Banks	Feb-11	$ 15.00
	1-934230278	Bitter by Danette Majette	Feb-11	$ 15.00
	1-934230299	Married to a Balla by Jackie D.	May-11	$ 15.00
	1-934230308	The Dirty Divorce Part 3 by Miss KP	Jun-11	$ 15.00
	1-934230316	Next Door Nympho By CJ Hudson	Jun-11	$ 15.00
	1-934230286	Bedroom Gangsta by J. Tremble	Sep-11	$ 15.00
	1-934230340	Another One Night Stand by Kendall Banks	Oct-11	$15.00
	1-934230359	The Available Wife Part 2 by Carla Pennington	Nov-11	$ 15.00
	1-934230332	Wealthy & Wicked by Chris Renee	Jan-12	$ 15.00
	1-934230375	Life After a Balla by Jackie D.	Mar-12	$ 15.00
			Total for Books	$

* Prison Orders- Please allow up to three (3) weeks for delivery.

Please Note: We are not held responsible for returned prison orders. Make sure the facility will receive books before ordering.

Shipping Charges (add $4.95 for 1-4 books*) $ _____

Total Enclosed (add lines) $ _____

*Shipping and Handling of 5-10 books is $8.95, please contact us if your order is more than 10 books. (301)362-6508